Murder
Most
Fowl

ALSO BY DONNA ANDREWS

Murder Most Fowl

A Meg Langslow Mystery

Donna Andrews

MINOTAUR BOOKS

NEW YORK

First published in the United States by Minotaur Books, an imprint of St. Martin's Publishing Group.

MURDER MOST FOWL. Copyright © 2021 by Donna Andrews. All rights reserved. Printed in the United States of America. For information, address St. Martin's Publishing Group, 120 Broadway, New York, NY 10271.

www.minotaurbooks.com

The Library of Congress Cataloging-in-Publication Data is available upon request.

ISBN 978-1-250-76016-6 (hardcover)
ISBN 978-1-250-76017-3 (ebook)

Our books may be purchased in bulk for promotional, educational, or business use. Please contact your local bookseller or the Macmillan Corporate and Premium Sales Department at 1-800-221-7945, extension 5442, or by email at MacmillanSpecialMarkets@macmillan.com.

First Edition: 2021

10 9 8 7 6 5 4 3 2 1

Murder
Most
Fowl

Chapter 1

Thursday

"Mom?"

I kept my eyes firmly closed and focused on breathing in and out in the slow, deliberate way that was supposed to make you feel better when you were stressed. One . . . two . . .

"Mom," Jamie repeated. "I know when you're doing your yoga breathing we're not supposed to interrupt you unless there's actual bleeding involved."

"Or open flames," his twin brother, Josh, added.

"But I kind of think this might qualify," Jamie went on.

My eyes flew open.

All I could see for a second were the muddy shins and baggy knees of the woolen hose they were wearing as part of their medieval costumes. I craned my neck to see upward, past the well-worn leather doublets to their faces. Josh was leaning on his longbow as if it were a staff. Jamie had his slung over his left shoulder. Neither appeared to be injured. But they both looked . . . anxious. And that wasn't a look I saw very often on the faces of my not-quite-teenage sons.

"What's wrong?" I asked.

They exchanged a glance. Were they deciding what to tell me? Or just sorting out who had to do the telling?

"We think we found a body," Josh said.

"A dead body," Jamie clarified.

I opened my mouth to chide them for interrupting my

yoga breathing with what was obviously a bad practical joke. But I could see by their expressions that it wasn't a joke.

"Where?" I asked. "And who?"

"Out here in the woods," Jamie said.

"And we have no idea who," Josh said. "All we can see is the hands."

"One of the hands," Jamie corrected. "Kind of sticking up out of the ground. And maybe some fingers from the other hand."

"Show me." I sprang to my feet. I'd been sitting cross-legged by the side of a tiny stream in the woods behind our house, trying to relax by focusing on my breath—and the peaceful sounds of the water, the bird calls, and the occasional distant baaing of our neighbor Seth Early's sheep.

Clearly relaxation wasn't in my immediate future. I should check out what they'd found.

They both seemed a little less anxious now that I was taking their report seriously.

"Lead on, Macduff," I said.

"That's 'lay on, Macduff,'" Jamie corrected. "'And damn'd be him that first cries, *Hold, enough!*'"

I should know better than to try quoting lines from *Macbeth* when their father was currently directing a production of it. A production in which they both had small roles.

"'Exeunt, fighting.'" Josh was quoting the stage directions that followed Jamie's lines. "'Alarums.'"

"I'm impressed," I said. "Now show me this body."

The boys set off, and I could barely keep up with them. Not really surprising, since they were now eye to eye with me at five foot ten. And more of their height was leg, so they set a faster pace and were in danger of leaving me behind.

But characteristically, Jamie would glance back occasionally, notice that I was falling behind, and tug at Josh's sleeve to slow him down. And Josh slowed down a lot more readily than usual—that, combined with their expressions, told me that they were putting a brave front on something that had genuinely shaken them.

So I tried my best to keep up the pace. It helped that the last stretch was a slight downhill slope, and we arrived together at the edge of a small clearing.

"Over by that fallen log," Josh whispered.

Jamie merely pointed.

I looked across the clearing and felt the hairs rise on the back of my neck. They weren't pulling some kind of strange prank. There really were two hands poking up out of the half-rotted leaves covering the ground. Only the tips of three fingers of the left hand showed, but all five fingers of the right protruded, and even a little bit of the back of the hand. The fingers were long and slender, but twisted, contorted, as if their owner had died while reaching out to grab something in panic . . . or in agony. And they were deadly pale—the nails were, at least. Almost silvery. The flesh, though, was a little darker. In fact, it had a blueish-gray tint. Decay? Or was it just a trick of the light—the day was quite cloudy, and the branches of the huge oaks and maples at the edges of the clearing met overhead, so not much light made it in.

The boys each inched a little closer, as if having me along made them bolder, and I grabbed one with each hand.

"Keep your distance," I said. "We don't know what she died of."

"She?" Josh echoed. He took a step back.

"Mom's right." Jamie retreated several steps. "Definitely not a man. The fingers are too small."

"Could be a kid," Josh suggested.

Once I was sure they'd stay put I pulled out my phone and called 911.

"What's wrong now, Meg?" Odd. Debbie Ann, the dispatcher, made it sound as if I'd called her at least once already today. Maybe she was just having a bad morning.

"Josh and Jamie found a dead body in the woods behind our house," I said. "I have no idea exactly where we are, but I'll send the boys out to the road. They can lead whoever you send back here. I'll keep watch."

The boys nodded and dashed off. I wasn't exactly thrilled at being left alone with those creepy hands, but it was better than having to leave the boys alone with them.

"Oh, dear," Debbie Ann said. "Do you know who it is?"

Along with her words I could hear the rattle of keys that meant she was sending out a text message to one of the deputies. Or maybe all of the deputies. The more the merrier.

"No idea," I said. "All I can see is a pair of hands, sticking up out of the ground. So it's not just dead but dead and buried, only not very competently."

"Horrible," she said. "Vern's five minutes away, and the chief was already on his way out to Camp Birnam, so he's going to stop by—he might even beat Vern."

"The chief's back from his family camping trip, then?" I felt a surge of relief. And then guilt. I hated the idea that on his first day back in town the chief would have to cope with a dead body—and probably a not-very-recent one at that. Although I was also glad that he'd be here to handle whatever happened.

But wait—

"Why was the chief headed out to Camp Birnam?" I asked. "I mean, if you can tell me. I'm not exactly responsible for the place, but—"

"But you've been trying to keep them in line." She sighed. "I know. Seth Early called up just now, madder than a wet hen. He thinks that the reenactor folks out there have stolen some of his sheep."

I closed my eyes and muttered a few words that I hoped

the boys hadn't picked up from me. For that matter, I made sure Debbie Ann couldn't catch them.

"I hope someone told the chief that wasn't our idea," I said. "Having a bunch of medieval reenactors camping out in the woods. We only let them set up that wretched camp to please the History Department. And if he wants them gone—"

"He's probably already heard about them." Debbie Ann's tone was soothing. "And if he hasn't already heard how hard you've been trying to keep them from causing trouble, I'll tell him myself. FYI, Horace is on his way, too."

"Good." I nodded, even though she couldn't see me. My cousin Horace Hollingsworth was both a deputy and Caerphilly's one trained crime-scene investigator.

"Do you think this body could have something to do with them?" she went on. "The reenactors, that is."

I opened my eyes and studied the hands again.

"I can't imagine it would," I said. "If it turns out that any of the reenactors are responsible, we'll evict the whole lot, but I have a hard time imagining that. And if you're worried about Seth—well, he can be a hothead, especially where his sheep are concerned, but I can't imagine him killing anyone and burying them in the woods. Not even a sheep thief."

"He'd just punch the thief in the nose and then come down to the station to turn himself in," Debbie Ann suggested, with a slight giggle.

"Yes." I thought of adding that the body was obviously not brand-new, and I'd probably have heard about it if any of the reenactors had gone missing for very long, but I wasn't sure that thought would help matters.

I heard the crashing noises of someone approaching through the woods. Possibly several someones, by the sound of it.

"I have visitors," I said.

"Keep them away from the crime scene if it's not Vern or the chief," Debbie Ann warned.

"I will."

But to my relief I spotted Josh approaching. He appeared to be repeatedly running ahead, then backtracking to rejoin another figure. The second figure, sturdy and clad in an impeccably clean khaki uniform, hiked stolidly forward, ignoring Josh's darting back and forth.

"It's the chief," I said to Debbie Ann. "I'll hang up now."

The chief already looked grim. Since the modest town of Caerphilly was not just the largest but the only town in our small, rural Virginia county, he didn't see that many dead bodies. Not nearly as many as when he'd been a homicide detective in Baltimore. But the ones he did see these days hit him harder, since they happened in "his" town. The expression on his round brown face suggested that the boys' find had already undone some of the benefits of his vacation.

"Where is this body?" he said as he drew near.

I stepped aside and pointed across the clearing.

He studied the hands in silence for a few seconds.

"Did any of you go over there?" He didn't take his eyes away from the hands.

"I didn't." I glanced at Josh.

"We didn't, either," he said. "It was pretty creepy. We went to find Mom."

"Good," the chief said. "Let's keep the scene undisturbed. Horace should be here soon. In the meantime—"

He jerked his head around, evidently noticing the same sounds I had. People crashing through the underbrush from two directions.

He sighed.

"With luck, that will be Horace and Vern," he said. "But if it's people coming to gawk—"

"We'll help you head them off. Josh, you go that way." I pointed to our right. "I'll go this way. The chief doesn't want anyone to mess up his crime scene, so don't let anyone go past you into the clearing."

Josh raced away. I circled around until I was roughly a third of the way around the periphery of the clearing. Josh did the same thing in the other direction. He took an arrow out of the quiver on his back and nocked it onto his bow. Then he glared at the woods around him, as if daring anyone to approach. I settled for crossing my arms over my chest and staring fiercely in the direction of the crashing noises nearest me.

To my relief, Jamie appeared, followed by Vern Shiffley, the chief's most senior deputy. Like all of the enormous Shiffley clan, Vern was tall and lanky, with a long, imperturbable face. He appeared to be merely ambling through the woods, but his strides covered ground, and Jamie was half running to keep up with him.

"Why don't you take over guarding this part of the perimeter?" I suggested when Vern drew near. "I'll go help the chief deal with them."

I nodded toward the other group, who were heading for where Chief Burke stood.

"Yeah," Vern said. "That crew's going to get on the chief's nerves in no time flat."

Actually, the two women, dressed in medieval peasant garb, in much the same drab earth tones Josh and Jamie were wearing, would probably behave themselves. But the tall man in the garish plaid kilt was another matter. He was the main reason I'd been out in the woods trying to calm myself with yoga breathing.

"I assume these are some of the people Debbie Ann told me about," the chief said in an undertone when I reached his side. "The ones having their costume party in your parents' woods."

"Not exactly a costume party," I said. "They've set up their idea of what an eleventh-century Scottish military camp would look like."

"Why?" he asked. "I mean, it might make sense in Scotland, but here in rural Virginia?"

"Eleventh-century Scotland is when—and where—the real-life Macbeth lived—the one on whom Shakespeare based his play."

"So this has something to do with the play Michael's directing?"

Before I could answer, the reenactors were upon us. The tall man in the gaudy black-and-yellow tartan stuck out one large and not-very-clean hand.

"Calum MacLeod," he said, in his annoyingly bad fake Scottish accent. "Chieftain of the Caerphilly sept of the Clan MacLeod, and leader of the war-band now encamped in Birnam Wood."

"Henry Burke," the chief said. "Chief of the Caerphilly Police Department and sheriff of Caerphilly County. I'd appreciate it if you'd stand over there and keep clear of my crime scene."

The chief's tone made it clear that, however politely worded, this was an order. Calum's face showed surprise and, just for a moment, a trace of rebellion. But then he did as he was told, gesturing imperiously at the two women to follow him. And it wasn't as if he'd have trouble gawking to his heart's content. The clearing was in a low spot, so that on all sides around it the ground rose like a shallow, tree-filled amphitheater.

"Chief! Chief!"

The chief and I turned to see two more figures racing down the gentle slope toward us. The chief's face brightened—no doubt because he recognized the lead figure as Dad. Since Dad was also the local medical examiner, no doubt his arrival would be timely. But the man following him—

"The guy with Dad is a documentary filmmaker and an avid blogger," I said quietly. "Also a jerk with no concept of privacy or boundaries. So unless you want pictures of your crime scene popping up all over the Web—"

"His name?"

"Damien Goodwin," I said.

The chief strode a few paces toward the approaching figures.

"Mr. Goodwin! Stay where you are!"

Goodwin slowed down but didn't completely stop. Vern, as if anticipating the chief's next order, loped in Goodwin's direction, his long, rangy stride quickly taking him to where he could intercept Goodwin if needed.

"Dr. Langslow," the chief went on. "I could use your assistance."

Dad almost skipped the rest of the way to the chief's side.

"I hear you've got a murder!" he said.

"A body," the chief corrected. "So far we have no cause to suspect homicide." His smile was a little strained. I was never sure whether Dad's obsession with murder was the cause or result of his avid consumption of crime novels, but it was a source of great annoyance to the chief, in spite of how highly he valued Dad's skill as a doctor and a medical examiner. "Over there." The chief gestured toward the clearing, and the three of us turned back toward it.

Behind us, Goodwin was arguing with Vern.

"You have no right to take away my camera!" Goodwin was shouting. "Seizure of private property! Suppression of my First Amendment rights! Freedom of the press!"

"You're not allowed to film here," the chief said over his shoulder.

"I have permission from the owner," Goodwin said. "I'm within my rights—"

"That permission is rescinded until further notice," I said. "Right, Dad?"

"Sorry—what?" Dad was taking his binoculars out of their case. Trust a birder never to venture into the woods unprepared. He probably also had a battered copy of the Peterson Guide in one pocket, to supplement the dozen or so birding apps on his iPhone.

"We don't want this Mr. Goodwin taking unauthorized pictures of our crime scene, now do we?" the chief said. The "our" was definitely a kind of flattery.

"Perish the thought." I shuddered with deliberate drama. "So you're temporarily rescinding Mr. Goodwin's permission to film in this part of the woods, right, Dad?"

"Oh, of course. Of course." He was staring at the hands through his binoculars. "Damien! Go away for now."

Goodwin subsided, grumbling.

"See that he keeps his cell phone in his pocket," I called to Vern. "He's just as dangerous with that as the camera."

I tried to ignore the renewed wrangling between Vern and Goodwin.

"Oh, my goodness," Dad said. "How amazing!"

Chapter 2

Dad chuckled—not a typical reaction for anyone who'd just spotted a dead body and what might be a crime scene. Especially not Dad, whose joy at being involved in murder cases was always tempered with sorrow for the victim and even pity for the guilty.

"Horace should be here in five minutes," the chief said. "After he does a little preliminary work on the surrounding area, you can—"

"No need for Horace." Dad took the binoculars from his face and darted toward the body.

"Dr. Langslow!" The chief took a step to follow, then stopped, visibly torn between the desire to keep Dad from trampling the crime scene and reluctance to add his footsteps to Dad's.

Dad stopped just short of the spooky hands. He pulled out his phone and took several pictures of them, leaning to get different angles.

"You can relax," he said. "Definitely not a murder. In fact, not even a body."

I had to restrain a gasp of horror as he reached down and snapped off one of the contorted fingers—the smallest of the fingertips. The chief actually did gasp.

Dad turned around, held up the finger, and beamed at us.

"It's a fungus." He ambled back in our direction. "*Xylaria polymorpha*. Commonly known as 'dead-man's-fingers,' or sometimes 'dead-man's-toes.' So called because that's often what they look like. I have to say, though, I've never seen a more lifelike example."

He handed the pseudo finger to the chief, who didn't exactly flinch—but you could tell he found it a lot less charming than Dad did.

"Very interesting." He handed the fungus back to Dad after a brief examination.

"Does it grow on dead people?" Josh's tone suggested that he hadn't yet given up the hope of finding a body. Was Dad's obsession with crime fiction having too much influence on the boys? Should I suggest that he ease up on talk of crime scenes and autopsies around them?

"Not on dead bodies—only dead trees." Dad pointed toward where the remaining fingers were still poking out of the earth. "Notice it's right around the trunk of that fallen maple. What we're seeing is just the top of it. It's a saprobic fungus—lives on dead or rotting plant matter. So underground, it's feeding on the tree."

"Is it poisonous?" Jamie asked.

"Now, that I don't know for sure." Dad's expression suggested that not knowing bothered him. I'd have to keep an eye out to make sure he didn't decide to find out, using himself as a test subject. "Some sources merely list it as inedible. Others say it's edible, but unexciting. But I've also found a source saying it contains amatoxin and phallotoxin—two of the compounds that make *Amanita phalloides* so toxic."

"*Amanita phalloides*," Josh repeated. "You mean—"

"The death . . . cap . . . mushroom!" Jamie intoned. He and Josh both looked at the benighted fungus with renewed interest.

Yes, I should definitely have a talk with Dad. And Grandfather. Not quite into their teens yet, and already the boys had picked up not only the mystery bug but also the annoying family habit of learning and using the Latin names for things that had perfectly good English equivalents.

"It's not a crime scene, so I don't see why I can't film it," I heard Goodwin saying.

"It's okay," I said over my shoulder. "Unless the chief minds." I couldn't think of any downside to having Goodwin film the fungus. In fact, maybe it would be a good thing if he had something else to distract him if the chief was about to head over to Camp Birnam to investigate Seth Early's sheep-stealing accusation.

"Be my guest," Chief Burke said.

"Stand clear and let me get some good long shots of them!" Goodwin ordered.

Actually, no one seemed all that eager to get closer to the harmless but sinister-looking fungus. Even the boys were content, for the moment, to examine the sample Dad had brought to the chief.

"Amazing," Goodwin was muttering, as he circled around the periphery of the clearing, intently filming. I could see the chief studying him with a slight frown on his face. Goodwin was dressed entirely in black—black jeans, black pullover sweater, black ankle boots. His black hair was close-cropped, and a neatly trimmed goatee adorned his face. He'd probably have looked chic and with-it on the streets of Manhattan or Hollywood, but out here in the woods of Caerphilly, "pretentious" and "city slicker" were the first words that came to mind.

"Truly amazing!" Goodwin paused, and looked up. "Now let's reenact the discovery. Who found them?"

"We did," Josh said.

Goodwin's face fell. I'd made it painfully clear to him that he did not have Michael's or my permission to film our sons—and recruited several relatives who were lawyers to hammer the point home. Goodwin wasn't pleased at this obstacle to his filming, but I was pleased to note that he'd stopped trying to change my mind.

"Actually, I noticed the presence of the . . . um . . . *Amazonia porphyria* a few days ago," MacLeod said.

The boys mostly suppressed their amusement over how he'd mangled the Latin name.

"Of course, since I knew what it was, I didna call in the constabulary," he went on. "But I'd be happy to re-create my initial experience for you."

"Go for it," Goodwin said.

MacLeod strolled into the clearing, swinging his walking stick. He stopped halfway across, pretended to spot the fungus, and did a double take so broad that the boys had to suppress more giggling.

The chief was on his phone, giving Debbie Ann an update on the situation.

"Yes, everyone can stand down," he said. "Yes . . . yes, Dr. Langslow got some photos, and I think Vern did, too. . . . No, it was a completely valid call. It had me fooled, too. . . . Yes. I'll be heading up there now."

He hung up and turned his gaze to where MacLeod was doing a second reenactment of his alleged discovery of the fungus.

"He's one of the reenactors staying up at this Camp Birnam place?" he asked me, in an undertone.

"He's their chief," I said. "Possibly self-appointed. Pain in the—"

I glanced around to see if either of the two female re-enactors were within earshot, but they had already started back for their camp.

"Pain in the neck," I finished. "I've already had one argument with him this morning. One of their bagpipers woke up early and decided to practice. Instead of telling him to shut up, MacLeod sent him marching down the road in the direction of our house."

"Ouch," the chief said.

We watched for a few minutes, until Goodwin tired of filming. He'd noticed that Dad was expounding many facts about the dead-man's-fingers to the boys. Dad had been one of the filmmaker's favorite subjects from day one. I drew close enough to take a few pictures with my own phone.

MacLeod, realizing that he was no longer the center of attention, turned to leave.

"Before you go," the chief called.

But either MacLeod didn't hear him or he pretended not to, striding off in the same direction the two women reenactors had taken.

The chief made a small annoyed noise, not quite a growl.

"Enlighten me," he said in an undertone. "Why do we have all these people in funny costumes camping out here in your parents' woods? And causing a lot of trouble while I was gone, from what little news Vern's had time to tell me. Not sure I understand what they have to do with Michael's play."

"It's a long story."

"The longer I talk to you, the longer I can put off visiting this Calum McCalum person."

"Calum MacLeod," I said. "And yes, putting off talking to him would be the smart thing to do. I try to avoid him as much as possible myself."

"Let's stretch our legs, then, and leave them to it." He nodded slightly at where Dad was still giving his mycology lesson to the twins. And mugging for the camera. Damien Goodwin was standing right behind Josh and Jamie, which not only gave him the best view of Dad but ensured that he could keep the boys out of his frame. I made a mental note to call my lawyer cousin Festus and thank him for doing such a great job of helping me scare Goodwin into good behavior.

"Incidentally, I brought Adam with me," the chief said. "Dropped him off at the house before I got the call to come out here. I gather the plan is for him to tag along to rehearsal with Josh and Jamie. I suppose I should tell them."

Adam Jones Burke was the youngest of the three grand-sons that the chief and his wife, Minerva, had taken in after the boys' parents' tragic death in an auto accident. Adam, Josh, and Jamie, along with their friend Mason, had long formed what we called the Four Musketeers. The twins had been counting the days until Adam's return from vacation.

"Unless you took his phone away, I suspect they already know he's here," I said. "And have made plans to connect."

"You're probably right," he said. "And he seemed happy enough eating a second breakfast with all the actors. So let's head in the general direction of this Camp Birnam place while we talk. I have to drop by there before too long. But we can take it slowly."

"Can do." I suppressed a sigh. I'd rather have been heading back to the house. Or in any direction other than the one toward Camp Birnam.

"It all started with the play Michael's directing for Arena Stage," I began.

"The production of *Macbeth*," the chief said. "And I thought he was going to be directing it up in D.C. Isn't that where Arena's located?"

"It will play up in D.C. on Arena's main stage," I said. "But they're rehearsing it down here."

"Much nicer for all of you." The chief nodded his ap-proval.

Actually, the boys had been quite miffed at missing the opportunity to live in the nation's capital for a couple of months. I tried not to imagine what kind of trouble they could have gotten into if we had agreed to do that.

"Michael and the Arena management got in touch with the Caerphilly College Building and Grounds Department so they could rent some rehearsal space in the drama build-ing," I went on. "And that's when things started getting complicated. There's a very senior professor in the English Department who's supposedly a Shakespeare expert."

"Supposedly? Not exactly a ringing endorsement."

"He's a nutcase." I sighed. "Tenured, unfortunately, and a good friend of both the English Department chair and the head of the Building and Grounds Department."

"A nutcase with clout. So the interdepartmental feud's still going on then? Hasn't it been almost a decade since Drama broke away from English to be its own department?"

"More than a decade," I said. I thought of asking how he'd heard about the feud—did the whole town know? Then again, maybe it wasn't surprising—the chief didn't miss much that went on in his town. And come to think of it, I might have vented to him about it myself. "But these are people who consider anyone newer than Chaucer a modern writer. Ten years is nothing to them. Anyway, Dr. Desmond Philpotts was trying to keep Michael from using any Caerphilly College facilities unless he agreed to replace the commonly accepted text of *Macbeth* with his so-called more authoritative version."

"Authoritative how?" the chief asked. "Does he think he can improve on what Shakespeare wrote? He's not one of those people who try to censor out anything the least bit off-color, is he?"

"No, his particular theory is that the published version of the play wasn't authentic to what Shakespeare wrote," I explained. "Remember that back in Shakespeare's day, they didn't print a lot of copies of a play and hand them out to the cast. They copied the scripts by hand, which cost a lot of money, and for that matter paper wasn't cheap. So most of the actors only got what they call sides—their lines and cues. And lines changed over time, with or without the playwright's permission. Most scholars consider the First Folio, a collection published in 1623, the primary source for Shakespeare's plays. But by the time that came out there were probably a lot of random copies floating around, so there's plenty of room for scholars to squabble."

"Can't Michael just use this First Folio version, though?" the chief asked. "I mean, regardless of what he wrote earlier, isn't it safe to assume that what he had them print was the final version—or at least the latest, greatest one?"

"He didn't have them print it," I said. "He was dead by then. By six or seven years."

"Ah." The chief nodded. "So who knows what he would have wanted."

"Dr. Philpotts thinks he does," I said. "He thinks Shakespeare's original version was nothing like what got published in 1623. Every other Shakespearean scholar in the known universe thinks he's a loon, but he's determined. And unfortunately his version leaves out most of the poetry and all of the drama. Michael knew trying to put that on would be a disaster."

"I can see Michael hasn't been having much fun," the chief said. "But I don't quite see what this has to do with those nutjobs in costume."

"Sorry," I said. "I told you it was a long story. Michael had to do something to fend off the ridiculous demands from the English Department. So he joined forces with the History Department. In return for their political support against the English Department, he agreed to partner with them on some projects. Which is why we have a bunch of history grad students hanging around the house roping the cast and crew into projects on costume and cooking and manners, both in the Elizabethan era, when the play was written, and the medieval period, when the events it's based on took place. And history professors showing up regularly to lecture everyone on Tudor politics and economics and the roots of colonialism. And it's thanks to the History Department that we have Damien Goodwin, the filmmaker—in addition to documenting the progress of the play he does video of all their projects and lectures. And for those more interested in the medieval side, a so-called authentic eleventh-century Scottish military encampment out there in the woods."

"I see." The chief's expression was thoughtful. He'd probably already deduced that I wasn't thrilled about having the reenactors underfoot. Or Goodwin, for that matter. I felt a sudden rush of hope. Michael and I had already decided that we had to get rid of both Goodwin and the reenactors, but we hadn't yet figured out how to do it without upsetting the delicate and useful alliance between History and Drama. But if the chief decided they were a threat to the citizens he was sworn to protect and serve, he might solve the problem for us.

"So the reenactors are history students?" he asked.

"A few of them might be," I said. "But most of them are just avid members of a group that likes doing historical reenactments."

"The Society for Creative Anachronism?" the chief asked. "I've heard of them. Scadians, they call themselves."

"I know Scadians," I said. "My grandmother gets a lot of them at the renaissance faire she runs. I wouldn't mind having a bunch of them around. No, these clowns call themselves the DARK—the Dystopian Alternate Realities Krew. I never heard of them before they showed up here, but from what I've been able to find out, I gather they got kicked out of the SCA for being oblivious to any kind of rules, especially when it comes to health and safety."

"Great." He shook his head. "And they've been stealing Seth's sheep."

"They might not be actually stealing them," I said. "You know how Seth's sheep get around—on any given day at least half of them are out exploring the countryside. Camp Birnam's well within their range."

"Yes, a few of them make it all the way into town occasionally," the chief said. "Camp Birnam—that's from the play, right? *Macbeth*."

"Yes." I assumed a dramatic pose and quoted the famous lines. "'Macbeth shall never vanquish'd be until / Great Birnam wood to high Dunsinane hill / Shall come against him.' They've taken to calling our house Dunsinane, by the way, which can be a little confusing if you're not hip to the lingo."

"Speaking of your house—I assume that's why you've got so many extra cars all up and down the road. You're letting the reenactors park there."

"No, we make them park out near their camp. The cars at our house belong to the cast and crew. Professor Philpotts did manage to sabotage our efforts to get cheap rooms for them in the dorms, so most of them are staying at our house. It's only for a few more weeks," I added. Not that the chief would care how long our houseguests would be staying, but reminding myself it was a short-term headache helped keep me sane.

"And I hear you've been having trouble with someone playing destructive pranks."

"Yes." Clearly Vern had briefed him well. "I've been thinking of it as sabotage, actually. Or vandalism. At least so far it's been mostly small things."

"Such as?"

I pulled out my notebook-that-tells-me-when-to-breathe, as I call my trusty combined to-do list and calendar, and turned to my record of what the vandal had done. "They started by painting blood-red footprints on our front walk," I said. "You can probably still see traces of that. Then they knocked several hundred books off the library shelves. Stole lingerie from several female cast members, tied them into garlands, and decorated the library shelves. Poured red paint over one actor's script so it was almost unreadable. Smashed a birthday cake to bits and poured strawberry jelly all over it, like blood."

"I'm not liking all the emphasis on red," the chief said. "Given its very natural association with blood. Is that it?"

"We found a poisonous snake in one of the bathrooms, but that could have wandered in on its own. And there has been some graffiti."

"Yes, Vern told me about the racial epithets the vandal spray-painted on your walls," the chief said. "In red. He also warned me that we were keeping that a secret to help catch the perpetrator, though I'm not sure how that's going to work. Wouldn't everyone in your house have seen them already?"

"No," I said. "It was in the long hallway going down to the library. I found them one day when the cast and crew were all at rehearsal, and once Vern had photographed them for his report, he helped me repaint the hallway before anyone else got home."

"He didn't mention that," the chief said. "Glad he did."

"So far no one's been hurt by anything the vandal has done," I said. "And apart from the graffiti, there's been very little property damage. But it feels menacing, as if whoever is doing it was angry. And getting angrier."

"Any idea who could be doing it?"

"If you're wondering if I suspect the reenactors we're about to visit, the answer would be yes," I said. "But I have nothing to back up that suspicion. And remember, we've got dozens of unfamiliar faces coming and going—not only the reenactors but also the cast and crew and all those history students and professors. If the vandalism was aimed primarily at me, I'd be even more suspicious of the reenactors. They're camping on Mother and Dad's land, but whenever they get up to anything dangerous or annoying, like playing their bagpipes in the middle of the night or trying to start a forest fire, I'm the one who ends up dealing with them. I hear they call me The Enforcer. But it hasn't really targeted me, and I have no evidence against them. Or anyone else. We haven't had any incidents in two days now, but that's mainly because once everyone takes off for rehearsal I stay home and patrol the house all day."

"You shouldn't have to do that," the chief observed. "Now that I'm back, I'll see what I can do. Meanwhile I detect signs of life ahead of us. I assume we're arriving at Camp Birnam."

Chapter 3

Signs of life. What did the chief mean by that? Was he referring to the children, either clad in drab homespun rags or stark naked, who were running around in a vigorous game of tag? The droning and squawking noises emitted by one of the camp's several amateur bagpipers? Or the odors we could detect, now that we were downwind of camp—a combination of cooking smells and the privies?

"Before we go in," I said, "I should warn you. Do not say the word 'Macbeth' while you're here."

"Why not?" He stopped and frowned slightly.

"A lot of them attended a lecture Michael gave about the history of the play," I said. "And unfortunately, he mentioned how it's considered bad luck to say it in a theater unless you're actually performing or rehearsing the play. Long-standing actor's superstition."

"Except they're not actually actors." He frowned.

"No, and even if they were, why would it matter out here, since we're not actually in a theater. But they don't seem to get the distinction. Or maybe they just enjoy having conniption fits whenever anyone says the name. Logic does not apply with them."

"I'm not sure how investigating an alleged sheep theft could possibly lead to a discussion of Elizabethan drama, but I'll be careful."

"You can call it *The Scottish Play*," I said. "Or *The Bard's Play*. If you're talking about the character or the historical figure Shakespeare based him on, say the Scottish King. Mackers is also an acceptable substitute. His wife is Lady

M, and for heaven's sake, don't quote any lines from it. Or from any of Shakespeare's other plays—they're a lot more superstitious than they are knowledgeable. They gave me what-for the other day for daring to say 'to be or not to be,' which any fool should know is from *Hamlet,* not *The Scottish Play.*"

The chief frowned in the direction of the camp for a long moment. Then he glanced at me and nodded.

"Thank you for the warning." He smiled unexpectedly. "So since I suddenly feel the urge to quote the bard, I should get it out of my system now."

I smiled back and cocked my head to show I was listening attentively.

"'We must not make a scarecrow of the law,'" he said. "'Uneasy lies the head that wears a crown.' 'There is a tide in the affairs of men.' 'To thine own self be true.' 'Never a borrower or a lender be.' 'The evil that men do lives after them; the good is oft interred with their bones.' 'Will all great Neptune's ocean wash this blood clean from my hand?'"

He paused and frowned slightly, as if waiting to see if any more quotes were going to bubble up out of his memory. Then he nodded, assumed a serious expression, and strode toward the camp.

I hurried to follow him. I'd had over two weeks' experience keeping the Birnamites in line. Which made me arguably their least favorite person in the county, but still, I should do what I could to help keep the peace.

And if the chief ended up tossing a few of the worst miscreants in jail, I wanted to be there to see it.

As we drew near the encampment, I kept my eyes on the chief. I'd seen the place plenty of times and was curious to see how he reacted.

He frowned when he saw the huts—half a dozen of them, made of logs, branches, and vines, built in a semicircle around the fire pit. The fire pit was actually looking pretty good, mainly because I'd sicced the fire marshal on the Birnamites and they'd had to stop lighting huge, messy open fires. The huts were a disaster. Evidently the campers were devoid of any carpentry or engineering skills. Two of the huts had collapsed and the other four were so obviously destined to follow suit that the Birnamites had given up trying to inhabit them. Instead, they slept and sheltered from what little rain we'd had in a dozen nondescript canvas tents, arranged in a second, larger ring behind the huts.

The pile on the site of the farthest collapsed hut had grown noticeably smaller. Had they given up and began using their building materials for fuel? I might be relieved if they did—I'd worry less about the half-dozen children living in the camp, who probably saw the huts as perfect for playing hide-and-seek in. But if they'd reverted to lighting real fires, the fire marshal wouldn't be happy—due to the drought we were under a countywide burn ban.

MacLeod was sitting by the fire pit on a kind of throne made of hay bales covered over with moth-eaten furs. He watched discontentedly as a woman in drab homespun stirred the large kettle that was cooking over a small anachronistic camp stove—hidden in the middle of a bunch of logs in an unsuccessful attempt to make it look as if they were cooking over a forbidden open fire. I'd made the mistake of sampling one of their stews during an earlier visit. If what I'd tasted was typical of the camp cuisine, no wonder he kept sneaking down to our house to insinuate himself into the crowd and get some of the food prepared for the *Macbeth* cast and crew and our visiting relatives. He looked as if he was contemplating another visit.

The chief stood for a few minutes, studying the camp and its inhabitants.

The bagpiper was drawing near, playing either "Scotland the Brave" or a slow-tempo version of the theme from *Gilligan's Island*. I could tell the chief was as relieved as I was when MacLeod shooed him away.

"Is that what I think it is?" The chief was pointing to something beyond the fire pit—a rail fence. I was relieved to see that it probably accounted for the materials scavenged from the fallen hut. The fence enclosed a small, roughly circular pen. And inside the pen—

"Seth's sheep," I said.

I followed the chief over to the pen. He tried to lean his elbows on the top rail of the fence, but it collapsed under even that slight pressure, knocking down one entire four-foot stretch of the pen.

The occupants of the pen—two burly Lincoln sheep and a small fawn-colored heifer—looked longingly at the opening we'd made in the side of the pen. But since they were all three tied with short ropes to some of the larger logs that made up the other sides of the fence, there was no way they could escape.

"Yes, those are two of Seth's sheep," I said. "And that's one of Dad's prized Guernseys in there with them."

I pulled out my phone and texted Josh and Jamie, asking them to come up to Camp Birnam ASAP to take home some stray animals.

The chief scowled. He turned around and strode over to where MacLeod had suddenly become intensely interested in watching the progress of the stew.

"Mr. MacLeod," he said. "Kindly explain what these animals are doing here."

MacLeod looked up with an unconvincing look of innocent surprise.

"They just wandered into camp," he said, waving one hand vaguely as if to suggest he was only just barely aware of the animals' existence.

"Hmph." A sturdy middle-aged woman was standing nearby, her hands on her hips, watching. Her costume was cleaner and noticeably less drab and shapeless than those worn by most of the camp's inhabitants. I didn't know her full name—I'd heard some of the other reenactors call her Sally—but I'd already marked her down as one of the few sane occupants of the camp—and possibly someone who was gunning to dethrone MacLeod.

"We had no notion where they came from." MacLeod lifted his chin and tried on a look of noble self-sacrifice. "So we built a shelter to keep them safe until we figured out if they belonged to anyone."

"If they belonged to anyone," the chief echoed. "I don't know how things worked in medieval Scotland—and I don't much care. Here in twenty-first-century America, a farm animal that escapes from its pasture does not become the property of whoever runs across it."

"Oh, we weren't going to keep them," MacLeod protested. "But we were hoping maybe the owners would let us borrow them for the few weeks we'll be staying here. They add such a note of authenticity to the camp."

"That's up to the owners to decide," the chief said. "We'll be returning these animals. And if any more show up here, I expect you to return them yourself."

"But we're not from around here! How are we supposed to know who owns every animal we run across?"

"Fair enough," the chief said. "If you don't know who the owner is, you can notify the police, and we'll take care of it."

"But how can we notify you?" MacLeod's tone was starting to sound distinctly whiny. "We're miles away from town, with no means of communication!"

The chief frowned at him for a good fifteen or twenty seconds.

"If you're so dedicated to this historical accuracy thing that you've left your cell phones at home . . ." he began finally.

Several of the reenactors cringed and covered their ears as if he'd uttered an obscenity. Sally, the sane one, rolled her eyes at their antics. She was growing on me.

" . . . then you can send a messenger down to Meg and Michael's house," the chief went on. "That can't be more than a ten-minute walk, and there's nearly always some-one there. In case there isn't, you can leave a note. Meg will make sure there's a pencil and paper on her back porch in case you don't keep any around here."

"Gladly," I said. "Of course, the literacy rate was prob-ably pretty low in eleventh-century Scotland, so I expect most of them have given up reading and writing for the duration. But you can still draw, right?" I said, turning to the crowd. "Even if it's just little stick figures with wool or horns and an udder. Do your best, and we'll get the idea."

Smothered laughter broke out here and there in the crowd. MacLeod frowned thunderously, though I had no idea if he was annoyed at what I'd said or the fact that some of his followers were laughing at it.

"Meanwhile, let's lead these poor creatures back where they belong." The chief frowned again, and I suspected he wasn't keen on leading any of them himself. "Meg, I don't suppose—"

"I already texted Josh and Jamie," I said. "They should be here any minute. They can take the sheep back to Seth, and I'll manage the cow."

"But I'm sure Dr. Langslow wouldn't mind our keep-ing the cow," MacLeod said. "Just for the time being. He wouldna want us to be without fresh milk for the bairns."

"I have no idea how Dad feels about it," I said. "But Mother was not amused when she heard about this. She wants her favorite cow back."

I had no idea if Mother went in for favorites among their livestock, though if she did, this one would be a con-tender—a pretty little Guernsey with a soft fawn coat. But I knew Mother found the reenactors annoying and would back me up if I claimed she'd sent me on a mission to re-trieve her favorite cow.

Some of the reenactors turned pale, gasped, took a step or two away from the pen, or fled to the tents. I deduced that they'd met Mother in one of her previous missions to civilize the camp.

"And incidentally," I went on, "if you succeeded in getting milk from this particular cow, you'd have accomplished a miracle. She's actually a heifer—less than two years old. Too young to breed, and cows only give milk after they've given birth. I hope you didn't waste much time trying."

From the way MacLeod's face flamed beet red, and the titters from the back of the crowd, I suspected he had.

Just then the boys came racing up, with Vern loping along behind them.

"There you are," I said. "Some animals have wandered up here to Camp Birnam—can you help me take them home, please?"

"Wandered?" Josh favored the Birnamites, and especially their leader, with a suspicious frown.

Jamie just walked over to the makeshift pen and began shifting the bits of fallen fence, to make an easier path for the animals to leave. Josh gave MacLeod a final long, level scowl before going over to help. Several Birnamite men pitched in, although they kept glancing anxiously at their leader.

Vern nodded at the chief and then worked what I thought of as his magic trick of blending into the scenery. None of the Birnamites seemed to notice him, but he was there, ready to help if the chief needed him.

Meanwhile, the chief had been sniffing the air—perhaps a little ostentatiously, but I gathered he was trying to make a point.

"Has the county health inspector checked out this place?" he asked.

"She's taken to dropping by daily," I said.

"We have her to thank for those noxious pest holes," MacLeod said, in a tone of righteous indignation.

"Noxious pest holes?" The chief glanced over at the ramshackle huts with a puzzled expression.

"The porta-potties," I said. "They're camouflaged by that fence." I pointed to the fence, constructed with much the same materials as the huts, but a lot better made, since a couple of workmen from the Shiffley Construction Company had put it together.

"People survived without contraptions like that for millennia," MacLeod said.

"And untold numbers of them died from typhoid and dysentery," the chief said.

"They reek."

"They won't if you have them serviced regularly," I said. "As I know you've been told, by both the health inspector and my mother."

"Your mother's been up here?" the chief asked.

"Who do you think sicced the health inspector on them?" I said.

He smothered a grin.

"The rental company charges an arm and a leg for those things," MacLeod said. "And even more if you want them cleaned out. We are but poor peasants. A little bad smell won't kill us, and we have no Sassenach gold to pay for luxuries."

"Mr. MacLeod," the chief said. "You're a guest in this county and on Dr. and Mrs. Langslow's land. If you—"

"Help! Please! Help!"

Chapter 4

The shouts for help startled us, and we turned to see my cousin Rose Noire running into the center of camp, looking disheveled and alarmed.

"What's wrong?" the chief asked. "Are you all right?"

"It's not me—it's Vivian. Come quickly!"

She turned and ran back the way she'd come.

The chief set off in the same direction, and I hurried to follow him. Vern and the reenactors followed suit.

"Who's Vivian?" the chief said over his shoulder as we jogged.

"Beats me," I replied.

Ahead of us I saw something—a heap of logs, branches, and dead leaves that partly concealed another small pen. Rose Noire was scrambling over the fence that surrounded the second pen.

Inside the pen was a sheep. Probably another of Seth Early's prize Lincoln sheep, like the two we'd already found, but it was a little hard to tell. This sheep was missing most of her wool, and whoever had sheared her clearly had no idea how to do the job. Tufts and scraps of unsheared wool dotted her coat in a haphazard fashion—and, worse, small trickles of blood were running down her legs and body in an alarming number of places. Rose Noire was embracing the sheep, which seemed to be nestling against her in terror.

"Who's been torturing this poor sheep?" I demanded.

Nobody answered. The reenactors all looked uncomfortable, but they didn't say a thing. The only sound was the soft murmuring of Rose Noire's voice as she comforted the unhappy sheep.

"Ms. Langslow asked a question," the chief said. "One I'd like to hear the answer to myself. Who's responsible for what was done to this poor, unfortunate sheep?"

A few more seconds of silence, then someone spoke up.

"No one was trying to hurt her," a woman said. "They were just shearing her."

"And doing a da—a blasted lousy job," the chief said. "The poor thing's bleeding in half a dozen places."

"More like a dozen that I can see," I said. "And trembling like a leaf—she's probably been traumatized for life."

"So I'm asking again," the chief said. "Who attempted to shear this sheep?"

The reenactors just stood there, huddling a little closer together. Some of their faces began taking on stubborn looks.

"That's it," the chief snapped. "You're all detained for questioning."

A low murmuring rose from the crowd. The chief pulled out his phone, punched a few buttons, then, after a short pause, spoke into it.

"Debbie Ann? I'm down at that encampment behind the Waterston house . . . yes. Can you ask Maisie Shiffley to come down here with her school bus? I've got a whole passel of suspects to transport down to the jail."

A chorus of protests rose from the crowd. MacLeod stepped forward—or, more accurately, was shoved forward by half a dozen of his flock.

"You can't do this," he began.

"I most certainly can." The chief folded his arms and scowled at MacLeod—who wisely held his tongue.

"But what are you arresting us for?" a woman wailed.

"Theft of a farm animal's a class five felony," Vern said, in his most helpful tone. "Punishable by one to ten years in prison. And we're looking at four separate counts—that could really start to add up."

"We didn't steal anything!" another woman protested.

"Oh, they all walked into those pens on their own?" I asked.

"We were going to take them back," someone said. "We were just keeping them safe in the meantime."

"So you say," I muttered.

"Unfortunately, cruelty to animals is only a class one misdemeanor," Vern went on. "Too lenient, if you ask me."

"Grandfather agrees," I said. "He's been trekking down to Richmond regularly, lobbying the state legislature to have that increased."

"You tell him to let me know if there's anything we can do to help." The chief was as big an animal lover as anyone in the county.

"Still, it's up to a year in jail and a fine of up to twenty-five hundred dollars for each count." Vern smiled as if delighted by the prospect of booking the reenactors. And I could tell that his ability to quote from the Code of Virginia was having its usual demoralizing effect on the crowd.

"Ought to put them *under* the jail," the chief muttered.

"And what about the fleece?" I pointed to a ragged-looking pile of bloodstained wool just outside the make-shift pen. "Properly sheared, a Lincoln fleece can sell for several hundred dollars, but I doubt if any of that can be salvaged."

"Petit larceny, I should think," Vern said. "Another class one misdemeanor."

"And if you think a rural jury's going to be lenient on crimes like this—well, you'll see," I shrugged as if washing my hands of their fate.

"You've got that right," Vern said. "Half of the jury would probably have sheep of their own."

Actually there probably weren't more than fifteen or

twenty sheep owners in the county, but the reenactors wouldn't know that.

"It was all his fault," someone shouted.

"We told him it was a stupid idea," someone else called out.

"It's not fair, arresting us for something he did."

"Be a man, Calum!"

"Don't blame us for what he did."

Suddenly none of the reenactors would shut up. The chief raised his hand for silence, but it took quite a while before they noticed and figured out that they'd be better off complying. The chief continued to eye them until they all fell silent.

"Any of you who's willing to tell us what you know about this incident can go along with Deputy Shiffley," he said at last. "And he'll start taking your statements."

Vern nodded, turned on his heel, and began striding back toward the center of the camp. First a few, and a growing number of the reenactors followed him.

"The rest of you can come down to the station with me," the chief added.

More reenactors hurried to follow Vern. Even MacLeod, after a hasty glance at the chief, turned and started to follow.

"If I could have a word with you, Mr. MacLeod." The chief's voice wasn't loud, but it stopped MacLeod in his tracks.

The chief walked over to lean his arms along the top rail of the fence surrounding the tiny pen. At the last minute, remembering what had happened to the last fence, he changed his mind and folded his arms across his chest.

"You need any help getting that poor thing home?" he asked Rose Noire.

"If you and Meg could dismantle one side of that fence, I think we'll be fine," Rose Noire said.

"No problem," I said.

The pen was so badly constructed that the sheep could probably have freed herself if she hadn't been so shell-shocked by her ordeal. Rose Noire had done more than a little accidental demolition, just climbing over it a couple of times. While the chief and I tore it apart, Rose Noire busied herself removing a rope that had been tied around the sheep's neck—a little more tightly than seemed necessary. When she finally hurled it away, the chief picked it up and studied it for a moment. He pulled a brown paper evidence bag out of his pocket, tucked the rope into it, and then turned his eyes back to MacLeod.

"I'm going to take poor Vivian home," Rose Noire said. She draped an arm over the sheep's neck and the two of them set off at a sedate pace, in what I assumed was the direction of Seth's pastures.

"I'll go help the boys with the rest of the stolen livestock," I said.

MacLeod winced slightly.

"And you're on notice." I pointed my finger at him.

He assumed a completely implausible air of wounded innocence.

"If you cause one more bit of trouble, you're out of here," I said. "You and anyone else who aids and abets you."

"Not fair," he said. "You can't throw me out without a second chance! Just because—"

"You're on around your hundredth chance as far as I'm concerned," I said. "One more problem and you're out of here."

He looked mutinous, but he had the sense to shut up.

"Now then, Mr. MacLeod," the chief said. "I, too, have a few issues to discuss with you."

I left them to it.

Back in the center of camp I could see Vern talking to Sally the Sane, who was looking more and more like a potential rival leader. She wasn't raising her voice, but she was clearly angry about something, and kept pointing in the general direction of where the chief and MacLeod were still talking.

"What was Rose Noire so upset about?" Josh asked.

"We didn't see what was happening over there," Jamie explained. "We stayed here to guard the sheep and the heifer."

"Good thinking," I said. "I'll tell you on the way—let's take these poor animals home."

Josh handed me the end of a rope that he'd tied—very loosely, I was pleased to note—around the heifer's neck. Each of the boys was leading a sheep.

Once we were on our way, I texted Dad to see if he could touch base with Rose Noire and arrange to check on the injured sheep. Of course, technically Vivian needed a vet rather than a retired human doctor, but her injuries, though distressing, appeared superficial. Thanks to the boys, Dad had more experience than most doctors at patching up minor wounds. And given how much time he spent helping out at Grandfather's zoo or at the animal shelter run by Clarence Rutledge, the town vet, he could probably cope with a little ovine first aid.

And luckily texting Dad also ensured that we were well away from Camp Birnam before I told the boys what Rose Noire had been so upset about.

"What jerks!" Josh exclaimed. "Maybe we should stop hanging around that place."

"I think it's mostly Mr. MacLeod who's the jerk," Jamie said.

"But they should realize what a jerk he is," Josh said. "And stop . . . um . . ."

"Toadying to him?" I suggested.

"What does that mean?" Josh asked.

"It's a more polite way of saying 'sucking up,'" Jamie said. "Right, Mom?"

I nodded.

"That works, then," Josh said. "Toadying. Yeah. Why are they all still *toadying* to him?"

"I bet not as many will be doing it after this," Jamie suggested.

"Still, we should make sure Grandpa knows who did that to Mr. Early's sheep," Josh said.

"Grandpa will probably want to kick him out when he finds out," Jamie said.

"And if he does, I won't argue with him," I said.

"What if he takes a lot of the other reenactors with him?" Jamie asked. "Won't that upset the History Department?"

"Your dad will calm them down." And it probably wouldn't be that hard, I reflected. Saner heads in the History Department were already showing signs that they regretted recruiting the reenactors. "Look, if you guys want to steer clear of Camp Birnam altogether, that's fine with me."

"To tell you the truth, hanging out there isn't as much fun as we thought it would be," Jamie said.

"We thought it would be a lot like Great-Gran's renaissance faire," Josh said. "But it's not nearly as much fun."

"And not nearly as historically accurate," Jamie added. "And that's saying something."

I had to laugh—my grandmother Cordelia would be the first to admit that the Riverton Renaissance Faire was a deliberate compromise between historical accuracy and catering to the tourist dollar. I was relieved that she'd decided to schedule it in the fall this year, so we'd have a chance to spend some time there after the *Macbeth* run was finished.

"I confess, I wouldn't be upset if you decided to avoid Camp Birnam," I said. "The more I see of those people the less impressed I am. But if you do go there again—or if you see any of the Birnamites around—keep an eye on them. If you even suspect they're up to anything they shouldn't be doing, don't confront them—come and tell me or your dad. Or one of your grandparents."

"We'll sic Grandma on them," Josh suggested. "They're all terrified of her."

I made a mental note to ask someone exactly what had happened when Mother had visited Camp Birnam. I knew she'd found the sanitary conditions so horrible that after calling the county health inspector she'd had to spend the rest of the afternoon in bed with a cold compress over her forehead. But apparently before giving way to her horror she'd managed to give the camp's denizens a sufficiently blunt piece of her mind that they were still running scared.

They weren't quite that scared of me yet. Something I should work on.

We arrived back at our own backyard a lot faster than I'd have managed solo. I turned the heifer into the pen with our llama herd. The boys could lead her back to Mother and Dad's pasture when they got back from leading the sheep home. Or Dad could retrieve her.

The llamas were already clustered around something at the other end of their pen. I strolled over and found Rose Noire and Vivian, the wounded sheep.

"I thought we'd keep her here until she's healed a bit," Rose Noire said when she saw me arrive. "You know how protective Seth is of his flock."

"Good thinking," I said. "Maybe it's just as well the chief will be taking MacLeod down to the station."

I texted Dad to let him know where Vivian was, and headed for the house to get my day back on track.

I waved to the cast members who occupied several of our dozen or so picnic tables. Some were finishing late breakfasts. Some were merely sipping coffee and talking. I glanced at my watch. They'd take off for rehearsal soon, and they'd be gone all day. Michael and the boys would be going with them.

Leaving me stuck in the house by myself.

"Reframe that," I told myself. Rose Noire had been

nagging me about the importance of positive self-talk. She might have a point.

The cast and crew would be at rehearsal all day, leaving me free to enjoy the peace and quiet that was not to be had when they were underfoot.

And thanks to today's drama up at Camp Birnam, the odds were good that the reenactors would steer clear of Dunsinane for a day or so.

Rose Noire was right. This reframing thing already had me feeling more cheerful.

Michael emerged from the barn, spotted me, and dashed over.

"Have you got the creepy dagger?" he asked.

Chapter 5

"Which creepy dagger?" I asked. Michael had tasked me with making what he described as a "seriously creepy dagger" for the Macbeths to use when they murdered King Duncan—in fact, "seriously creepy" was the theme he was pushing for the costumes and sets as well. So far I'd done three prototype daggers, each creepier than the last. Michael loved them all and was having a hard time choosing, but I wasn't yet satisfied. "The one with the big red eye in the hilt, or—"

"Well, any of them for now," he said. "It's only rehearsal, but I want them to get used to working with real iron."

I led the way back to the barn, opened up one of the locked cabinets in which I kept tools and anything else I didn't want to disappear, and gave him his choice of the three daggers. He stood staring at them, and I'd have worried if I hadn't seen the satisfied smile on his face.

"I can't choose," he said. "I'll take all three."

"Just don't let anyone walk off with them. And I don't recommend using the snake one. It's sharp."

"They all look pretty sharp," he said.

"With the eye dagger and the bone dagger it's an optical illusion," I said. "But the snake's still too sharp for rehearsal use."

"Roger," he said. "But I'd rather take it as well—I'm still trying to decide which one we should use. And seeing them might help Roger and Maeve make progress on their sketches." Roger and Maeve were the set and costume designer, and I decided I didn't need to point out to him that they were very talented and would come up with fabulous ideas in time. After all, I'd had more notice than they had about the look he wanted, and I was still trying out multiple ideas

"Set a good example," I said as he packed up the daggers. "Don't let them see you running with them."

"Right." He headed outside, walking rather than running—but at a pace that would have made him a serious competitor in a race-walking event.

I glanced at my phone. Still an hour before rehearsal started, but he probably had half a hundred other things to do before taking off. I made sure my phone's ringer was on, in case he called or texted me to help with any of them. Then I strolled outside and gazed around.

Most of the cast and crew appeared to have finished breakfast. Some were sitting around, talking and tossing leftover bits of bread and fruit on the ground for our copper-brown Welsummer chickens. A few were studying scripts, or talking on their phones.

Tinkerbell, my brother Rob's huge but mild-mannered Irish Wolfhound, was ambling around casting long, soulful glances at the plates of anyone who still had scraps of meat, egg, cheese, or butter, and trying to convince them that she hadn't yet been fed today. Hadn't, in fact, been fed for months and was facing imminent starvation. As usual, she was getting a lot of handouts. Spike, our eight-and-a-half-pound mixed-breed fur ball, strutted around with a peevish expression on his face, occasionally giving a peremptory bark at someone he thought ought to be sharing their breakfast with him. Objectively speaking, he was cuter than Tink, but unfortunately for him, everyone had gotten to know him by now. Thanks to his fondness for biting hands that fed him, he no longer got nearly as many handouts as he had the first few days—and most of those came from people who were worried that he'd resort to chomping on their ankles and would toss tiny bits of food as far away from themselves as possible.

Macbeth was sitting apart from the others—actually, the actor playing Macbeth, but I was having a hard time learning so many names at once, and had fallen into the lazy habit of thinking of most people by the names of their characters. As usual, Macbeth appeared to be brooding angrily, occasionally scowling or grimacing. I'd have been alarmed if I hadn't figured out by now that he was mentally running over his lines, already fully immersed in his character.

The lovebirds—Duncan and the Third Witch—were giggling as they fed each other bits of fruit. The First Witch was sitting nearby in a lawn chair, with her eyes closed and a set of earbuds in her ears. She was swaying, waving her hands to the classical music only she could hear, and occasionally fingering the air during the cello solos.

Nearby were what I'd mentally dubbed the Odd Couple—Gina, the Second Witch, and Fawn, the costume assistant. Actually, I should probably start calling them the Odd Trio—lately they'd been joined at most meals by one of the reenactors, a pale young woman who seemed to have run out of fabric before finishing the bodice of her costume.

Although maybe the Mean Girls was a better name for them. I couldn't prove it—yet—but I doubted they were saying anything nice about anyone in their whispered, giggling conversations. I was keeping my eyes on them.

Right now they were giggling and appeared to be whispering about the only person still actually eating—Celia Rivers, the actor who played Lady Macbeth. And I wasn't sure what she was doing qualified as eating. She had a half-full cup of vanilla yogurt on the table in front of her and half a slice of dry toast. Every so often she'd break off a bit of toast and nibble it or scoop up a tiny dollop of yogurt on her spoon and lift it carefully to her mouth, wincing as she did so. She'd been having gastrointestinal problems since shortly after arriving here. Or maybe she'd been already suffering them when she arrived.

I suspected stress was causing her problems. And not just the stress of tackling one of the biggest roles of her career. Most of the cast were either delighted at the chance to summer in Caerphilly or at least unbothered by it. Celia, not so much. She didn't like being away from her comfortable apartment in Arlington, and all her usual routines and comforts. She seemed indifferent if not actually hostile to the joys of living out in the country. And while she tried to hide it, she obviously hated living in such close proximity to several dozen other people.

"She's high-strung," one of the other actors had said shortly after they'd all arrived.

"You're a nicer person than I am," another actor had said. "I'd have said high maintenance."

And then they'd giggled and moved on to gossip about other cast members, but I took mental notes. I'd need to find a way to keep Celia happy to ensure the success of the play. Happy and healthy.

And so far I wasn't having much success. I'd actually sicced Dad on her—what if her recurring abdominal cramping and pain weren't due to stress after all? What if she actually had a medical problem? One that threatened not only the success of the play but her own well-being?

But getting her to talk about her symptoms was like pulling teeth, and Dad had had only limited success in persuading her to undergo the various diagnostic procedures he wanted to run.

At least she was eating something today, I told myself. And not actually doubled over in pain. And since she reacted so badly when anyone asked about her health, claiming that having everyone fussing over her made her feel worse, I repressed my urge to ask how she was feeling or cajole her into talking to Dad.

Maybe I should take my nephew Kevin's advice and leave her alone. Early on, I'd tried to enlist him to make her feel more at home. He was a scary-smart tech guru, still in his twenties and already managing a major department at Mutant Wizards, the computer company run by my brother, Rob. Between acting jobs, Celia did some sort of computer programming that was in sufficiently high demand that she could almost always pick up a well-paid short-term gig when she needed one. I figured maybe Kevin could communicate with her better than we low-tech peons could. And he was handy, since he was currently living in our basement—ostensibly until he could find a suitable place of his own, but given how tight Caerphilly's real estate market was and how indifferent Kevin was to his surroundings, provided he had enough space and electricity for all his computers, I wasn't expecting him to move out anytime soon. We'd made him responsible for all our household technology and would have considered that more than enough repayment, even if he hadn't been scrupulous about contributing to the household expenses. And he hadn't protested when I'd enlisted him to help with Celia.

"She's lonely," I'd said. "See if you can coax her out of her shell."

But alas! what I thought was a brilliant way to make Celia feel welcome failed completely.

"I actually tried, you know," Kevin told me a few days later. "But if you ask me, she's not the least bit lonely. She just likes being alone."

Maybe he was right. Or maybe being a fellow techie didn't endear him to her. By that time, I'd figured out that she didn't want to talk about what she did between acting jobs. Most likely, not being able to work full time in the theater and earn her living from her acting embarrassed her.

So I should probably stop trying to play hostess, at least with her.

Instead I went into the kitchen, poured myself a tall glass of lemonade, and went out to sit on the back porch and enjoy the morning. It would get hot later, but right now it was pleasant enough. I could close my eyes, lean back, and—

"Meg? Can we talk?"

I opened my eyes. Rose Noire was standing beside the porch, looking up at me.

"Sure," I said. "How's, um . . . Vivian doing?" I'd begun to wonder—did Seth name all his sheep? Or was that Rose Noire's idea?

"She'll be fine," Rose Noire said. "The cuts are minor, and the llamas are calming her down."

Yes, over in the llama pen I could see Vivian's mostly naked form, dwarfed by the two llamas that were standing, one on each side of her, like woolly bodyguards. They were probably humming to her.

"I'm going to give her a proper shearing later—take off all those little stray tufts and streaks that horrible man missed. With luck Seth won't ever know how much she suffered."

"He's going to wonder what happened to her fleece," I pointed out.

"Oh, I'll tell him they sheared her," she said. "And mangled the fleece so badly it was unusable. He just doesn't need to know that she was injured—that would send him over the edge. But that's not what I wanted to talk about."

"I'm all ears." I kept my eyes open, but leaned back against the pillar and sipped.

"And so is everyone else here," she said, glancing around the yard. "Let's find someplace more private."

She dashed away, assuming I'd follow. I suspected, from the direction she was taking, that her idea of "someplace more private" was the herb-drying shed and greenhouse she had built just across the fence, in the pasture Mother and Dad let her use for her organic herb farm.

I caught up with her and we made our way together past

the barn and through the small cluster of tents housing the cast and crew members who either enjoyed camping out or had spoken up too late to snag a place in one of our spare bedrooms. As soon as we passed through the gate onto Mother and Dad's land and she was surrounded by her beloved plants, she felt secure enough to speak up.

"I'm worried about them," Rose Noire whispered. Her eyes darted around as if she were still anxious about eavesdroppers.

"Who?"

"The chickens?"

"Which chickens?"

"All of them."

I glanced around. I assumed the chickens in question were the ones we could see—our black Sumatrans, who lived over here in Rose Noire's herb garden and were even now foraging for bugs among the herbs. On the other side of the fence, the larger and more mild-mannered Welsummers were no doubt doing much the same thing in my vegetable garden and flower beds. But they were out of sight, so I assumed Rose Noire was talking about the Sumatrans.

Now that cockfighting—for which they'd originally been bred—was illegal, Sumatrans were lucky to be such decorative creatures. They were too small to be much use for meat—not that we could ever bring ourselves to eat any of our own chickens. They displayed great cunning at hiding the relatively small number of eggs they laid. And anyone who tried to collect those eggs had better be wearing heavy gauntlets, because when the hens were feeling broody—which seemed to be most of the time with Sumatrans—they defended their nests vigorously. But we won ribbons with them so regularly at the county and state fairs that we had no difficulty selling any surplus chicks to people who wanted them as show animals or just as pets. And I had to admit, they looked beautiful with the sun bringing out a beetle-green sheen on their glossy black feathers as they hunted and pecked up and down the rows, devouring any bugs not repelled by the essential oils that were Rose Noire's only form of pesticide.

They were decorative and feisty. I liked them. I thought Rose Noire did, too.

"Why are you worried about the chickens?" I asked.

"I think there's something sinister going on." Her expression showed that she wasn't joking. Or if she was, her ability to do so with a completely deadpan expression had improved miraculously.

"What is it you think the chickens are up to?" I asked, finally—keeping my voice too low for the Sumatrans to hear.

"I don't think the chickens are up to anything." Her look and tone were both exasperated. "I think someone has sinister designs on them."

"Ah," I said. "What kind of sinister designs? And who do you suspect? The Birnamites?" I suspected all of the reenactors were too squeamish to attempt adding a Sumatran to one of their noxious stews, which was a good thing—but if I was wrong . . .

"I don't know." Rose Noire looked troubled. Her eyes followed Napoleon, the rooster, as he strutted through the rows of lavender plants, looking as if he knew how handsome his long, trailing tail feathers were. "It could be some of them. But there could also be someone from the show involved."

"Involved in what?" I reminded myself that Rose Noire had good instincts, but I hated even the idea that one of the cast or crew could have designs on our fowl. And I wished she'd stop being melodramatic and just tell me what she was worried about.

"I went up to look at that fungus the boys found," she

said. "And while I was out there in the woods, I did a little looking around for herbs."

I nodded. So far this sounded like a typical day in the life of an organic herbalist.

"And I found something." She turned and led the way into her herbal workroom. I paused just inside the door to inhale the rich, almost overwhelming mixture of odors. A lot of lavender in the mix today, which was probably a good thing. I could use its calming influence, and by the look of it, so could Rose Noire.

She went over to a cabinet she kept locked—the cabinet where she kept any herbs she considered dangerous. I still hadn't figured out whether this only meant plants that were technically poisonous, or if she read the plants' auras and confined any she suspected of evil intent.

She unlocked the cabinet, took out something, and stood looking down at it. Then, as if suddenly making up her mind to trust me, she thrust out her hand, holding up the object for me to look at.

It was a piece of old paper—maybe even parchment. It looked as if it had been torn from a larger sheet of paper, or possibly out of a book. Both sides were covered with a mixture of words and pictures. The words were in a cramped Gothic script that made it hard to recognize the letters. It took me a minute or two to puzzle out enough of them to realize that the writing was in Latin.

"I think it's a spell," Rose Noire half whispered. "And not a very nice one."

I nodded absently. I was pretty sure Rose Noire understood even less Latin than I did, but maybe she didn't need to. The pictures were bad enough—creepy little line drawings that were very evocative despite—or perhaps because of—their simple, almost primitive style. An upside-down pentagram. A flask with smoke billowing out of it. A horned devil with a grotesquely leering face.

Rose Noire turned the paper over so I could see the other side. More cramped, almost unreadable words in black letter. More drawings.

Including one in which another horned devil was holding a knife to the throat of a startled rooster.

Chapter 6

I looked up from the scrap of paper and glanced out the window to where Napoleon was strutting among the hens. I felt a sudden surge of fierce protectiveness.

"Not very nice, whatever it is," I said.

The paper was an unhealthy-looking yellowy beige, mottled with age spots, and the writing on it looked as if it had originally been black and then faded over time to a dull matte brown. It looked old. Ancient. But . . .

"May I take a closer look?" I held out my hand.

She nodded and gave me the slip of paper. The second I touched it I knew it wasn't as old as it looked. The paper was too sturdy.

"Let's take a look at something." I led the way over to her worktable. There, among the mortars and pestles, knives, shredders, beakers, retorts, and other more utilitarian tools of the herbal trade that littered its surface, I knew I'd find a relatively powerful handheld magnifying glass. I grabbed that, turned on her task light, and made a closer examination of the shred of paper.

"It looks like a page from a grimoire," she said. "Which is—"

"Which is what magicians call the book they write their spells in," I said. "I know."

"Are you finding any clues to who wrote it?" she asked.

"You mean who printed it," I said. "This isn't handwritten—it's printed. Four-color offset printing. Look at it with the magnifying glass and you can see the tiny little dots that make up the colors. And see where the paper was torn—the antique parchment color is printed on, too—the actual paper is much lighter."

She frowned, and did as I said, taking a much longer look than I had before raising her head and nodding.

"You're right," she said. "But that doesn't make it any less nasty."

"Actually, if you ask me, the fact that someone printed this makes it more nasty rather than less," I said. "Especially since this is obviously high-quality printing—look how authentic the water stains and foxing are. Someone spent good money to produce this nasty thing. If you want my guess, it was torn out of a book. A book someone also spent good money to buy."

"Do you think that will make it easier for us to find who it belongs to?" Rose Noire asked. "Because I found this out in the woods, in a clearing—and given what else I saw out there, I'm worried."

"What else did you see?" I asked.

"The remains of a fire," she said. "And I think someone was cooking over it—brewing something. I saw the marks where they set the cauldron. And if it was something they got from that, I'm worried." She pointed at the scrap of paper.

"So you think someone's casting a spell?"

"Or brewing a potion. And whatever it is—well, I got a very bad feeling from that clearing. Someone is working evil out there in the woods. There's danger approaching."

I nodded absently. I wasn't as worried as Rose Noire about the possibility that someone was trying to brew nasty potions or cast wicked spells out in our woods. But it was bad enough if someone was sneaking around lighting fires in the middle of a drought. And if someone was planning to sacrifice one of our chickens as part of their sick game . . .

"As I said, I bet this came from a book," I said.

"Not a book in your library." She shivered slightly.

"Not that I know of," I said. "And if anything this nasty somehow found its way in, we'll be evicting it posthaste. But if we could find out what book this comes from, and what the cover looks like—"

"Then we can look around to see who has a copy and figure out who's doing this." She looked cheerful for a minute, then her face fell. "But I have no idea how we can even begin to figure out what book it's from."

"Neither do I, but I know who might."

I moved aside several baskets of herbs to clear a space on her worktable and centered the little paper on it. I pulled out my phone and took a couple of pictures, making sure they were good and sharp. Then I turned the paper over and took several more shots of the other side.

"Who are you going to send those to?" Rose Noire asked.

"To Dad," I said. "His Latin should be good enough to translate the text. And to Ms. Ellie Draper, because if you want to know anything about a book, you ask a librarian."

"Yes!" Rose Noire clapped her hands with delight. "I knew you'd know what to do."

"I assume you're okay with bringing them in on this and swearing them to secrecy."

She nodded vigorously, so I opened up my email program and began typing a message to Dad and Ms. Ellie. I normally tried to avoid typing emails with my thumbs, but I didn't want to wait until I got back to my laptop before sending out my pictures. I'd probably get interrupted half a dozen times on my way there.

When I finished drafting my email, including a stern warning to keep this to themselves, and had attached the best of my pictures, I glanced up at Rose Noire.

"I say we include Chief Burke on this," I said.

"Oh." She frowned. "What can he do? It's not as if casting evil spells is illegal."

"No," I said. "But stealing and slaughtering other peoples' livestock is illegal. And so is setting an open fire in the woods when we're in the middle of a drought and the whole county's under a fire ban. And besides, anyone who would even consider sacrificing a chicken—well, if they're up to something, I think it would be a good idea if he knew."

She nodded. I added the chief's email to the cc field and hit SEND.

"Isn't there anything else we can do?" she said.

"I don't know," I said. "Let me think about it. Meanwhile, mind if I keep this?"

"I'll be relieved to have it away from me," she said. "But don't carry it about with you—you don't want that bad energy around. Lock it up somewhere."

"I'll lock it in my office when I get back there—but meanwhile . . ." I paused and took a deep breath. I might regret this. "Why don't you show me where you found it?"

"Perfect!" She started out the door.

"Take your herb-gathering basket," I called out. "Let's at least do what we can not to alert whoever's doing this to the fact that we're onto them."

"Oh, good idea." She came back inside, picked up two large wicker baskets, and handed one to me. "It's not that far."

I dropped the scrap of paper into my basket—maybe Rose Noire was having an undue effect on me, but I was just as happy not to keep touching the thing—and followed.

Rose Noire headed for the woods once we left her herb shed. I noticed she was veering to the right, and we'd have turned left to go to Camp Birnam—this could mean the clearing in which she'd found the scrap of paper and the fire remains wasn't all that near the reenactors. Was that a good thing—a sign, perhaps, that they weren't involved in whatever nastiness was going on? Or just a sign that the perpetrator was smart enough to put some distance between the camp and whatever they were up to?

And once we got inside the woods, Rose Noire steered more to the left. I had to smile. Evidently she'd picked up on the advisability of cunning.

And maybe wherever she was taking me wasn't as far from Camp Birnam as I'd thought.

I noticed she kept looking at her phone. At first I was annoyed—couldn't she focus on our mission? Then I realized she was using a navigation program to find her way. In spite of how shaken she was by her find, she'd had the presence of mind to save her location so she could find her way back to it.

Why hadn't I thought of doing that? When I remembered how much time I'd spent circling around in the woods lately, I wanted to kick myself.

We eventually arrived at a small clearing with the blackened remains of a fire in its center.

"I found the paper over there, under some of the leaves," she whispered, pointing to one side of the clearing.

I examined where the fire had been. And while I was no wood-wise tracker, I thought I could detect signs that there had been more than one fire there. Some of the charred bits of wood seemed to have disintegrated more than others. And there were several sets of indentations in a triangular pattern around the ashes—from the legs of a cauldron?

I pulled out my phone and fiddled with it until I figured out how to capture my location. Then I sent it to Chief Burke, followed it up with a picture of the campfire, and suggested that someone who knew about such things could find some useful information from it.

"Thanks," he texted back. "Vern's on his way to check it out."

I relayed this bit of information to Rose Noire.

"Good." She looked less worried. "But I think we need to do more than just have Vern check it out. We need to stake this place out tonight."

"Bad idea," I said. "If you believe whoever's been lighting this campfire is doing something seriously evil, you should leave catching them to the police."

"Even if the police believed in casting evil spells, doing it isn't against the law," she said. "The police won't do anything about it."

"Casting evil spells may not be against the law," I said. "But right now lighting open fires certainly is, and the police will take that very seriously."

"I hadn't thought of that." She looked surprised.

"For that matter, stealing other people's poultry is pretty illegal, too," I added. "I can try to convince the chief that because of your expert knowledge of magic, you're worried that someone might be planning to steal some of our chickens and sacrifice them out here in the clearing. Remember, the chief's an animal lover—he'd want to stop that. And he's already pretty ticked at the Birnamites, so if he thought they were up to something out here, it's even more likely he'll do something."

"We don't know that it's the Birnamites," Rose Noire pointed out.

"And if they're not out here cooking up evil potions, they won't get arrested for breaking the fire ban," I said. "We just use the chief's suspicion of them to help convince him to stake this place out."

"Good," she said. "I knew you'd find a way to deal with this."

"So you'll put your own stakeout on hold while I enlist the police."

"Of course." She nodded. "Well, I think as long as I'm out here, I'll do a little herb gathering."

"I'm going to head back to the house," I said. "I need to compose a persuasive email to the chief, and besides, I don't want to be gone too long, in case our vandal drops by." I retrieved the scrap of paper and held out the basket I was carrying. "You want this?"

She took the basket and hiked off—heading away from Camp Birnam, unless my sense of direction was totally off.

And I hoped it wasn't. I headed in the general direction of Camp Birnam, although that wasn't my goal.

I wanted to take another look at the dead-man's-fingers.

After a couple of minutes I realized I could hear bagpipes in the distance. Curious how well the sound carried. I headed toward the sound and, after a while, things began to look familiar—the clearing where we'd found the fungus was in a sort of depression, like a gently sloping natural amphitheater, so I just headed downhill till I found it.

The fungus was still there, untouched. And creepy as ever.

The first thing I did was pull out my phone and save my location so I could find my way back if I needed to. Then I took a few pictures of the fungus from across the clearing. And then a few more pictures from six feet away. I finally lay down on my stomach in the leaves and took a whole bunch of close-ups from ground level, trying out different angles.

An idea was forming in my brain.

I sat back, clicked through the pictures, and nodded with satisfaction. If one of the Birnamites came along this afternoon and picked the fungi or kicked them to bits, all was not lost. I'd captured how incredibly creepy they were.

I found I was holding out my right hand, trying to imitate the exact pose the fungal fingers were holding.

What if it wasn't a hand . . . but the hilt of a dagger?

"That's it," I said aloud. "One seriously creepy dagger coming up."

I scrambled to my feet and headed in what I hoped was the fastest way home. I also hoped the vandal wouldn't show up today. I was planning to spend the afternoon out in my forge, creating a dagger with the dead-man's-fingers for a hilt.

I arrived back at the house without too much delay—
just in time to give Michael a kiss before he and the boys
jumped into the Twinmobile and set out for rehearsal. Not
enough time to tell him about my creepy dagger inspiration, but that was okay. Better to wait until I saw how it
turned out.

In fact, I'd wait to start my work until the house had
cleared out. I strolled into the front yard to watch the
daily exodus of the cast and crew. Damien Goodwin's
travel trailer was parked a little way down the road—I saw
the filmmaker testing his door, to make sure it had locked
properly. So far his precautions seemed to have prevented
the vandal from doing any damage to his equipment, and
he was determined to keep it that way. Of course, there
was always the possibility that he was the vandal himself,
in which case he was doing an admirable job of pretending to be worried.

And thank goodness I'd managed to evict Goodwin's
trailer from our driveway and force him to move away from
the house. Only two hundred feet away, unfortunately,
since that was the length of the largest industrial-weight
extension cord we'd found, but it was better than having
him right under our noses, aiming his cameras at our windows. And waking up the whole household whenever he
whiled away his insomniac hours with music or movies—
his taste in music ran to heavy metal and he seemed to
prefer movies full of car crashes and screaming.

He was getting into his truck now, and glancing around
as if waiting for someone to join him. Various actors and
crew members were running back and forth, fetching forgotten items. Some of them were crammed rather tightly
into the available cars and vans, but I noticed no one
asked Goodwin for a ride.

I waited until the last car had disappeared down the
road to town. I went out, unlocked my office, and deposited the little scrap of paper in a drawer that I also kept

locked. Then I sat down at my laptop to compose an email to the chief. I decided on honesty.

"Rose Noire was planning on staking out the clearing where someone's been lighting fires—the one Vern's checking out," it ran. "I think I convinced her that she should avoid interfering with any stakeout you might be planning. Is there any possibility you might consider doing one? Assuming Vern thinks the fires are recent and frequent enough to warrant it, of course. From what she knows about magic, she's convinced someone is planning to steal one of our chickens to sacrifice in some kind of evil ritual. And even if she's wrong on that, someone's definitely lighting fires out there."

I sent the email and added an item in my notebook-that-tells-me-when-to-breathe, a reminder to check back with the chief later in the day if I hadn't heard from him. Actually, I thought there was next to zero chance he wouldn't reply, whether or not he thought an official stakeout was a good idea. But if Rose Noire asked, I could honestly say that not only had I emailed the chief, I had set myself a reminder to bug him.

When I came out of my office, I cast a longing glance across the barn at my workspace. But if I was going to disappear into my smithy for the day, it was more important than ever to check the house first.

I started on the third floor and checked to make sure all the bedrooms were locked, along with the door to the attic. I locked the few bedroom doors that were unlocked or, worse, hanging open. If their occupants had been careless enough to leave their keys in their rooms, they'd have to hunt me down to get in. It would teach them to be more careful.

I did the same on the second floor. On the ground floor, I made sure the door to Kevin's basement lair was locked, along with a few strategic closets and cupboards.

Not much I could do about the main rooms, but I hurried down the long corridor to the library.

Which was only slightly untidy. I resisted the impulse to make it completely tidy, because I was determined to enforce the rule that if the cast and crew wanted to use it as their lounge, they were responsible for picking up after themselves. I only broke down and tidied there if I saw something that would cause damage or draw bugs if left till later, like spilled liquid or uneaten food. My quick glance around showed nothing of the kind. That would probably change when the cast came back from rehearsal. I sighed, turned to go—and started as the library door suddenly flew open.

Chapter 7

"Sorry!" It was Tanya, the young, light-skinned African American woman who was playing Lady Macduff. "I didn't mean to startle you."

"Not a problem," I said. "I just thought everybody had left for rehearsal."

This, of course, was her cue to explain why she hadn't, but she was looking around with exactly the kind of expression I liked to see on visitors to the library.

"I love this room," she said. "I have to confess, I had serious library envy when I first walked in here."

"I'm glad we decided not to tear it down," I said.

"Tear it down?" She looked horrified. "Why would you ever do that?"

"Believe me, it didn't look anything like this when we first bought the house," I said. "A previous owner with serious social aspirations built this wing on to serve as a ballroom. But eventually they lost all their money—or ran out of it doing projects like this. The first time we saw this room, the windows were boarded up, the roof leaked like a sprinkler system, the floor had fallen into the basement, and a whole colony of bats had moved in. The sensible thing would have been to tear it down—but Michael and I both looked into that big wreck of a space and said, in unison, 'This would make a perfect library!' Took a while before we could afford to repair it and fix it up like this, but I'm glad we did."

"So am I." She gazed around and nodded in absent-minded appreciation. I took a moment to appreciate it myself. I suppressed the urge to explain that in the normal course of things Michael and I would still be saving up to refurbish the library, and she'd be looking at a big, empty space with maybe a dozen IKEA bookshelves and a few thrift store tables and chairs. Maybe later, when I was feeling more at leisure, I'd tell the whole story—how, thanks to bad financial management by a crooked former mayor, the Caerphilly Public Library building had fallen into the hostile hands of the town's creditors. And how Randall Shiffley, who was now both the town's mayor and the owner of its leading construction company, had made us an offer we couldn't refuse—that if we'd shelter the books until the forces of reform could either recapture the library building or erect another, he'd renovate the room to our specifications.

Our specifications were ambitious enough that we'd been willing to put up with several years of hosting the town library to achieve them. Sturdy oak bookshelves covered most of the walls, from the polished oak floors to the soaring twenty-foot ceilings. In one corner, a wrought-iron staircase—my handiwork—led up to the balcony, and four library ladders—two upstairs and two down—gave access to all of the books. The shelves were interrupted here and there with small reading alcoves, and the main body of the room contained three sturdy Mission-style oak tables, a lot of comfortable oak desk chairs, and half a dozen comfy armchairs. A large-screen TV stood on a stand in front of the shelves along one wall—the wall that separated the library from Michael's office. A new addition, and probably one that would only last until rehearsals were over. We preferred the library as a TV-free zone, but having one here acted as a magnet for the cast and crew and kept our living room more of a family zone. In the wall opposite the TV screen a pair of French doors led out into the sunroom and the backyard beyond.

And I took a few minutes to appreciate the newest

addition—Mother, who did all our decorating, had hung several large quilts from the oak railings that surrounded the balcony—all of them fairly modern and featuring some of the jewel tones Michael and I loved—a lot of teal, with accents of indigo and lime green. The quilt Michael and the boys had given me for Christmas held pride of place where you could see it as soon as you walked into the library.

"I should stop appreciating and get busy," Tanya said, with a sigh. "Michael sent me back to get that Ian McKellen Shakespeare DVD he's been raving about. He wants to show us something from it later, and he said if it wasn't in the player in the library maybe you'd know where it was."

"Not here," I said, checking the player. "But I bet it's in his office." I led the way out and down a short hallway to the office. I'd planned on checking that door anyway. Now I unlocked it and stopped in. Sure enough, a DVD whose cover featured the handsome, brooding face of a very young Ian McKellen was lying in the middle of the otherwise clear space in the middle of Michael's desk.

"Victory," I said as I handed her the DVD.

"Yay." She turned and began heading back toward the main hallway. I locked the office again and followed.

"Remind him that I could always bring it over next time," I said, falling into step beside her. "No need for the cast to run errands."

"It's okay," she said. "I volunteered. The second we got there, I realized I'd left my lunch behind in the kitchen—I can pick that up while I'm here. And we're starting at the top today, so since my big scene isn't until act four, it made sense for me to come back. And—oh! Someone's here."

Yes, someone was at the far end of the hallway, peering through the doorway from the foyer: a middle-aged, balding man in new-looking blue jeans and a tweed jacket with leather elbow patches. A vaguely familiar face, but not one of the cast and crew, so what was he doing poking around our house?

"May I help you?" I called out.

"Mrs. Waterston! I knocked, but no one answered."

I recognized him now. Professor Cohen, from the History Department.

"Sorry," I said. "I was back in the library. Did you ring the doorbell? We've set it up so it can be heard all over the house. If it's not working, I need to get it fixed."

"Sorry—I didn't think to." He looked abashed for a moment, then brightened. "I just wanted to know if tomorrow would be convenient for my lecture."

"As long as it's in the afternoon," I said. "Theater people are night owls, you know."

"How about three o'clock," he said. "I've already told my graduate seminar to keep that time available—I want them all to attend."

"Three o'clock?" Tanya echoed. "But—" She stopped herself and tried to fade into the woodwork.

"That should work fine." Fine for me, at least. I wondered if Professor Cohen frequently required his students to attend extra sessions late on Friday afternoons and, if so, how dismally low he scored in that survey in which the students got to grade their professors. Not my problem, though. I pulled out my notebook-that-tells-me-when-to-breathe. "And what's the title again?"

"'The Role of the Other in Elizabethan Society,'" the professor proclaimed, in what I recognized as his lecture voice. "I'll be touching on *Macbeth,* of course, along with *The Merchant of Venice, Othello, Twelfth Night*—it's really surprising how much you can find on the subject in Shakespeare."

"I'm sure." I was never all that surprised at a professor's ability to see his own pet subject anywhere he looked. I began moving toward the front door, the better to ease him out of it.

"You still have the setup to show my PowerPoint slides from my laptop on the big-screen television?" the professor asked, anxiously.

"Yes, of course." I scribbled a reminder in my notebook to arrange having someone around who knew how to connect the laptop to our TV, since it had been my experience that few Caerphilly College professors had mastered this feat. "And email me if you think of anything else you need."

I succeeded in ushering Professor Cohen out the door without making it seem quite as if I were giving him the bum's rush. And I locked the door behind him. We couldn't exactly lock up the whole house—cast and crew members might wander back at any time, and we certainly didn't want to lock out the volunteers Mother rounded up to help out with the cooking. But at least if we locked the front door, the history professors and other random passersby might give up and go home.

"You need anything else?" I asked Tanya. "Before I head out to do some work in my forge?"

"Um—so there's a lecture at three o'clock tomorrow," Tanya said. "Should I spread the word? I guess this Professor Cohen is one of those influential faculty members we have to stay on good terms with."

"And three o'clock tomorrow will be right in the middle of rehearsal." I could easily figure out what she wanted to say. "I know. Don't worry about it."

"I mean, theoretically, some of us could come back and attend," she said. "It's not as if the lectures aren't interesting. Your dad's for example—fascinating!"

"Which one did you catch?" I asked. "The one about poisons, or the one about really horrible stuff doctors used to do to people because they thought it would cure them?"

"Both." She laughed. "I suspect Professor Cohen isn't

as interesting as your dad, but still, those of us who aren't in whatever scene is being rehearsed could come. Me, for example, as long as we're not rehearsing my scene. I only have the one, you know."

"A very important scene," I pointed out. As Lady Macduff she did appear in only a single scene—but it was a powerful and pivotal one. I knew Michael had fretted during the auditions about finding an actor strong enough to do it justice, and yet willing to take on a part that was technically only one scene long. And he was very happy with his choice of Tanya.

In fact, he was starting to wonder if he'd made a mistake, casting her as Lady Macduff and Celia as Lady Macbeth. Having Tanya around was the main reason he wasn't panicking about the possibility that Celia's increasingly severe stomach problems would force her to drop out of the production.

"An important scene, yes," Tanya said. "But we could schedule rehearsing it after Professor Cohen's lecture."

"And what if Celia has another attack and Michael needs you to read her lines?" I asked. "Don't worry—we have a plan."

I had pulled out my phone and was calling Mother as I spoke.

"Good morning, dear," Mother said.

"Morning," I said. "Can you call in the ringers for tomorrow at three?"

"Ringers?" Tanya echoed softly.

"Of course, dear," Mother said. "What's on the program?"

"A lecture by Professor Harold Cohen on the role of the other in Elizabethan society."

"The other in Elizabethan society?" Mother repeated. "The other what?"

"Professor Cohen just said 'the other,'" I said. "He mentioned that he'd be touching on *Othello, Twelfth Night,* and

The Merchant of Venice along with *Macbeth,* so I expect by 'the other' he means anyone who isn't white, male, English, and a member in good standing of the Church of England. You might have better luck recruiting if you gloss over the topic and mention that we'll be grilling afterward—hot dogs, hamburgers, portobello mushrooms, and bratwursts. And we're expecting more bushels of Silver Queen corn today."

"That should work nicely. I'll go make a few calls."

I hung up to find Tanya staring at me.

"So that's why we haven't had to sit through any lectures this week," she said. "You've been recruiting ringers."

"Mother's been doing the recruiting," I said. "And it's a win-win. She and Dad have rather a lot of visiting relatives underfoot at the moment—relatives who would probably be underfoot here at our house if we weren't full up with actors."

"Oh dear," she said. "Is displacing the visiting relatives a good thing or a bad thing?"

"A good thing," I said. "The cast and crew are a lot less picky about their meals than the family, and I feel absolutely no responsibility for keeping any of you amused. Actually, I wouldn't worry all that much about amusing the relatives, either, but Mother would, and she'd be nagging me to entertain them. She loves being able to send them over here for dinner and an improving lecture. Of course, the visiting relatives trend a little gray so, if possible, we also recruit some of the college kids who are working as interns out at Grandfather's zoo."

"And your grandfather's okay with that?"

"Either he's okay with it or he sees the wisdom of keeping Mother happy," I said. "And the interns' work is mostly hard physical labor done outdoors in the heat, so they're usually delighted to come here where they can rest in air conditioning for a few hours."

"And if there's a lecture here, I guess Damien Goodwin will have to show up and film it," she said with obvious satisfaction. "Having a guaranteed hour or two without him at rehearsal will make everyone happy. Even the worst hams among us are getting a little disenchanted with having him around all the time."

"Sufficiently disenchanted that we should kick him out?" I asked. "Because just so you know—it wasn't Michael's idea to have him here in the first place. The History Department foisted him on us, and while we want to keep on their good side, if need be I'll figure out some way to dislodge him."

"So far most of the cast are still basking in the joy of being on camera," she said. "But given how obnoxious he is, I can see us getting to a point where he's not just a minor distraction but a full-blown obstacle to getting our work done."

"And when you think we've arrived at that point, or getting close, let me know and I'll see what I can do."

"Will do." She chuckled. "And you got him to stop trying to film your sons—how did you manage that?"

"I told him that Michael and I did not give him permission to photograph the boys," I said.

"That's it?"

"Well, I picked the right moment to tell him," I said. "When he was sitting at a picnic table with my cousin Festus, the infamous crusading attorney, and four other relatives who also happen to be lawyers."

"You have five lawyers in your family?" She seemed surprised—or was it appalled?

"We have a lot more than that," I said. "It's a big family. And both strong verbal skills and a fondness for debating seem to run in it. Anyway, I briefed them on the problem, gave Goodwin my ultimatum, and then for the rest of the meal they had a high old time, speculating on what criminal charges he could face if he ignored my orders, and how much they could get from him in a civil suit. The next time he saw Josh and Jamie he ran so fast in the other direction that he probably achieved a personal best in the hundred-yard dash."

"Awesome," she said. "Next time he annoys me, I'll ask for your help. Anyway, thanks for finding the DVD. I'll head back to rehearsal now."

But when she opened the door, we found another visitor just lifting his hand to knock. Another professor, this one tall and thin and sporting a goatee that made him look almost dapper. He seemed surprised and even a little bit annoyed to have the door whisked away from his knuckles. I composed my face into a more welcoming expression and smiled at the chairman of the History Department.

Chapter 8

"Dean Braxton, so nice to see you." Which wasn't entirely a lie. His timing wasn't optimal, but as deans went, he was rather nice. And the History Department was Drama's ally at the moment. "Come in. May I help you?"

"Bye," Tanya murmured, and slipped past him.

"Michael said we were welcome to watch the rehearsals," Dean Braxton said. "But when I went over to the Drama Department today, Professor Philpotts was there in the main theater. He seemed to be directing his own play. I'm not sure what it was, but it definitely wasn't *Macbeth*."

"*Gorboduc*," I said, ushering him into the living room. "Also known as *The Tragedie of Ferrex and Porrex*."

"Ah." He frowned and perched on the arm of one of the sofas, which I took as a welcome sign that he didn't plan to stay long. "By Sackville and Norton. From a slightly earlier period than Shakespeare, if memory serves."

"Around 1560," I said, nodding. "I've read it, and while I'm admittedly no expert, I suspect it's of more interest to historians than audiences."

"That was my impression," the dean said. "But why is Philpotts directing *any* kind of a play?"

I suppressed my instinctive response, which would be either "because he can" or "because he knows how annoying it is."

"You'd have to ask him," I said instead. "I'm not really up on the English Department's plans and programs."

"Because he doesn't seem to be very good at it, if you ask me."

His tone gave away his irritation, and I couldn't help laughing.

"He really isn't," Braxton went on, with a rueful chuckle. "He's got five or six actors on stage, stiff as boards, bellowing blank verse at each other like . . . like . . . like nothing I've ever seen in a theater. Why is he there, taking up space that Michael could make better use of?"

"The discussions he had with Michael over the different versions of *Macbeth* seem to have stirred up his theatrical ambitions," I said, deciding it was safe to be a little more forthcoming. "And apparently he put in his request to Buildings and Grounds before Michael did."

"Balderdash," he said, though without heat. "He's miffed that Michael won't use his mutant *Macbeth* script, so he's used his clout to play dog in the manger. I know his games."

I didn't argue with him.

"But if Michael's not at the theater—and I gather he's not here, is he?" The dean looked puzzled.

"No," I said. "He's out at the zoo."

"The Caerphilly Zoo?"

"Yes." I sat on the opposite sofa, hoping to set a good example and inspire him to stop perching on the sofa arm, which might not be as sturdy as it looked. He wasn't fat, but he was solidly built and only an inch or so short of Michael's six foot four, so he was no lightweight. "My grandfather owns it, you know," I went on. "And when we found out Dr. Philpotts had booked the Drama Department's space for the whole period Michael needed for his rehearsals, Grandfather offered to let him use the zoo's amphitheater."

"I think I've seen your grandfather's falconry demonstrations there," Dean Braxton said. "It's a nice facility, but isn't rehearsing out of doors a little difficult?"

"Less so in June than it would have been in winter," I said. "Grandfather's rigged up a canvas awning to cover the stage and a few rows of seats. And if they get a really heavy rain, they can come back here and rehearse in the barn or the library."

I made a mental note to check the weather for this afternoon. If it looked like rain, I should probably shoot Michael an email. Tell him I'd be working in the barn, and if he needed to come back, to take the crew to the library so I could have the barn to myself.

"If you really want to catch some of the rehearsal, you're welcome to go out to the zoo," I said, focusing back on the dean. "I can arrange to have a pass waiting for you there."

"Well, if you're sure it's no trouble." He stood, and I was relieved to see that the sofa arm was still intact. "I could head over there now."

"Just ask at the ticket booth," I said.

I ushered him out and then texted my contact at the zoo to arrange the pass. I made sure the front door was locked again, and hurried back through the kitchen and out to the barn.

Considering that half a dozen cast and crew members had taken up residence there, the barn was reasonably tidy. Still, I was glad of the floor-to-ceiling metal grate I'd put up to keep people out of my work space when I wasn't in it. Actors tend to see any objects that happen to be lying around as props, and I didn't want to find out what they'd get up to if they gained access to my forge. They'd start mock fights with the swords and daggers—for that matter, with the andirons and candlesticks. They'd try to lift the anvil and end up dropping it on each other's toes. They'd whack things with the hammers. They'd chase each other around the room with the bellows. At least, those were the sorts of things the boys had been prone to when younger, and I was under no illusion that the actors were mature enough to be immune to the same temptations.

I started by transferring my pictures of the creepy fungus from my phone to my laptop and printing out a couple of the best. And then I pulled out my sketchbook and began planning.

Should I use a blade like a Malay kris, with its multiple wavy curves? Or would that be overkill? The hilt needed to be the focus. Maybe the contrast between the sinuous, twisted lines of the fungus fingers and a plain, straight blade would be more effective.

I grabbed one of each type of blade and set them on my worktable. I could decide later.

This was definitely going to be a mixed-media piece. I'd use clay to sculpt the fingers that made up the hilt. Once I had them perfect, I could make a mold and cast them in something. Metal, if Michael thought it needed to be really durable. Some kind of resin or polymer if we needed to make the weight more manageable.

Decisions for another day. I shoved the materials problem aside, hunted out the container of clay I used for such projects, and began sculpting the creepy fingers.

A few minutes passed by. Or possibly a few hours—I had no idea. I'd achieved a pretty creepy set of fingers that also worked as a hilt, and was grappling with the problem of how to make a graceful transition from hilt to blade when—

Someone cleared their throat behind me.

Maybe if I ignored them, they'd go away.

I focused back on my clay.

"Excuse me." A man's voice, high and peevish. "But there's no one up at the house."

Okay, ignoring wasn't going to work. I drew a damp cloth over my dagger-hilt prototype. Then I turned and saw a small, plump, bespectacled man in a badly fitting gray suit. He'd managed to pause in a spot that left his face in shadow, but the general shape of him looked familiar.

"What do you need?" I asked. It sounded ungracious, but I was pretty sure he was one of Professor Philpotts's minions from the English Department, and they'd long ago worn out their welcome.

"I need to talk to Mr. Waterston," the man said. I recognized him now. Professor Kroger. From the English Department. Someone from any other department would either say "Dr. Waterston" or play it safe with "Professor Waterston" if he didn't know for sure that Michael had a PhD. The English Department still held a grudge against the professors who'd seceded from it to form the Drama Department and frequently descended to such petty tactics.

"Dr. Waterston is out." I glanced around my worktable until I spotted a pen and a pad of paper. I picked them up and walked over to offer them to my visitor. "You're welcome to leave him a message."

"I need to talk to him *now*." He ignored the pen and paper in my outstretched hand. "Where is he?"

"Sorry," I dropped the pen and paper on the ground near his feet and walked back over to my worktable. "He's at rehearsal."

"But I need to talk to him now."

The whiny tone got to me all of a sudden. I lost it, just a little, and grabbed up one of my bigger hammers before whirling back to answer him.

"And I need to get some work done!" I shook the hammer slightly and tried not to giggle when Kroger flinched. "If you have a legitimate need to see Dr. Waterston, try calling or emailing to find out when and where he'll be available, instead of showing up here, intending to interrupt his working day and interrupting mine instead."

Kroger took a step or two back, but alas—he didn't leave.

"I tried to call just now and got no answer," he said.

"He's probably in the middle of rehearsal," I said. "How would you feel if he called you when you were lecturing one of your classes and had a hissy fit when you didn't answer?"

I could tell he didn't like the "hissy fit" part. Too bad. He drew himself up and tried to look dignified.

"I just wanted to give him the courtesy of a warning," he said. "We're going to file a complaint against him with the Grievance Committee."

"Really." I kept my tone blasé and let my eyes wander back to my worktable, feigning complete disinterest in his remarks—although actually I realized it was a good idea to find out what he and Philpotts were up to.

"He deliberately set out to sabotage our production of *Gorboduc*," Kroger exclaimed. "I know very well he did everything he could to keep all the really talented actors from auditioning for us."

"I'm very sorry that you're being forced to work with talentless actors." I thought I deserved an Oscar for being able to say this with a straight face. "But for your information, Michael did the best he could to spread the word about your production and encourage students in the department to try out for it. Unfortunately, you announced your auditions so late in the semester that most of the students who might have been interested had already found paying jobs for the summer."

I could see Kroger was struggling to find a comeback to that. I decided not to mention the fact that even actors who hadn't lined up a job might have been reluctant to audition for a director who had, as far as we knew, never before directed a play. And I definitely shouldn't bring up how universally despised Professor Philpotts was in the Drama Department for his tendency to grade papers much more harshly if he knew the authors were drama majors.

"And now we're having trouble finding anyone to run the lights and sound and such," Kroger said.

"I can understand that," I said. "Students with skills in those areas usually have no trouble finding well-paid summer jobs."

"That doesn't help us, now, does it?" Kroger retorted.

"Have you considered approaching Michael with a civil request that he help you find a seasoned tech crew for your production?" I asked. "Because if your goal is solving that problem, storming in flinging accusations and threatening to file grievances isn't exactly the most effective tactic, is it? Of course, if all you want to do is cause trouble, go ahead. I'm sure Michael will find it very annoying, having to hunt out copies of all the memos he sent out to the Drama Department faculty and student body, giving people a heads-up about your show. All those mentions in the departmental newsletter. All the emails he sent to students and former students, telling them about the opportunity."

Kroger looked troubled, and I smiled blandly at him. Smiling was that much easier, since I knew very well that those memos, newsletter articles, and emails really did exist. Sadly, thanks to the English Department, Michael had become a seasoned veteran of the internecine warfare that constituted academic politics at Caerphilly College.

"Perhaps you could tell him we'd like to discuss the issue," Kroger said finally. Clearly, he found it painful to be so civil.

"Can do," I said.

He turned on his heel and strode out of the barn. I followed him outside and stood watching until he'd climbed into his car and driven off. After all, he was a suspect for the vandalism, like everyone else. I resisted the temptation to consider him one of the main suspects—after all, I might be a little biased against the English Department.

And it occurred to me that he could have had the run of the house while I was working on my dagger.

With a sigh I put down my hammer and went for a tour of inspection.

I started with the livestock. I grabbed a handful of poultry feed, imitated the "chook-chook-chook" call that Rose Noire used to call the flock for meals, and when the Welsummers had arrived, counted to make sure they were all there.

The llamas were all lying down at the far end of their

pen, with Vivian, the naked sheep, nestled among them. Evidently, I'd been working long enough for Rose Noire to make good her plan of shearing Vivian completely. You could still see all the cuts and scratches, but they looked smaller and already somewhat healed.

I couldn't see anything amiss in the tents. Some of them looked as if they'd been ransacked by careless burglars, but that was the way they usually looked.

The black Sumatrans were all present and accounted for, and nothing seemed amiss in Rose Noire's shed.

Inside the house, all the doors that were supposed to be locked still were. And nothing looked any different, until I got to the library. I was pretty sure I'd left the door closed, but now it was hanging open. I walked noiselessly to the door and peered in.

Chapter 9

Damien Goodwin stood on one of the tall library ladders. He appeared to be putting something on a high shelf. Something other than the books that belonged there.

"Looking for something?" I asked.

He started, but only slightly.

"A new angle." He climbed two rungs higher, turned until his back was to the ladder, made sure he was safely braced, then reached around behind him and grabbed the object he'd placed on the shelf. A camera, of course. He put his eye to the viewfinder and panned the camera around the room.

"For tomorrow's lecture?" I asked.

He nodded absently, not taking his eye from the camera.

"Not here," he said finally. "Too much backlight."

He climbed down the ladder, moved it a few feet to his right, climbed up again, and repeated the process.

"Maybe," he muttered. "What does this Professor Cohen look like, anyway?"

"Professorial," I said. "You've filmed him before. Last Friday. 'Class Consciousness Examined through the Lens of Shakespeare's Comedies.'"

"Oh, him." He grimaced. "Yeah, I'll definitely need a new angle. I don't suppose you could talk some of these guys into giving their talks out at Camp Birnam, could you?"

"I could ask," I said. "Probably not Professor Cohen, though. He'd be lost without his PowerPoint presentation."

"Bummer. Maybe he could do it in costume?"

"Dream on."

He nodded. Then he looked around and frowned.

"The room's not set up yet for tonight's sneak preview," he said.

"Sneak preview of what?" If I sounded suspicious—I was.

"Some of the footage I've taken over the past ten days. I cleared it with Michael," he said quickly, anticipating my next question. "So we need to have the room set up auditorium style." He looked at me with a peevish expression, as if he thought I should have taken care of it already.

"We can worry about that after dinner," I said. "If everyone pitches in it will only take a few minutes."

He didn't look happy with that answer but he seemed to be gradually learning the futility of arguing with me. He shrugged.

"See you later," he said, and left the room.

I planned to check with Michael to make sure he really had given the okay for Goodwin to show some of his footage. Not that I could think of any reason why it was a bad idea. So why was my initial reaction to it so negative?

Because it would mean watching Damien Goodwin show off, and a little of him went a long way.

Before I left, I did a quick inspection of the library— after all, Goodwin was a suspect for the vandalism. But I found no signs that the perpetrator had struck again.

Maybe he'd been planning something and I'd arrived in time to avert it. Or maybe I was suspecting him unjustly. After all, he did have a lot to keep him busy, what with trying to document the play, the professors, and Camp Birnam. And the fact that I disliked him didn't make him that much more likely a suspect.

But no—I wasn't suspecting him unjustly. I remembered when we'd found Celia's script spattered with blood-red paint. He'd filmed her reaction—all our reactions—with a fierce, predatory look on his face. He was always on the lookout for drama. If we weren't providing enough of it, I could easily see him trying to create some.

In fact, come to think of it, he'd been around to film the discovery of just about everything the vandal had done. He'd been right on my heels when I heard the uproar in the library and ran in to find women's undergarments festooning all the upper shelves. I'd shoved him out as soon as I saw what was happening, but I bet he'd managed to get some good shots. I didn't worry as much about chasing him out when we found the vandal had knocked several hundred books off the library shelves. He'd actually been the one to discover the bloody footprints on the front walk.

The jury was still out on whether vandal had put the copperhead in the half bath off the kitchen—it's hard enough to keep wildlife out of an old house, even if you don't have several dozen people going in and out and leaving doors and windows open half the time. But Goodwin had certainly enjoyed filming the action when Dad and Michael trapped the snake and carried it off to the zoo.

And the birthday cake. Rose Noire had made a large chocolate cake to celebrate two birthdays—Russ, the actor playing Banquo, and one of the spear carriers. We were picnicking outdoors that evening, and a couple of people slipped into the kitchen to fetch the cake. Their shrieks had brought us running, and we found them staring at the remains of the cake. Someone had split it in two with a meat cleaver, and then poured a whole jar of strawberry jelly over the remains, so it looked as if the cake had bled all over the kitchen table. Goodwin had been all over that.

Was it a coincidence that the vandal's feats had been more visually interesting than they were destructive?

And speaking of vandals . . . had I locked up my work space after Professor Kroger interrupted me?

I headed back out to the barn. And no, I hadn't locked up.

I pulled out my phone and checked the time. I could

probably do a little work on my dagger before Michael and the cast got home. I still had to solve the problem of how to finish off the hilt and attach the blade—everything I'd tried before looked awkward and just stuck together. But I've always been a big believer in turning your subconscious loose on knotty problems. Evidently while I'd been jousting with Professor Kroger, inspecting the house, and chatting with Goodwin, my subconscious had come up with what just might be a good idea. I decided to work on it while I had it clear in my head.

I'd just finished provisionally attaching my creepy fungus finger hilt to a long, menacing dagger blade and was inspecting the join when—

"Oh, my God! That's awesome!"

I started so violently that I dropped the dagger and nicked my left forefinger in the process.

Michael controlled his excitement long enough to run for the first-aid kit I kept nearby. The cut wasn't that bad, so I told him I'd do my own patching up. While I swabbed my wound with an alcohol wipe and wrapped a bandage around it, he examined the fungus dagger and exclaimed over it.

"This is undoubtedly the best one yet!" he said. "In fact, I think it just might be the ultimate creepy dagger. Where's Roger—I need for him to see it."

"Be careful with it," I called after him as he ran out, dagger in hand, in search of Roger, the set designer. I knew he and Roger had both been getting a little frustrated—Roger because Michael hadn't yet approved any of his rough sketches for the set, and Michael because Roger didn't seem to be catching on to the whole "seriously creepy" theme.

I began cleaning up my work area—which took a little longer than usual, thanks to the bandage. About the time I finished, Michael and Roger came running back in, with Josh, Jamie, and Tanya trailing along behind.

"This is fabulous!" Roger exclaimed. "Michael says you have some more pictures of this fungus?"

I pulled out my phone, opened up the photo app, and handed it to Roger.

"This is it!" he exclaimed. "This is what I need for the set design! Can you show me where this is? I want to do some sketches from life."

"I should stay here at the house to keep watch on the dinner crew," I said. "But I've got the coordinates—you could use your phone's GPS program to guide you there."

"Um . . ." Roger blinked and looked anxious. "Could you show me how to do that?"

I'd forgotten. Roger wasn't tech-savvy.

"It's okay, Mom," Josh said. "We can take him out there and still be back in time for dinner."

"We can't just leave him out there," Jamie protested. "He'll get lost."

I glanced at Roger, who didn't seem particularly insulted by Jamie's comment.

"Jamie's right," I said. "Try to teach him the way there, but if he's not sure he can get back on his own, stay with him. You still have an hour before dinnertime and if you're late I'll make sure we don't run out of any of your favorites."

The trio set off at a breakneck pace.

Michael was still playing with the creepy fungus dagger, trying out different grips and angles. Tanya was watching with more than casual interest. Not surprising. She'd almost certainly get a chance to wield it in rehearsal. Maybe in some performances, if Celia's health continued dodgy.

Was it disloyal to hope she got the chance? When Michael had first cast Celia, we'd both thought her perfect for Lady Macbeth. She was tall—roughly my height, five ten—with the trim, athletic body and the angular, high-cheekboned face of a model. She had a stately presence that made her plausible as a noblewoman and then a queen—but she also had the physical and emotional force to make her believable as a killer.

Tanya was very different. She was a little shorter, and much slighter—still athletic, but with more of a graceful, willowy presence. Her round-cheeked face was pleasant and friendly rather than beautiful. Looking at her, I'd thought her destined to progress from ingenue roles through young mothers to sensible housewives. But now that I'd seen her perform, even if only in rehearsal, I knew better. She became a different person when she stepped into the role of Lady Macbeth—sinister, powerful, and ambitious. It was impressive. And quite possibly better than anything Celia would ever come up with.

"It's perfect." Michael made a quick stabbing motion with the dagger, interrupting my thoughts.

"Careful," I said. "It's a little too perfect at the moment. I tried several blades on it, and the one that seemed just right was one I'd made for the bloodthirsty market."

"The what?" Tanya looked up at me, startled.

"Most of the weapons I make are for show," I said. "People buy them to wear with a costume or hang on the wall for decoration."

"Or wave around onstage," Michael added.

"Right," I said. "So I do my best to make it so the blade looks sharp but isn't really going to do major damage if you whack your finger with it. But some people want a knife that looks historic and also actually cuts. I sell a lot of knives to craftspeople like leather workers or carpenters who want to look authentic when they're doing demonstrations at renaissance faires or Civil War reenactments. Or reenactors who want to cut up their meat and vegetables with historically accurate utensils."

"So we have to be really careful with this one," Tanya said.

"I can dull it down before tomorrow's rehearsal," I said. "It would probably be safer to leave it here till then. Plus the hilt's only made of clay. It could break if you're too rough with it."

"I'll just take it up to the house to show everyone at dinner," Michael said. "And then we can lock it up for the night."

"Don't blame me when people start slicing off each other's fingers," I said.

They dashed out, and I wasn't even sure they heard me.

I finished tidying my workspace and locked up before following.

Up at the house, Rose Noire and a large flock of visiting relatives were preparing dinner. Since it was a Thursday night, the meal would be relatively simple by Hollingsworth family standards. Country ham for the carnivores. Enough macaroni and cheese for everyone. Big vats of tossed salad. Fresh baked rolls. And the usual variety of pies, cakes, and cookies for dessert.

Outside in the yard, Michael was showing off the creepy fungus dagger to the cast and crew—and having a hard time keeping it in his own hands. I wondered if I should fetch my first-aid kit from the barn, just to be prepared. Everyone seemed enchanted by the dagger.

Almost everyone. Celia was watching from afar. She didn't look enchanted. She looked . . . wistful. As if she didn't want to get too excited about a shiny new toy that she might not be around much longer to play with.

And oh, lord—Rose Noire was scurrying up to her holding a steaming mug of some liquid. While her intentions were only the best, Rose Noire's herbal teas were legendary for their horrible tastes. I went over to Celia's table, trying to look nonchalant.

"And what are you giving Celia?" I asked Rose Noire. "Are you sure it's something Dad approves of?"

"Only ginger tea," Rose Noire said. "From fresh ginger root. I wanted to add several other things that could be helpful, but your dad vetoed them. He just wants her to try the straight ginger."

"That's okay then." I turned to Celia. "Give it a try. Really helped my morning sickness when I was pregnant with Josh and Jamie."

"I'm not pregnant!" Celia's tone was not just defensive but downright angry.

"I wasn't suggesting you were," I said. "Just remembering how it helped me when nothing else worked. It's good for any kind of stomach problems. We give it to the boys when they're recovering from minor stomach bugs, and it's not bad for hangovers, either."

Celia grimaced, but she picked up the cup and sipped.

Rose Noire scurried away to see about something in the kitchen, stranding me there with Celia. I racked my brain for something to say. She seemed perfectly content to sip her ginger tea and stare into space. Why couldn't I follow her example?

Maybe because I was the hostess.

"How did rehearsal go?" I asked. It was the most innocuous thing I could think of.

"Fine." She glanced at me and frowned slightly. "I managed to do my part. Didn't need for anyone to fill in for me, if that's what you were asking."

"I was just hoping you all had a good rehearsal," I said. "Michael's always more fun to have around when the show's going well."

She smiled slightly at that and lapsed back into silence, gazing across the backyard at the group gathered around Michael and the dagger.

I pretended to do the same while studying her out of the corner of my eye. What if she was pregnant? Women often suffered the most from morning sickness during the first trimester. As long as she could get past that, pregnancy needn't keep her from playing Lady Macbeth.

Michael might like the macabre note of having a pregnant murderess.

But along with the nausea she was also having cramping and abdominal pains, which would not bode well for any pregnancy. I made a mental note to ask Dad if he'd considered this possibility.

And I could see why he was so worried. She'd visibly lost weight in the last two weeks. There were dark smudges beneath her eyes, and a certain curiously vulnerable translucence to her eyelids.

And it was all very well to say she wasn't my problem and she was a grown-up who could take care of herself. She was under our roof, and from what I'd seen, she wasn't doing such a great job of taking care of herself.

"Look," I said. "Tonight's menu doesn't seem like a good option for an unsettled stomach. Is there anything you'd rather have instead? A little clear soup? Crackers? Rice?"

"I don't want to cause any extra work," she said.

"But you also don't want to eat something that's going to upset your stomach, do you?" I asked. "Because that would cause even more extra work, and problems for the play to boot. Besides, just between you and me—that passel of visiting relatives we've got out in the kitchen to do the work includes Aunt Penelope, who should be kept busy so she doesn't get up to something extreme like rearranging the entire pantry the way she'd have done it. She actually started doing that the last time we didn't manage to find enough for her to do. Let's go into the kitchen, and I'll put her in charge of fixing whatever your heart desires. If you can keep her occupied, it would actually be doing me a favor."

She studied me for a few moments, then nodded.

"If you're sure," she said.

"Follow me."

Inside the kitchen, a dozen aunts and cousins were busily slicing ham, chopping up vegetables, and hauling baking sheets of rolls and biscuits in and out of the oven, under Aunt Penelope's direction. Normally Mother would have been bossing the crew, but perhaps she decided with Aunt Penelope in charge, she could afford to take a night off. For that matter, with Aunt Penelope in charge, I'd be happier if I could stay out of the kitchen myself, so after introducing her to Celia I grabbed a handful of carrot and apple slices for the llamas and went back outside.

Michael joined me while I was feeding treats to the llamas. The llamas and Vivian.

"So why is there a naked sheep in with the llamas?" he asked as he leaned against the top rail of the fence. "Or do I even want to know?"

"Camp Birnam strikes again." I filled him in on the Birnamites' latest iniquities. Although I suspected they were mostly Calum MacLeod's iniquities. When I was finished, Michael reached over and patted Vivian's head.

"Poor thing," he said as he fed her a bit of carrot. "I suppose I should talk to Dean Braxton. Try to convince him that maybe the authentic medieval Scottish military camp has outlived its usefulness."

"Did it ever have any usefulness?" I asked. "Actually, I think it would be pretty harmless if MacLeod wasn't in charge. Can you have him declared persona non grata? There's an older woman there, Sally something, who would probably take over if he left. Not sure if she's his arch rival or his second-in-command or what, but she's levelheaded."

"I'll suggest as much," he said.

"Speaking of people we wouldn't mind getting rid of," I went on, "did you really give Goodwin the okay to show some of his footage tonight?"

"Yes—why?" He turned and looked worried. "Do you think it's a bad idea?"

"I have no objection," I said. "I just wanted to make sure he really did clear it with you. I can see him telling me you approved it, and telling you I did."

"So can I." He laughed ruefully. "I couldn't see any harm in it. I can find a way to veto it if you think it's a bad idea. Could be useful, though."

"Yes, which is why I'm okay with letting him go ahead," I said. "I'm curious to see what he's really up to."

"You think he's up to something other than making some kind of documentary?" Michael looked slightly alarmed.

"No, but what kind of documentary is he making?" I asked. "I mean, depending on how he chooses to slant it, you could all look like geniuses or idiots."

"Yeah. Exactly." He sighed. "That's why I think it could be useful to see what he's up to. Not so much for me—I think I'm savvy enough to avoid doing anything really ridiculous on camera."

"Not to mention the fact that if he really ticks you off, he could find himself out on his ear," I said.

"Out on his ear and on the wrong side of your mother's entire family." Michael chuckled. "I wouldn't risk it. But it might be a good thing for the rest of the crew to see what he's up to. Figure out that the camera is not always their friend. Because some of them are clueless about that."

"Ouch," I said.

"Yeah. Tonight could be interesting."

Just then the dinner bell rang, and we went to join the line for the buffet. I was relieved to see that the boys had returned in time to take their usual places at the very head of the line.

When the meal was over, I put out a call for volunteers to set up chairs in the library. I made a token appearance to help with the cleanup in the kitchen before heading down to see what Goodwin was up to.

Chapter 10

Evidently Goodwin had done a reasonably good job of getting out the word about his event. Several history professors showed up, along with a handful of their grad students. A large contingent of reenactors had walked down from Camp Birnam, although I suspected some of them were less interested in seeing Goodwin's video than in grabbing the opportunity to use indoor plumbing for a change. Most of our visiting relatives were present, along with every single one of the *Macbeth* cast and crew.

Dad showed up bearing the official Caerphilly popcorn machine—it was technically the property of the New Life Baptist Church, but when they weren't using it they willingly lent it out to anyone who was holding a festival, picnic, or party. Josh and Jamie took charge of feeding batches of kernels into it and handing around the bowls of popped corn. Rose Noire brewed up vats of iced tea, including—as usual—rather more gallons of healthy caffeine-free herbal tea than were really needed. But—again, as usual—the crowd would almost certainly turn to the herbal brews when the regular kind ran low, so nothing would go to waste.

"I gather Mother's not coming?" I asked when I could get Dad's attention.

"Ladies Interfaith Council meeting," he said. "She said to tell you she's sorry she can't come over to help out."

"To tell the truth, I'm relieved," I said. "Call me a worrywart, but from what I've seen of Goodwin, this evening's entertainment might not be to her taste."

"Oh, I'm sure everything will be fine." Dad was frowning slightly, and his voice sounded a little over-hearty, as if he, too, had his suspicions.

"But just in case it isn't, at least Mother's not here to be upset. Anything else we can deal with."

"True." His face lightened and he hurried off to greet a history professor who shared his fascination with medieval medicine.

Most of the attendees had gathered as close as possible to the TV screen, which meant that the crowd was thickest at the end of the library next to Michael's office. I took a place at the opposite end of the room, just to the left of the French doors that led to the sunroom—it seemed like a good vantage point for keeping an eye on everybody. I was curious to see Goodwin's footage, but even more curious to find out how everyone reacted to whatever they were about to see. Although I had to admit, my observation post was also the next best thing to avoiding Goodwin's presence entirely, since he was up front near the TV, fussing with the computer from which he'd be showing his video.

Michael came over to join me and we leaned against the bookshelves in companionable silence.

MacLeod was there—did that mean the chief had let him go without charging him? Or was he out on bail? I'd find out later. But clearly things were not as they had been at Camp Birnam. The reenactors were clustered around Sally the Sane, who seemed to be riding herd on the rowdier ones. MacLeod kept to himself, merely nodding to people as he passed them. I didn't notice many of them nodding back. He took a post to the right of the French doors and tried to look like a man in search of solitude instead of a shunned outcast.

A little after seven, Goodwin stood up in front of the TV screen and clapped his hands for the crowd to quiet down. He was dressed in what I suspected was his version of formal wear: reasonably clean, rip-free black jeans, a black UCLA Film School hoodie, and black cowboy boots made, as he was fond of boasting, out of caiman belly.

"Thank you all for coming," he said when he could make himself heard. "I know you've all been dying for me to tell you more about what I've been doing."

"I think it's more that he's dying to tell us," I murmured, softly enough that only Michael could hear.

Michael suppressed a chuckle.

"I think it's time to share my concept for the project," Goodwin went on.

"I'm delighted to know he has one," Michael said, out of the side of his mouth.

"Are you ready?" Goodwin exclaimed.

If he was hoping to generate enthusiasm, he was doomed to disappointment. The only sound from the crowd was the crunching of popcorn.

"Just get on with it," one of the actors called out.

"The concept—is you!" Goodwin beamed at us as if expecting us to cheer and applaud at this announcement.

The crunching continued.

"All of you!" He looked anxious at the lack of response. "Instead of coming in with a bunch of preconceived notions, I decided to let you, my subjects, decide the course of the project."

"In other words," Michael muttered. "He hasn't a clue what he's doing."

I nodded.

"So with that as my concept," Goodwin went on. "Well, I'll let you see for yourself. Can someone hit the lights?"

Josh and Jamie obliged, and since it was still light outside Michael drew the curtains over the French doors. Goodwin went over to the laptop he'd hooked up to the TV and fiddled with it briefly. A title graphic appeared on screen, announcing "Another Dam Good Production!" Although a close look revealed a tiny "ien" after the "Dam," and "win!" after Good.

Goodwin stepped back until he was leaning against the bookshelves. The TV screen illuminated his face slightly as he stared with fierce concentration at his audience.

I focused back on the TV.

Goodwin's footage opened with a series of morning vignettes. Reenactors emerged from their tents, some already in costume, most in the twenty-first-century garments they'd slept in—t-shirts, cut-off jeans, athletic shorts, and the like. A few retreated when they realized they were being filmed or held up their hands to shield their faces. Most just glowered and shambled off-screen in search of the camp's badly brewed coffee. Then came a sequence shot in much lower light, although you could still recognize MacLeod emerging from a tent, looking around furtively, adjusting his pants, and scurrying off.

"Oops! Wrong tent!" someone called out, and there was derisive laughter from most of the reenactors. A woman reenactor stood up, shoved through the chairs around her, and ran out the French doors into the sunroom— and presumably from there into the yard. A man rose and followed.

"Someone should go after her," a reenactor said.

"And him," another added.

"Ssh," several people hissed from various parts of the audience.

Four more reenactors departed, including Sally the Sane.

MacLeod pressed back against the bookshelves behind him as if trying to melt into them.

On-screen, the scene had changed to morning in our backyard. Rose Noire was scattering feed for an eager swarm of Welsummers. I was proud of how well they looked, so plump and lively, with such a healthy sheen on their chestnut and brown feathers. Actors and crew members crawled out of their tents. A few clowned for the camera. Most ignored it. Michael appeared, setting out boxes of doughnuts on one of the picnic tables, attracting an eager swarm of hungry humans. The resemblance between the humans and the Welsummers was amusing, but also pretty obvious, after the tenth time Goodwin cut back and forth between them.

Back to Camp Birnam, where the reenactors were building their huts. Goodwin must have spent a whole day out there, filming the slow, laborious construction process. He'd added a soundtrack, a lush orchestral piece that sounded both heroic and vaguely familiar. Of course. The music was from *Witness*—the scene where the Amish community so competently erected a barn in a single day.

The reenactors would have flunked Amish barn-building. But they finally finished a hut, and began a wild victory dance around it.

The hut promptly collapsed.

A quick montage followed, of huts falling down, with or without occupants who had to be rescued from the rubble.

And Goodwin had been there when Mother inspected the camp. He got a lovely close-up of her, standing in the middle of the camp, sweeping her gaze around, and uttering words that would sound completely harmless coming from anyone else.

"This is *not* acceptable."

Next Goodwin showed Mother in action, and I had to admit that the ominous shark music from *Jaws* was an amusing touch. Mother discovering that the reenactors' open campfire had started a fire. Mother declaring that the huts were unsafe for human habitation—and the hut in question collapsing in the middle of MacLeod's claim that he'd let his own mother sleep in it. Mother laying down the law that no, an open trench was not a suitable form of sanitation, and if they weren't willing to acquire and use porta-potties, they could pack up and leave this instant.

By this time the reenactors were growing a little mutinous and resentful, so they were probably just as happy to see Goodwin turn his attention from them to the *Macbeth* cast and crew.

I braced myself.

He started off with a montage of small, embarrassing moments. An actor flubbing a line. Another actor tripping and falling flat on his face. Did the man sit around waiting for people to yawn, fart, or scratch themselves? I winced when I saw Macbeth proclaiming "Is this a dagger I see before me / the handle toward my hand?" I knew what happened next—the dagger's blade came loose and plummeted to the ground, almost skewering the actor's foot. Which would not have happened if the prop master hadn't taken an unfinished dagger from the forge while my back was turned.

More actors mangling lines and taking pratfalls, going on far too long. Still, I had to hand it to him—he'd caught an embarrassing moment for nearly every member of the cast or crew. That took dedication.

Everyone breathed easier when the scene shifted to the finding of the dead-man's-fingers. I focused even more intently, ready to pounce if he had any forbidden footage of the boys. But while I occasionally spotted a bit of shin or the tip of a longbow, he'd done a good job of either not filming them or editing them out.

He mostly focused on Dad. At first, I thought Goodwin would let him off lightly—the footage showed Dad discoursing about *Xylaria polymorpha* with great eloquence and charm. Then the angle shifted, and we all burst out laughing, because it looked as if Dad were about to pick his nose with the eerie little fungus finger. Dad found this as funny as the rest of us, so if Goodwin was trying to upset him, he'd failed utterly.

Then the professors got their turn in the spotlight. Professor Cohen had a nervous habit of stepping back and forth the whole time he talked. On film it was ten times more distracting, especially when Goodwin speeded up the tempo and added a jazz piano rendition of "The Charleston," making it look as if the professor were dancing with the jerky movements of a silent movie.

Apart from a few nervous titters, nobody laughed. I felt a brief surge of pride and fondness for the audience.

I glanced over to where the delegation from the History Department was sitting. Professor Cohen didn't look happy. And neither did Dean Braxton. Maybe even a good thing, that—Goodwin just might have made it that much easier for us to get rid of him.

Especially since Goodwin followed his cruel depiction of Professor Cohen with a short clip of Dean Braxton. Nothing to laugh at there—the dean was a polished, eloquent lecturer.

But by now I knew to expect the sudden, petty sting. The footage started with a close shot of the Dean lecturing here in the library. Then the camera slowly pulled back, and another sound gradually drowned out his voice—the sound of snoring.

I remembered the incident. The man was an elderly visiting cousin, who'd nodded off briefly and snored almost inaudibly. Goodwin had jacked up the volume on the snoring—in fact, he'd probably dubbed in someone else's loud snores—the sounds were ever so slightly out of sync with the gentle flapping of the cousin's lips.

The audience didn't react much. Dean Braxton had steepled his fingers and was tapping his chin with his two forefingers, a thoughtful look on his face.

I focused back on the screen in time to see the stout but dapper form of Professor Philpotts appear, standing on our front step. He was dressed in a three-piece suit, and thanks to his bushy mustache, round face, and wire-rimmed glasses he looked alarmingly like Theodore Roosevelt. He knocked on the door—what did all these people have against doorbells? Evidently someone had left the door open, and it swung in when he knocked. Philpotts stood frozen for a few long moments. Then he looked around—left, right, over his shoulder. Evidently Goodwin was well hidden—in fact, I was beginning to suspect that he'd planted hidden cameras in strategic places around the house. Philpotts pushed the door open and cautiously stepped inside. We saw the door slowly pulled closed behind him, and then . . . just a long static shot of the closed door. I probably wasn't the only person who was wondering what Philpotts was up to inside. Was he the vandal?

Goodwin could tell us the date he'd taken that shot. Even if he didn't remember, all his video was in digital format, and the date would be right on the files. It would be interesting to learn if Philpotts's unsupervised visit corresponded with any acts of vandalism. Interesting to me, and also to Chief Burke. Even if Philpotts wasn't the vandal, he'd become a bloody nuisance. Maybe having to answer questions from the chief about his whereabouts during the vandalism incidents would make him less likely to show up here.

I'd worry about that later. On-screen, another history professor was lecturing. Her delivery wasn't exactly Oscar-worthy, but it was quite competent. Why was Goodwin showing it?

Aha. He wasn't focusing on the professor. After a short close-up, the camera switched to a shot of her audience, listening with reasonably pleased or intent expressions. And then the French doors at the back of the shot opened and a face appeared. It was Russ, the actor who played Banquo. The camera zoomed in to show him standing frozen briefly, with a look of alarm and dismay on his face. Then he ducked back into the sunroom, closing the door behind him.

What was that all about? I glanced up to see Michael's reaction, but his puzzled expression mirrored mine.

The screen now showed our backyard, where the actors

playing Macbeth and Macduff were working under Michael's direction on their final sword fight. Suddenly the camera zoomed in to focus on something in the background: Banquo ducking furtively into the sunroom and from there into the library. The camera stayed focused on the sunroom for what felt like an eternity, with just the sounds of wooden swords clacking in the background, and then Banquo emerged from the library, and glanced right and left before half-tiptoeing across the sunroom to the outside door. There, he repeated the furtive glancing in both directions before slipping out and skulking off into the distance.

"What's he up to, anyway?" Michael murmured.

"The vandal hit in the library," I murmured back. "Several times."

Michael frowned and studied Banquo.

Banquo's fellow actors were teasing him.

"Is that where you hid the body?"

"Forget Shakespeare, dude; you'd be perfect as Snidely Whiplash."

On-screen, Goodwin was showing a montage—several more shots of Banquo furtively entering or emerging from the library, from both the outside and inside doors, ending up with a scene inside the library, with Banquo surprised halfway up one of the library ladders, a guilty expression on his face.

I made a mental note to tell the chief about this, too.

Chapter 11

I glanced over at Banquo, who didn't seem amused by his castmate's teasing. In fact, he breathed a visible sigh of relief when the show moved on.

To the three witches, stirring their cauldron and reciting the familiar "Double, double toil and trouble; Fire burn, and cauldron bubble." An early rehearsal, obviously—before Michael had introduced the idea of having them sing their lines. The video moved to Michael and the witches gathered around the piano arguing over how the tune should go.

"No, no," Michael was saying. "'When shall we three meet again' is G-A-B-G-A-F-F. Go up on the next line. 'In thunder, lightning or in rain' is G-G-A-B-G-A-F-C. Up to the C, and hold it." He pointed to the ceiling with his left hand while thumping out the note sequence with his right, and the witches followed along.

Then a rehearsal scene where they sang their lines. The first witch's powerful voice danced between the second witch's rich contralto and the third witch's high soprano, with its eerie combination of bell-like tone and throbbing vibrato. And they wore ragged gray cloaks, the better to rehearse their blocking, which was so complicated it almost amounted to choreography. The whole effect was so damned spooky that a chill ran down my spine, and a smattering of applause broke out in the audience.

Then another scene, in lower light, so the picture quality wasn't nearly as good. Three cloaked figures standing around a cauldron, but not the witches from the play.

Possibly the second witch—I heard what sounded like her low, throaty chuckle. But neither of the others could be the first witch, who at six feet had two inches on me, and was so rail thin that she looked even taller. Nor were any petite enough to be the third witch. And the cloaks weren't the ragged, slightly luminous gray cloaks the witches wore—just ordinary cloaks. The wearers could easily be some of the reenactors.

Flames rose up beneath the cauldron. One figure pulled something out from under her cloak and dipped it into the cauldron. She raised her hand again, revealing a small glass bottle. The camera began to pull out, and tree trunks appeared, framing the scene at the cauldron. It was a clearing in the woods—probably the one Rose Noire and I had seen earlier in the day.

As we watched, one cloaked figure noticed that some leaves had caught fire, and stamped them out. Maybe Rose Noire was right. Someone might be casting spells out in the woods. Someone was certainly being damned careless with an open fire.

Another low-light scene with MacLeod and two of his henchmen along a wire fence. Quite possibly the fence that divided our yard from Mother and Dad's farm, although admittedly most of the fences in our part of the county looked pretty much the same. Then they crept past Rose Noire's combination herb-drying shed and greenhouse—there was nothing else even remotely like that for miles. They weren't far from the Sumatrans' coop—was Rose Noire right that someone had sinister designs on our fowl? Someone like MacLeod?

They crept on, body language telegraphing that they were up to something sinister. I breathed a sigh of relief when they left both Rose Noire's shed and the Sumatrans' coop behind and arrived at another fence. This time, thanks to the landmarks they'd been passing, I recognized the fence between Rose Noire's herb farm from the pasture where Dad kept his heritage-breed sheep and cows.

If I were Goodwin, I'd edit down the scene of the three of them trying to get over, under, or through the wire fence. Fifteen seconds or so would have gotten across the point: these were three city slickers who'd never met a wire fence before. The whole audience uttered an audible sigh of relief when they finally spotted the gate a hundred feet away and headed for it.

And while they'd been fumbling at the fence, I'd spotted the rope they carried, so I wasn't surprised when they captured the friendly Guernsey heifer and led her away. More footage showed them back at their camp, shoving her into the tiny pen. And a shot of two reenactors tugging on ropes tied around the necks of two of Seth's Lincoln sheep, leading them through the camp and into the pen.

I checked my watch. Too late to call or text Chief Burke. But I'd definitely email him before bed.

A pity Goodwin hadn't captured MacLeod attempting to milk the heifer. But he did manage footage of the sheep shearing. More fodder for Chief Burke's investigation. MacLeod hopped into the pen and strutted up to Vivian, shears in hand, only to receive a solid kick in the shins from the anxious sheep.

The audience cheered. But their mood in the room soured when two reenactors stepped forward to hold Vivian down. I scanned the audience until I spotted Rose Noire. The naked anger on her face shocked and alarmed me. A few minutes ago I'd have sworn Rose Noire would never harm another living creature. Right now I wasn't so sure.

I was relieved that Goodwin didn't show much of the actual shearing. Enough to make it clear that MacLeod had no idea what he was doing, though, and that only luck had saved poor Vivian from more serious injury. And that he showed absolutely no concern about her pain or fear.

Rose Noire's wasn't the only angry face in the audience. Sally the Sane had returned and was glaring at MacLeod.

I wondered if he was smart enough to regret making bail.

If I were him, I'd request police protection.

I was still focused on him, wondering if he'd sneak out before the lights came up, when I was startled to hear my own voice coming through the speakers.

"Who's been torturing this poor sheep?"

Cheers and applause. I glanced back at the screen, where I was standing with my hands on my hips, fixing MacLeod with a gimlet stare.

I realized, to my astonishment, that I looked a lot like Mother.

Not physically, of course. Mother was tall, slender, elegant, and still improbably blond. I'd inherited the height, of course, both from her and from Dad's parents, but I was a brunette, and even Michael, still my biggest fan, would chuckle if someone tried to call me slender or elegant.

But still, there was something in our manner that pegged us as mother and daughter. MacLeod seemed more wary of me than of the chief, which was a tactical mistake on his part.

I was glad when Goodwin focused again on the actors. Some footage taken of a rehearsal out at the zoo amphitheater. Michael stood beside the stage, wholly focused, as Celia delivered Lady Macbeth's soliloquy from act 1, scene 5. But just as she got to "yet do I fear thy nature / It is too full o' the milk of human kindness," her voice suddenly rose into a piercing shriek as she doubled over and clutched her abdomen.

More scenes of Celia followed. Celia pausing to brace herself until a wave of pain passed. Celia shrieking or groaning. Celia leaping up from the dinner table and running for the nearest bathroom. Celia leaping up from the picnic table to retch in the shrubbery. And alternating with these, scenes of Celia pacing up and down here in the library, talking on her cell phone with a look of unhinged anger on her face. You couldn't hear what she was saying, which might have been a good thing . . . except the reason you couldn't hear her was that Goodwin had again dubbed in music: the Wicked Witch of the West's theme music from *The Wizard of Oz*. He'd even matched one of the witch's cackles with a moment when Celia was laughing on screen.

"Enough!" Celia leaped out of her seat, strode forward, and jerked the TV's plug out of the electrical outlet. "This is *not* okay. I am *not* sitting still for this." With each "not" she aimed a short, sharp kick at the stand on which the TV was sitting.

"No, wait—" Goodwin scrambled forward and dropped to his knees by the electrical outlet and began fumbling for the plug. Bad idea—for a second, I thought Celia was going to aim a kick at him. But instead, she took a step or two toward the laptop from which Goodwin had been streaming his footage. She picked it up, whacked it against the library table a couple of times, then threw it onto the floor and stomped on it, hard.

"What the hell—" Goodwin shouted.

Celia kicked at the laptop, propelling it a foot or so in his direction, then turned and headed for the door. She ploughed into Macbeth and Banquo, almost knocking them down, and after that everyone else scrambled to get out of her way.

She slammed the library door, and everyone else in the room was so quiet that we could hear her steps disappearing down the hallway.

The lights came on, and I saw Jamie standing beside the switch, looking slightly anxious.

"Someone should go after her," I muttered. I scanned the crowd, trying to remember which of the cast and crew members she was closest to. And coming up empty. I couldn't remember her socializing with any of them.

And worse, they all knew what I was thinking—the women cast members, anyway—and were all avoiding my eyes.

I glanced over at Rose Noire.

"Can you come with me?" I asked.

She nodded. We left the library together and went in search of Celia.

She didn't answer when I knocked on the door of her room—a bedroom on the third floor, tiny, but nicely furnished. Its size was actually a plus at the moment, since it was too small to hold more than a single occupant. She tended to retreat there instead of socializing with the rest of the cast—maybe because of her stomach problems. Or maybe she just wasn't very sociable.

But I listened at the door and I was positive she wasn't there now. She wasn't locked in any of the bathrooms. She wasn't in the living room or the dining room or the kitchen. Or the yard. Or the barn. She hadn't fled to commune with the llamas, as many cast members had taken to doing at times of stress.

We stood in the backyard, uncertain what to do. Evidently the gathering in the library had broken up after Celia's exit. We saw a large crowd of reenactors setting off to walk back to their camp, and the cast and crew members who slept in tents or in the barn were drifting outside.

"She could be anywhere," I said.

"Doesn't she drive that odd-looking car?" Rose Noire asked. "Sort of copper colored?"

I pulled out my phone and opened up the list of cast and crew I'd compiled. It included information about their cars, so we could keep from towing anyone who had actually been invited to park on our property.

"An orange Mini Cooper." I read out the license number. We inspected the cars in our driveway and the ones parked up and down the road that ran past our house. No orange Mini Cooper.

"If she took her car, she really could be anywhere by now." Rose Noire looked exhausted. "What can we do?"

"She's a grown woman and should be able to take care of herself." I could tell from Rose Noire's expression that she found this unsatisfactory. I did, too.

I thought about it a moment. Then I pulled out my phone and called my cousin Horace.

Chapter 12

"I could use your advice," I said, after Horace and I had exchanged greetings.

"My advice?" He sounded startled.

"On a police matter," I said. "Or more accurately, on whether or not something is a police matter."

"Oh, that's okay, then." He sounded more confident.

I explained what had happened during the evening, as succinctly as possible. It still took a while.

"The chief will definitely want to see Goodwin's video," Horace said.

"I figured as much," I said. "I'll email him about it tonight. But meanwhile, what should I do about Celia?"

"Do you think she's a danger to herself or others?" he asked.

"Not deliberately," I said. "But yes, if she's driving around in the same mood she was in when she stormed out of the library—"

"Let me have the make, model, and license plate number, if you have it," he said. "Because knowing you, I bet you do. I'll get the word out informally to keep an eye open. If we spot her, we can make sure she comes to no harm."

"Thanks." I rattled off the information he wanted.

"Any idea where she might go?" he asked. "Does she have friends in town?"

"I'm not even sure she has friends out here." I thought for a moment. "She stayed at the Caerphilly Inn the first night or two she got here, until we organized a room for her. I suppose it's possible she might go back there."

"It's not as if there are any other hotels in town that she could try," he said. "Okay, I'll start by going over to the Inn right now to see if she's there. And if she's not, I'll get the word out to anyone else who's on patrol."

With that we signed off.

"I guess that's all we can do," Rose Noire said. "If you need me, I'll be in my shed."

"If you were planning to sneak out of your shed to stake out that clearing," I began.

"I'm too tired," she said. "Besides, you told the chief about the clearing, right?"

"Yes," I said. "I haven't heard back from him yet, so I have no idea if he's staking it out. Of course, I haven't checked email in quite a few hours."

"But he wouldn't come right out and tell you he's staking it out," she said. "If he were here, he might hint, but he wouldn't come right out and say it. He'll want to keep it confidential."

I wasn't sure how a few private emails between me and the chief would threaten the confidentiality of any surveillance operation. But I knew better than to ask. She was planning to stay out of the woods tonight—that was all I cared about.

"Don't stay out in the shed too late," I said. "You look beat."

"I'm going to sleep there," she said. "To keep an eye on the Sumatrans—I've got them all cooped up in my workroom."

I tried not to think about what her workroom would look like after thirteen chickens had roosted there overnight.

"What about the Welsummers?" I asked.

"I put them in that little portable coop in the middle of

the llama pen," she said. "They won't come to any harm with the llamas watching over them."

"Good thinking," I said. "Sleep well."

I watched as she trudged off in the direction of her shed. It occurred to me that I could probably get the boys excited about guarding the Sumatrans and let Rose Noire sleep in her own bed.

Tomorrow night. Guarding the chickens was probably going to be a long-haul project. We'd take turns.

I headed back inside.

The house was settling down. The relatives who'd volunteered for KP duty were finishing up in the kitchen. The rest of the relatives, along with the cast and crew, had disappeared and were presumably in bed. Well, most of them. In the library I found Michael and the boys watching _Raiders of the Lost Ark_.

They looked a little guilty when I walked in, but I noticed none of them reached for the remote.

"We were just testing the TV to make sure it wasn't damaged when Lady Macbeth pulled the plug out," Jamie said, without taking his eyes off the screen.

"Seems to be working," I said. "What about Mr. Goodwin's computer?"

"He was kind of mad about that," Josh said.

"Kind of?" I echoed.

"I'd call it annoyed," Michael said. "Not really all that mad, strangely enough. The laptop's screen cracked when Celia knocked it off the table, but evidently it wasn't his main one. It's an old one he uses in situations when he doesn't want to risk his main one, which is much newer and fancier."

"So maybe he wasn't completely surprised that someone reacted badly to his video," I said. "Maybe he's had this happen before."

The boys snickered softly.

"Sounds likely," Michael said. "And he doesn't keep any

data on that laptop. The video he was showing was on a portable hard drive. She didn't do any damage to that. And even if she had, it was a compilation. He'd still have all the original footage."

"Which was not on the laptop?"

"Evidently not," Michael said.

"Well, at least he's gone," I said, glancing around. "Unless he's hiding up on the balcony."

"No, he packed up all his gear pretty quickly after Celia stormed out," Michael said. "The boys and I helped him fend off some of the people who weren't too pleased with him, and saw him safely back to his trailer." He suddenly succumbed to an enormous yawn. "Guys, why don't we watch the rest of this tomorrow?"

"Let's just watch until the end of the 'Well of Souls' scene," Jamie suggested.

"Snakes. Why did it have to be snakes?" Josh said, in a surprisingly good imitation of Harrison Ford's voice.

"Take this. Wave it at anything that slithers," Jamie replied, in an equally spot-on impersonation.

"Okay, we'll watch to the end of the 'Well of Souls,'" Michael said. "And then, bed."

I glanced at the clock. Almost midnight. I left them to it.

It was definitely too late to call the chief. But I could send him an email about Goodwin's video. I trudged out to the barn, where I routinely left my laptop locked up in my office.

Outside the yard was quiet. Deserted. Almost deserted. I spotted two women leaving the barn and heading for the tents—probably returning from using the bathrooms we'd installed in the barn to cut down on traffic into the house when we held big gatherings in the yard. They were giggling over something. Something they didn't want overheard—when I got close to them, they scattered in much the same way our chickens would if Spike got loose and tried to chase them. Inside the barn I found two of the men who were sleeping there still up, sipping beers, muttering about Goodwin. When they saw me they fell silent.

I hoped Goodwin had the common sense to lie low for a while.

I decided to grab my laptop, lock up my office again, and retreat to the bedroom. I could write my email there.

And I decided it was a good thing I'd come out to the barn. My work space was open again. I could have sworn I'd managed to close it when I'd finished with the dagger.

The prop master. I'd given her the key to return the daggers. I'd have a word with her tomorrow. At least the door was only a little ajar, so probably no one but me would notice, but still—with the vandal on the loose, this was no time to get careless. I glanced inside and saw nothing obviously amiss, so—

Wait. Where was my creepy dagger? The new one modeled on the dead-man's-fingers. I did a quick but thorough search. It wasn't here.

When had I last seen it? When Michael was showing it off before dinner. He probably had it. Or he'd given it to the prop master, and she'd locked it up with the rest of the rehearsal props, instead of returning it here.

I'd worry about it tomorrow. I locked up and turned off the light—producing sighs of relief from a couple of the people who'd set up their sleeping bags in the stalls.

On my way back, I saw a light coming from Goodwin's trailer.

Maybe I should talk to him. Warn him that the chief would be asking for a copy of his footage on the sheep and cow thefts. If I could make it sound as if giving the police his video would make him the center of attention, I could increase the likelihood that he'd cooperate.

And I could suggest that he make himself scarce tomorrow. Maybe for a few days, until people had a chance to cool off.

So I took a detour over to the trailer and knocked on the door. No answer. I tried the doorknob. The door was locked.

"Damien," I called. "It's Meg Langslow. Could I talk to you for a minute?"

No answer. And I heard no stirring inside.

He could be asleep. Or pretending to be. Or he could be out somewhere. Not far away—his truck was still in the driveway.

I knocked once more, waited another long minute or so, and then gave up. I'd tackle him in the morning.

I took another look up and down the line of cars. Celia's orange Mini Cooper was still missing.

When I got upstairs, I threw on my nightgown and gave my teeth a barely adequate brushing. Then I opened up the laptop and composed an email to the chief.

"Damien Goodwin showed us some of the footage he's been shooting over the last few days," I began. "He actually has video showing the reenactors taking Mother and Dad's heifer from their pasture and leading it back to their camp. And video of MacLeod shearing one of Seth's poor sheep. And possibly some video that might suggest who's responsible for the vandalism. He seems to be making himself scarce at the moment—I think he had unflattering footage of nearly everyone in the neighborhood, and everyone's pretty ticked at him. If I see him in the morning, should I suggest that he share the compromising video with you? Or would you rather tackle him yourself?"

Michael came in as I was hitting the SEND button.

"Celia still AWOL?" he asked.

"As far as I know," I said. "Her car's still gone."

"Damn." He slumped down on the bed, looking exhausted. "Maybe Goodwin's show was the last straw. Maybe she said the hell with this and headed back to D.C."

"I don't think she had time to pack," I said. "Still—you want me to check on her? I could knock, and if she doesn't answer, I could even open up her room to see if she's hiding in there?"

"No." He shook his head. "We'll find out soon enough. She's a grown-up; I don't think it's unreasonable to expect her to act like one. Either she'll calm down and show up for rehearsal in the morning, or Tanya will get another chance to rehearse her part. I'm not going to worry about it now."

He got up and ambled into the bathroom, shedding clothes along the way. I considered crawling out of bed and shoving his clothes in the hamper. And should I ask him if he knew where the latest creepy dagger was?

No. I'd worry about all that tomorrow.

I think I was asleep before Michael finished brushing his teeth.

And I was definitely fast asleep at 4:00 A.M. when my cell phone rang. Normally I don't answer unless I know who's calling and want to hear from them, but I was so focused on stopping the noise before it woke Michael that I answered without checking to see who was calling. I muttered a terse "hello" into the receiver.

A male voice launched into a tirade of obscenity-laced invective.

I pressed the END button.

Then I looked at the screen. NAME UNAVAILABLE, followed by a phone number. A local phone number, but not one I recognized.

The phone rang again. NAME UNAVAILABLE again, with the same number. Probably some drunk, misremembering the number of his ex-wife, ex-boss, ex-buddy—whoever he was drinking to forget. I pressed the button that would refuse the call and then blocked the number before going back to sleep.

Chapter 13

Friday

I woke up at what the cast and crew would consider the ungodly and even mythical hour of 6:00 A.M. When I saw the time my first impulse was to turn over and go back to sleep, but then I realized that I actually felt pretty rested, in spite of my late bedtime and that annoying middle-of-the-night wrong number. Not fully rested but still—not dog tired, and very much in the mood to take advantage of the peace and quiet of the early morning.

Well, maybe it was more like too restless to sleep, but I was in a good mood. If need be, I could nap once they all left for rehearsal.

Most nights the theater crowd would stay up late—talking, singing, helping each other run lines, watching movies and arguing loudly about their merits, joining the ongoing Dungeons & Dragons games my nephew Kevin ran every weekend, and generally playing hard to make up for the long hours of hard work they put in at rehearsal. Most nights I didn't even try to keep up with them—and for that matter, most nights Michael didn't either. I had to break up the party once or twice—like that evening when shortly after midnight they all donned the LED headlamps we keep around in case of power out-ages and began playing a noisy game of Xtreme Croquet in the backyard. And then there was the evening when they'd encouraged a visiting bagpiper from Camp Birnam instead of chasing him away. But those were exceptions. Most of the time they were reasonably considerate. Still, even when they found quiet things to do, I had a hard time going to sleep, knowing so many people were busy doing fun things downstairs. Was it simply a desire to join in the fun? Was it more a case of resentment that they were still able to lead the night-owl life I'd had to give up in my effort to become a socially responsible adult? Had I become so much the adult that I worried about how much damage they might be doing in my absence?

I couldn't say. All I knew was that all too often I tossed and turned for hours, my senses alert for any sound of what was happening in the rest of the house, so that I missed out on both rest and recreation.

But not last night. I'd slept well. However disastrous Damien Goodwin's watch party had been in some respects, it had had one useful side effect—even after they'd calmed down a bit, no one had been in the mood to party. From what I had seen almost everyone had been in bed by mid-night. With any luck they'd still sleep late—out of habit, plus surely most of them were dangerously sleep deprived by now. But even if they all awakened earlier than usual, if I got up now I could enjoy the peace and quiet for a few hours.

I left Michael still out for the count, his not-quite snores slow, deep, and even. I threw on my jeans and a purple FRIENDS OF THE CAERPHILLY ZOO t-shirt and slipped downstairs.

No sleeping forms on the sofas in the living room. No insomniacs studying their lines in the dining room. No zombie-like night owls struggling with the coffee maker in the kitchen. I could almost pretend we weren't hosting several dozen houseguests and campers.

I poured myself a glass of iced tea from the pitcher in the fridge and sat down at the kitchen table to contemplate the day—which was the highfalutin term I used for my morning ritual of checking my calendar and my notebook-that-tells-me-when-to-breathe, planning how I'd spend the hours ahead. Although with school out and the cast and crew underfoot, I knew better than to make the kind of detailed plans that required precise timing and long stretches of uninterrupted solitude.

Come to think of it, I'd long since given up making those kinds of plans—since around the time the twins were born.

Top of my list was making sure everyone would get fed. I made a note to inventory the refrigerators out in the barn, where we kept a supply of food so the cast and crew could fend for themselves at breakfast and lunchtime. I smiled when I read an email from Mother saying that she had recruited both the necessary ringers for today's lecture and a crew of volunteers to cook dinner. Delegating a task to Mother was as reliable as doing it myself, and a lot less work. I smiled even more broadly when I read an email from Chief Burke thanking me for notifying him about the existence of potentially useful video footage and noting that he'd be dropping by later that morning to see Mr. Goodwin.

Maybe I should confront Goodwin himself and see if I could get my own copy of that footage. Because the more I thought about it, the more convinced I was that Goodwin's footage might hold a clue to the identity of our vandal. And not just the footage he'd shown us—what if he had other footage, as yet unseen, that caught the vandal in the act? I should talk to him.

In fact, maybe it would be a good idea to tackle him now—assuming I could find him. He kept odd hours, sometimes staying up all night and sleeping until mid-afternoon, and sometimes getting up before dawn—the better to catch embarrassing footage of the campers and reenactors when they were still half asleep.

I strolled over to a window from which I could catch a glimpse of his trailer. No lights on, but the door was hanging open. Which meant he was probably nearby. He was feckless about most things, but I'd never known him to forget locking up the trailer that contained all his fragile and expensive equipment.

So I picked up my iced tea and went out onto the back stoop, taking care to ease the screen door closed instead of letting it slam. No sign of life from any of the tents. No chickens scratching in the yard, which meant I was up even before Rose Noire, who usually let them out.

No, I was wrong on that last bit. There she was, sitting in a yoga pose near the fence that surrounded the llamas' enclosure. I wasn't often up this early—maybe she started every day by meditating with the llamas. Maybe that was what gave her the energy to accomplish the massive amount of work she got done every day both in our house and yard and over in her herb farm. I waved, but either she didn't notice or she was too focused on her breathing to respond.

And the llamas were still asleep near the other side of their enclosure. Two had their legs tucked under and their necks extended, in what llama fanciers called the kush position, and the other three were sprawled like cats basking in the sun. Since llamas were endlessly curious about human behavior, they usually woke up at the first sign of activity from the tents and spent most of the morning hanging their necks over the fence, observing our antics. I could see Harpo, the lightest sleeper, raising his head to see if I was doing anything worth watching and then stretching out on the ground again. And Vivian was still there, fast asleep, with her still-fluffy head and pink-skinned neck resting on Zeppo's fluffy belly.

I headed through the side yard toward the spot by the side of the road where Goodwin's trailer was parked.

He wasn't sitting in one of the folding lawn chairs he'd set up just outside the trailer's door. I knocked on the half-open door.

"Damien?" I called. "Are you there?"

No answer.

I waited a minute or so, then knocked and called again. Still no answer. Strange.

I'd stopped in a spot where the door blocked my view into the trailer—partly out of respect for Goodwin's privacy, but mostly because I wanted to avoid getting another view of him in the ragged SpongeBob SquarePants briefs that seemed to be his habitual nightwear. Now I shifted my position, nudged the door open a little more widely, and peered in.

"Uh-oh," I muttered.

Someone had ransacked the trailer. Or trashed it. Ransacked *and* trashed it. Every drawer and cabinet door hung open. Doritos, Cheerios, and crumpled papers were everywhere. And the floor was littered with bits of plastic and metal that had once been expensive pieces of video and computer equipment.

I pulled out my phone and dialed 911.

"Morning, Meg," Debbie Ann, the dispatcher, said. "What's the emergency?"

"I'm not sure it's an emergency," I said. "But our vandal seems to have struck again."

"Oh dear—what now?" In the background I could hear the rattle of keys as she typed in the message that would send a deputy heading our way.

"This time they hit the trailer that belongs to Damien Goodwin—the filmmaker who's been staying here."

"The annoying one."

"Yes." I got as close as I could to the open door. "Someone has totally trashed the inside of his trailer and smashed a lot of his expensive video equipment. You know, if Horace is on duty, it might be a good idea to send him out to see if he can get some useful forensic evidence from this mess. Because if this was done by the same person who did all the other things, they've really upped the ante this time."

"Roger. Does Mr. Goodwin have any idea when it happened?" Debbie Ann asked. "Or who did it?"

"He's not here." Suddenly the possible implications of that struck me. "Or if he is, he's not answering. I should go in and check. See if he's . . . asleep or injured or . . . something."

"Vern should be there in ten minutes," Debbie Ann said. "You should wait for him."

"And what if Goodwin's injured and needs help?" I took a deep breath. "I'm going in to check. I'll try not to mess things up more than I have to."

"You should wait," Debbie Ann said. "Or if you're hell-bent on going in, at least stay on the line with me."

She knew me too well.

My footsteps sounded unnaturally loud on the metal steps that led up to the trailer. I paused at the top to look around before inching into the main room. Doritos and broken glass crunched under my feet.

An inspiration hit me. I opened my phone's camera, switched it to video mode, and began panning it around the room.

To my right were a wall-mounted TV and several utilitarian wall-mounted metal shelves that had once held much of the equipment now strewn in pieces over the floor. Beyond that were the microwave, the sink, and a few overhead cabinets. The cabinet doors hung open. Someone had swept their contents—dishes, glasses, food—onto the floor and then topped the mess off with a few of the dirty dishes that had filled the sink.

The door to the bedroom was between the sink and the refrigerator. I'd work up to opening that in a minute.

The refrigerator's door hung open, and its contents—

mostly bottles of beer—had been thrown onto the floor. Several bottles had broken, and the room reeked.

To the left of the refrigerator, and almost directly across the trailer from me, was the dinette, situated in one of those pop-outs that provided more floor space when the trailer was parked. The last time I'd seen the dinette, the table and nearly all of the U-shaped banquette had been covered with papers and electronic gizmos. Now most of that had been swept to the floor.

The space between the dinette and the bathroom door held more electronic rubble. The bathroom door hung open. Goodwin wasn't in the tiny shower stall; he wasn't sitting on the compact toilet; and taking a few steps forward proved he wasn't cowering in the corner by the sink. That just left the bedroom.

"Meg? Everything okay?"

"So far." I stepped carefully across the debris on the floor and peeked into the bedroom. Goodwin wasn't on the unmade bed. He wasn't hiding in any of the corners. And the bed was flush with the floor—no space to hide under it. The doors to the overhead storage areas behind the bed were hanging open, and I could see that their contents had been dragged out. Piles of rumpled clothes and smashed electronic gear littered the floor, but none of the piles were large enough that he could be hiding under them.

"Pretty sure he's not here," I said into the phone. I retreated to the main room, where the beer stench, though pungent, was an improvement over the bedroom, which had that college dorm reek of unwashed laundry and musky aftershave. "I'll see if I can figure out where he is." I stepped back outside and took a deep breath of fresh air.

"Good idea," Debbie Ann said. "When Vern gets there he'll need to find out what Goodwin knows about this. I mean, for all we know, he could have smashed all his stuff in some kind of artistic temper tantrum."

"Maybe." I wasn't buying the idea. I could easily see Goodwin having a temper tantrum. I could even see him smashing stuff. But he'd make sure anything he smashed was either worthless or belonged to someone else.

"Meg?" I started, and turned to find Rose Noire standing just behind me. "Is something wrong?"

"Someone vandalized Goodwin's trailer last night." I gestured to the open doorway. "Don't go in," I added as she approached the steps. "Vern's on his way."

"Oh dear. Is Mr. Goodwin very upset?"

"No idea." I shrugged. "He's not here."

"Then where is he? What if something has happened to him?"

I shook my head. And then realized that perhaps I wasn't quite as awake as I thought I was. I pulled out my phone, scrolled down my contact list, and called Goodwin's number.

It rang four times, and then I heard his voice.

"Hello? Who's this? . . . What was that?"

I took one of those slow yoga breaths I knew Rose Noire would recommend if she knew how irritated I was. Goodwin had recorded a voice mail message that sounded for all the world as if he were answering the phone in a curt and annoyed manner and then uttering noncommittal responses to what his caller said. Only after thirty or forty seconds of vague comments did he get down to business, reveal that this was only his voice mail, and ask the caller to leave a message. The first time he'd fooled me. After that I'd given up waiting out his message. But I did this time, and when the beep finally came, I'd had plenty of time to plan what I was going to say.

"This is Meg Langslow," I said. "It looks as if someone has ransacked your trailer and damaged some of your video equipment. You might want to come back here to

see what can be salvaged, and maybe help the police figure out who did it."

Then I hung up and took another deep breath.

"Where could he be?" Rose Noire was visibly fretting. "I
have a bad feeling about this. I've been having a terrible
feeling of foreboding ever since I woke up."

Chapter 14

I wondered if Rose Noire really had awakened with a sense of foreboding or if she'd convinced herself it was so because she felt anxious now.

"Maybe he spent the night somewhere else," I suggested. "Or with someone else," I added, sensing that she was about to ask where.

"I can't imagine he's on that kind of terms with anyone around here." She grimaced slightly, as if to suggest she hoped no one we knew had such low standards.

"Maybe he lost his temper when he saw what had happened to his stuff," I suggested. "And went for a walk to cool off. Who knows? We'll find out when he shows up."

Just then a police cruiser pulled up and parked across the street from the trailer. Vern Shiffley stepped out.

"More trouble?" he asked.

"Or more of the same trouble we've been having." I gestured toward the trailer door. "Belongs to Damien Goodwin."

"That nosy filmmaker."

"Yes. I found the door open and the contents trashed."

Vern peeked through the door and shook his head.

"Maybe I should check inside," he said. "In case he's . . . hiding someplace in there."

"If you're worried that he might be injured or something, I already checked," I said. "He's not there. No one is. And there aren't a lot of places to hide. Here—I'll show you."

I held up my phone and started the video I'd taken of

my search. He hunched slightly and peered intently at the tiny screen.

"You're right," he said, when the video ended. "No way anyone could be hiding in there. Has anyone seen him recently?"

"I haven't seen him since last night." I glanced at Rose Noire, who shook her head. "He could still be lying low," I went on. "He showed us some of the video he's been taking over the last two weeks and none of it was very flattering to anybody. There was a big uproar. I'm wondering if one of them trashed his trailer out of revenge."

"You don't think it's whoever's been vandalizing things the last few days?"

"Also possible," I said. "But if it's the same person, they've certainly escalated, haven't they?"

"And graduated from misdemeanor to felony." Vern nodded. "Destruction of property. Burglary, unless he invited them in, and if any of my guests behaved like this, I'd be calling nine-one-one long before they finished. I expect the chief will send Horace over here to do a little forensic work—always makes Horace's day when he gets the chance to work a crime scene. Has anyone but you been in there?"

"Not that I know of," I said. "But anyone could have gone in before I got here."

"We can keep an eye out for anyone else whose shoes look like yours." He pointed down at my sneakers. I lifted one foot to look. Bits of food, plastic, and glass were embedded in the patterns on the sole.

"And we should check out Goodwin's soles when he shows up," Vern added.

"You're thinking he could have done this himself."

"Could be. Maybe he lost his temper and had to smash things. Got a cousin who does that."

"Seems out of character," I said. "Unless he's really worried about how negatively everyone reacted to his film. In that case, I can see him wanting to do something to make himself look like a victim and get our sympathy."

"Yup." Vern pulled out his cell phone and let Debbie Ann know that he had secured the scene and would wait for Horace's arrival. Then he returned to peering into the trailer.

"Speaking of that film of his—that reminds me," he said. "We found that lady you were so worried over—the one you told Horace about last night."

"Found her where?" I felt a twinge of guilt. I had forgotten about Celia's stormy exit, and hadn't checked to see if she was back.

"In a ditch less than half a mile from here," he said. "You know that nasty curve just down the road by Deacon Washington's driveway? Usually it's the tipsy ones who come a cropper there. I guess if you're driving while having a temper tantrum and forget to turn on your headlights, it has much the same effect."

"Yikes," I said. "Is she okay?"

"Far as they can tell," he said. "They kept her overnight for observation. And called your dad to come in and see her, for some reason."

"He's been treating her," I said. "Trying to, anyway. She's been having some kind of gastrointestinal problems. Stomach pains bad enough to double her over. If that happened while she was driving, it could account for the accident."

"It could," Vern said. "Could also explain why your dad was trying to talk her into having an endoscopy. Not the standard treatment for someone you think might have a concussion."

"Does she have a concussion?"

"Probably. I guess she's lucky you called Horace. The ditch is pretty deep there. Without the headlights, she was pretty much invisible from the road—as I had to remind your dad, who was kicking himself, saying that he must have driven right past her on his way home."

"At least half a dozen cars must have driven past her," I said. "Between the relatives and the history professors—they'd all have driven along that stretch."

"You pretty much had to get out of your car and walk over to peer down into the ditch to see her," Vern said. "I'm kind of used to doing that, though mostly only on Friday and Saturday nights. If I hadn't done it last night, we might not have found her till daylight."

"I'll warn Michael that she might not be available for rehearsal today," I said.

Horace's police cruiser pulled up and he parked behind Vern. He got out, a little more slowly than usual, as if he'd had a tiring night.

Rose Noire must have noticed the same thing.

"I'll get coffee," she said as she dashed away.

Horace was peering into the open door of the trailer.

"Is the owner around?" he asked.

"I haven't seen him since last night," I said.

"Should we maybe wait to get his permission?" Horace asked.

"We're a bit worried about him," Vern added. "Exigent circumstances."

"Have you checked to see if he's in there?" Horace sounded concerned.

"I did," I said.

"But Meg might not have your eye for noticing clues about his well-being or his whereabouts," Vern said.

Horace chuckled.

"This is Meg you're talking about," he said. "In case you hadn't noticed, she doesn't miss much. Okay, I'll start working the scene. Definitely worth doing, given the possibility that this could be the work of the same person responsible for all those other acts of vandalism. But Vern, can you stick around and keep an eye out? Just in case the owner shows up and pitches a fit about his reasonable expectation of privacy."

"Can do."

Just then Rose Noire returned with two mugs of coffee. Horace took one, thanked her, and began sipping it as he ambled back to his car—no doubt to fetch his forensic gear. Vern took the other, nodded his thanks, and sat down in one of Goodwin's lawn chairs to keep watch.

"Here." Rose Noire was holding out the Crocs I kept on the back porch to put on if I was going outside when the yard was wet and muddy. "In case Horace wants your shoes."

"Good idea," Vern said.

I slipped off my sneakers and donned the Crocs. I picked up one of the sneakers and studied what was embedded in the soles, so I'd know it if I saw someone else's shoes in the same shape. Then I set the sneakers on the ground beside Vern's chair.

Horace returned, pulled out a small camera, and began taking photos of the trailer steps.

"This could take a while," Vern said, nodding his head in Horace's direction.

I decided to interpret this as a subtle hint that my continued presence was unnecessary.

"Give me a buzz if you need anything," I said.

"I should go let the chickens out and give them their morning feed." Rose Noire turned to go. "It's way after their usual time, but I wanted to wait until there were more people awake."

"I think they'll be pretty safe with Horace and Vern here," I said as I fell into step beside her. "Even the Birnamites probably know better than to steal livestock under the very noses of the police. You want me to help?"

"That would be nice." We headed for her shed, since we kept the chicken feed in a bin just beside it. "You can do the Welsummers on your way back to the house. Did Vern say anything about that campfire out in the woods?" she asked.

"Not yet," I said. "We were kind of focused on the vandalism. But he'll be around for a while, watching Horace's back while he processes Goodwin's trailer. I could ask him—unless you'd rather."

"No, you do it," she said. "I think he takes you more seriously. I'm going to check with your dad and see how much longer they'll be keeping Celia. If she's staying in the hospital, she might like a few of her own things. And if she's coming home—well, it might be nice to make sure her room's in good shape. I could put on clean sheets, maybe collect her laundry—do a few of the things she's probably not going to feel up to doing for a day or so."

"If you have time, that would certainly be nice," I said. "And could you—"

I broke off, having suddenly noticed something in the distance.

"And could I what?" Rose Noire prompted. "Is something wrong?"

"Vultures." I pointed to the edge of the woods.

Rose Noire turned and peered in the direction I had indicated.

I could see two distinctive bird silhouettes gliding in the air near the edge of the woods. A third joined them and then they all three slowly circled downward and dropped out of sight.

"I know they're a little . . . lugubrious," she said. "But they're a vital part of the natural circle of life."

"You sound like Grandfather," I said. "Except that he'd call them an important component of the ecosystem. And he'd ask what we'd do if they weren't around to perform the important job of cleaning up carrion."

"I don't often agree with your grandfather," she said. "But about this, he's right. Why do they bother you so much?"

"They don't normally," I said. "I live in the country, too, remember? But given everything that went on yesterday,

I'd like to make sure the carrion they're cleaning up isn't a creature we're personally acquainted with. One of Seth's sheep or Dad's calves, for example."

"Oh dear." Suddenly she looked ashen. "Should we . . . ?"

"I'll just go over and take a quick look," I said. "You stay here and let the chickens out."

But she trailed along as I strode across her herb fields toward the fence that separated them from Mother and Dad's pasture. On the other side of the fence there was only a narrow strip of grassy open land between the herb fields and the woods—a sort of annex to the main pasture. Thanks to its proximity to the woods, this part of the pasture was shady in the afternoon, and Dad's sheep and cattle often retreated here on hot days. But it was usually empty this early in the morning.

I aimed for the gate the reenactors had used to get into the field yesterday and steal the heifer.

As we drew closer, I could see that the three vultures had landed on tree limbs and were looking down at something. We paused for a moment.

"Only those three, and I think they've only just arrived." Rose Noire sounded relieved that the natural circle of life was still on hold.

"Looks like it," I said. "Turkey vultures. I seem to recall Grandfather saying that they're hardly ever seen at night."

"Then maybe it's a good thing you were up so much earlier than usual," Rose Noire said, with the lark's typical dismissive attitude toward us night owls.

And she was looking at me expectantly. If she was waiting for me to trot out the Latin name for the vultures, she was out of luck. She'd have to hunt down Dad or Grandfather for that. I thought I was doing pretty well to have pegged them as turkey vultures.

"The gate's this way," I said instead, turning right and heading down along the fence.

Two of the vultures took flight when we came through

the gate. The third began to shuffle on his tree limb and followed their example as we drew closer to the edge of the woods. None of them went away entirely, though— they just retreated to higher branches and sat watching us.

"I don't think it's a sheep." Rose Noire had stopped and was peering ahead.

No. The shape the vultures had been studying was dark. Black. Seth didn't own any black sheep that I knew of. Dad's cows were either fawn-colored Guernseys or belted Galloways whose black color was bisected by a broad, highly visible white stripe around their bellies. And the shape was too big for a black Sumatran.

It looked like a human. Dressed all in black, including a black hoodie pulled up over his head. Two pale hands were the only skin visible.

"I think it's Damien Goodwin," Rose Noire whispered.

Chapter 15

"Yeah, it looks like Goodwin." I was already pulling out my phone.

Vern answered on the second ring.

"What's up, Meg?" he asked.

"I've found Damien Goodwin," I said.

"Is he okay with our doing forensics on his trailer?" Vern asked.

"He's in no position to object," I said. "I think he's dead."

A short pause.

"Where are you?" he asked. "And what do you mean, you think he's dead?"

"Well, I think it's Goodwin," I said. "But whoever it is I'm pretty sure he's dead, on account of the vultures."

"Vultures? Dear God."

"They only just got here. But I suspect they wouldn't be here at all if he'd merely gotten drunk and passed out or something like that. Black vultures might, because they hunt by sight, but these appear to be turkey vultures, and they hunt by smell, and the only smell that interests them is death. All those cartoons about people crawling through the desert dying of thirst with vultures circling overhead waiting for them to croak are so much nonsense, according to Grandfather. Sorry—I don't mean to babble."

"It's okay," Vern said. "Where is this probable dead guy?"

"He's here at the edge of the woods," I said. "Walk past the barn and look for the vultures perched in the trees. I'm going to check his pulse, just in case."

I had inched closer to the body. I realized that I was

trying to observe details I could tell Vern, while at the same time trying not to think too much about those details. I was becoming more and more sure it was Goodwin. He was lying facedown, with one arm flung out in front of him and one lying by his side, half under his body. There seemed to be blood on the grass around his head, but it was hard to tell without getting closer than I wanted to be. At least his hands seemed uninjured, which meant we'd arrived in time to keep the vultures from getting to him. I circled around until I was close enough to the outstretched hand to reach out and touch his wrist.

"He's cold," I said into the phone as I jerked my hand away. I steeled myself and reached out to grasp his wrist. "No pulse. Definitely dead. And there's blood on the ground around his head." I stepped back and gave in to the temptation to wipe my hand on the leg of my jeans.

Blood. I suddenly remembered my dagger—the missing creepy dagger, which I hadn't yet modified to make it less useful as a lethal weapon. What if—

No. I shouldn't jump to conclusions. Just because I saw blood didn't mean Goodwin had been stabbed. And even if he had been stabbed, there was no reason to assume my beautiful little dagger was the murder weapon. There were plenty of other cutting and stabbing implements available, including quite a few other examples of my handiwork.

"Call nine-one-one," Vern said. "I'm sending Horace over. I'll stay here and guard the trailer."

"Roger." As I dialed 911 I retreated to where Rose Noire was still standing, eyes wide.

"Meg, what's up now?" Debbie Ann said. Did I detect a note of anxiety in her voice, or was I projecting how I felt onto her?

"We found a dead body at the edge of the woods behind Rose Noire's shed," I said. "Damien Goodwin."

"That filmmaker guy? The one whose trailer was vandalized?"

"Yes. Horace is coming over here to take a look. We might need Dad. And I'm sure the chief will want to see."

"Do you have any idea what happened?" Behind her words I could hear the clicking of her keyboard.

"Not a clue," I said. "All I did was check for a pulse. I thought just in case he didn't keel over from natural causes, the chief's going to want Horace and Dad to help him figure out what happened."

"Was he someone you'd have expected to keel over from natural causes?" Debbie Ann asked. "I thought he was a young guy."

"Thirty-something, reasonably fit looking, and if he had any substance abuse issues he was pretty good at hiding them," I said.

"An overdose would be accidental, not natural," Debbie pointed out.

"I know." I wanted to add "accidental would still be preferable to either suicide or homicide," but she'd probably know that without my saying it. "Vern's here," I said instead. "I'll talk to you later."

Vern had joined us and was staring at Goodwin and shaking his head.

"What about Horace?" I said.

"He's grabbing some more stuff from his trunk. Aida just got here, so she's guarding the trailer. I thought I'd come over and check things out."

Or maybe he thought Rose Noire and I could use the moral support. I suspected he was right. Rose Noire had closed her eyes and was taking deep calming breaths.

"You positive it's this Goodwin fellow?" Vern asked.

"If it's not, it's someone exactly his size and shape, dressed exactly as he was the last time I saw him," I said. "Down to the boots, which are pretty distinctive."

Vern craned his neck to scrutinize the boots.

"Some kind of alligator?" he asked.

"Caiman, or so he says," I replied.

"Is that fancier than plain old alligator?" he asked.

"Must be," I said. "If you so much as glanced at them he'd tell you they were caiman."

"Ah." Vern said. "Well, I hope he got a good deal of enjoyment out of them while he could. Maybe we should send someone back to the road to direct Horace and the doc out here."

"I'll go." Rose Noire turned and began walking briskly.

Vern and I contemplated Goodwin's body in silence, with an occasional glance up at the persistent vultures.

"Probably a good thing you were up early and noticed Goodwin's door open," he said after a bit.

"I have no idea whether anyone went in there before I found it," I said.

"If anyone did, Horace will figure it out." Vern took a few steps to the right and leaned over to peer at Goodwin's feet. "Doesn't look as if he did it himself. The vandalizing, I mean."

"No Doritos and Cheerios sullying the soles of the caiman boots?"

"Yup." Vern nodded. "Of course, those boots don't have the same kind of deep tread as your sneakers, but you'd see something, especially on the heels. Horace can tell for sure—here he is, and the chief with him."

Horace arrived with his digital camera already clicking. For the present he was circling the body—he'd wait for Dad to pronounce before touching Goodwin.

"Any footprints or other signs leading up to the body?" the chief asked Vern. "Horace and I didn't see any, but we don't have your eye."

Useful to have one of the county's best hunters and trackers on your team.

"Not between the gate and here." Vern sounded apologetic, as if the lack of tracks were his fault. "Ground's baked dry from this drought, and Dr. Langslow's cows and sheep have cropped the grass pretty close. But if you don't need me for anything else, I thought I'd take a gander at the ground between here and the woods, and maybe a little way into the woods. Ground there might be better for signs."

The chief's eyes swept along the nearby line of trees.

"I get turned around out here in the country," he said. "What's in that direction—beyond the woods, I mean?"

"Caerphilly Creek if you go that-a-way." Vern pointed straight ahead. Then he shifted his hand to the left. "And if you head that way instead, you'll eventually run into Camp Birnam."

"I thought that might be the case." The chief nodded. "Yes, take a good close gander at the ground anywhere you think might be promising."

"What about that clearing in the woods where Rose Noire found the remains of a campfire?" I asked. "Which direction is that from here?"

Vern pointed again, about halfway between the directions he'd shown for Caerphilly Creek and Camp Birnam.

"I thought so," I said.

Vern nodded, and I deduced from his expression that he'd already been thinking about whether the clearing had a connection to the crime scene.

"Here's Dr. Langslow," he said. Then he turned and ambled slowly off, eyes scanning the ground.

The chief turned to greet Dad.

"Thanks for coming so quickly," he said.

"Of course!" Dad's voice reflected the truly mixed emotions I knew he'd be feeling right about now: Sadness at the premature and unnecessary death of another human being. Enthusiastic professional interest in finding out the cause of the death. The mystery reader's excitement at the possibility that this could be a real-life murder. And perhaps just a bit of gratitude toward Goodwin for managing to get himself bumped off on Dad's turf instead of in that of some rival and less appreciative medical examiner.

I shifted my position slightly so I could use my peripheral vision to get a vague idea of what Dad was doing without having to watch too closely. It wasn't so much that I was squeamish—I knew from many lively dinner table conversations what a medical examiner did at a death scene. But it depressed me a little when the subject was someone I knew, even someone as unlikeable as Goodwin.

"Poor man," Dad said. "Rigor well established. I'll get a temperature."

"So he's been dead a while," the chief said. "Any idea of the cause of death?"

"Blunt force trauma to the front of the skull," Dad said.

"Thank goodness," I muttered.

They all looked at me. Oddly.

"I was afraid it would turn out to be a stabbing," I explained. "Because I'm missing a knife. The creepy knife I made yesterday," I added to Dad.

"Oh dear," he said. "The one with the hilt that looks like the dead-man's-fingers?"

I nodded.

"Do you have reason to believe it was stolen?" the chief asked.

"Not really," I said. "I assumed it had gotten mixed in with the other props. It was one I was making for the play, but hadn't finished yet. Michael was waving it around yesterday at dinner, so the prop master could easily have taken charge of it. But then when I saw the blood, I was worried. The idea of someone using my work as a murder weapon . . ."

"Not the case here," Dad said. "Blunt force trauma— and completely the wrong shape to have been done with the hilt of your knife, in case you were worried."

I had been, and felt an immense surge of relief.

"In fact, it was something a lot closer to rectangular." Dad's expression showed puzzled interest. "But without any sharp edges."

"Interesting." The chief added a few words to his notebook. "Time of death?"

"We'll have a better idea after the autopsy." Dad pursed his lips and thought for a moment. Then he pulled out his phone and looked at something before continuing. "But for a rough estimate, sometime between eleven p.m. and one a.m."

"That would put it very soon after last night's festivities broke up," I said. "Michael and the boys helped Goodwin pack up his stuff and escorted him safely back to his trailer. So Michael might have some idea what time that was. Well before midnight, at any rate."

"Around eleven," Dad said. "I know because I helped them, and I texted your mother at ten fifty that I'd be home by midnight. That's why I was able to narrow down my estimate to a mere two hours."

"Useful," the chief said. "Can you tell whether or not he was killed here where we found him?"

"Not for sure—at least not yet," Dad said. "Seems probable, though. I'll have a better idea when we turn him over, but let's let Horace get a few more photos first."

"I'm going to check on the other part of our crime scene," the chief said. "Call me if you find anything I should see."

"Will do."

The chief turned to me.

"Things looked pretty quiet at your house when I got here. I gather the actors don't get up with the chickens."

"Left to their own devices, some of them would never see daylight." I pulled out my phone and checked the time. A little past eight. "But most of them will be crawling out of their tents in the next hour or two. Rehearsal starts at eleven today, and most of them try to eat a decent breakfast before they take off for it. I'm assuming you'll want to interview most of them."

"Alas, yes." He grimaced slightly. "But first I'd like to

hear from you. Let's give your dad and Horace some space."

"No problem." I turned and headed for the gate. I was curiously relieved to be putting some distance between me and Goodwin's body. I wondered if the chief felt the same way, or if he was just trying to be considerate of my feelings.

"Okay," the chief said as he fell into step beside me. "Fill me in. I gather there was some kind of dust-up last night that got at least one of your guests so mad that she drove off and wrecked her car in a ditch."

"Yikes," I said. "Is it really wrecked? Vern didn't mention that."

"It took a good bit of front-end damage," the chief said. "Not necessarily totaled, but fixing it won't be cheap. Osgood Shiffley towed it down to his garage. I hope Ms. Rivers is smart enough to realize her car's in the hands of a reliable, honest mechanic. You'd be surprised how often these out-of-towners pay through the nose to have their cars towed hundreds of miles. But that's neither here nor there. What got her so worked up in the first place?"

"Damien Goodwin insisted on having a get-together so he could show some of the video he's been shooting over the past week and a half," I said. "He had some really unflattering footage of her. Then again, he had some pretty unflattering footage of nearly everybody—possibly incriminating in at least one case."

"Meaning our light-fingered Mr. MacLeod," the chief said. "I saw your email. That isn't his real name, by the way. On his driver's license he's Christopher Miller."

"Not very Scottish sounding," I said. "I suppose that's the reason he's using an alias. I already knew the accent was faked. Anyway, as far as I can remember, he was the only person Goodwin caught on video doing something illegal— with the possible exception of the two reenactors who went along with him when he took Mother and Dad's heifer."

"Both of whom had already come forward and agreed

to testify against him in return for not being charged," the chief said. "From what you described the video would merely show them the wisdom of that decision."

"And even in his case, I find it hard to believe that he'd kill someone over it," I said. "I guess I'm wrong, because clearly someone did kill Goodwin. And maybe what happened to his trailer was the killer trying to destroy his video."

"We don't know for sure that the killer and the vandal are the same," the chief said. "I think it's highly likely, but you know what they say about making assumptions."

We'd reached Rose Noire's shed, and he gestured for me to sit in one of the wrought iron lawn chairs just outside its doors.

"Tell me everything you remember about the video he showed."

Chapter 16

Everything I could remember about Goodwin's video turned out to be quite a lot, but the chief listened intently and took copious notes. He did glance over occasionally to where Dad and Horace were at work—he'd deliberately chosen a chair that let him keep his eyes on what was happening out in the pasture. When I'd finished, he sat for a minute or so looking thoughtful.

"Why do you think Mr. Goodwin wanted to show his video?" he asked. "Or did you or Michael ask him to do it?"

"No, it was his idea," I said. "When I heard about it, I assumed it was because he wanted to show off. Now that I've seen it . . . I think he wanted to see how much trouble he could stir up."

"By showing people doing embarrassing or illegal things."

"Mostly," I said. "But in a couple of cases I think he wanted to see if people would react. Like Russ Brainard—the actor who plays Banquo in the play. Goodwin had this whole montage of pictures of the guy sneaking in and out of the library. Why? I mean, it was kind of funny how obviously furtive he was being. But was it more than that?"

"Didn't several of your vandalism problems occur in the library?"

"Exactly. So in addition to making poor Banquo look foolish, was Goodwin also fingering him as the vandal? Or at least saying 'Hey, this guy's acting all weird—check him out.'"

"It's possible." The chief was frowning thoughtfully. "But Mr. Goodwin could also be testing the waters. Maybe the message was for Mr. Brainard. He could be saying 'I have you on video going in and out of the site of some of the vandalisms. Maybe I've got actual incriminating footage I'm not showing.' If Banquo's reason for going in and out of the library were an innocent one, he wouldn't react. But if he were guilty . . ."

"You're thinking Goodwin could be a blackmailer?"

"I'm considering the possibility."

I thought about it briefly.

"I wouldn't put it past him," I said finally. "Even if he's not a classic blackmailer—you know, 'give me ten thousand dollars or I'll post this on all my social media'—he could be one of those people who likes having something on other people. Knowing he's got leverage if he wants something from them."

"Quite possible," the chief said. "And it's a dangerously slippery slope. After a while, merely having something you can hold over other people isn't so much of a thrill anymore, and along comes the temptation to get something of practical value out of what you know."

"Yeah." I glanced over at Goodwin's trailer. As trailers go, it wasn't impressive. The exterior paint was peeling and it had more than its share of dents. In fact, it was so unsightly that the first week it was here both Vern and Aida had assumed someone had abandoned it by the side of our road and had come close to having it towed to the junkyard. But I doubted that even a rundown-looking trailer came cheap. And he certainly spared no expense on his electronics. "For what it's worth," I went on, "I had wondered how a young filmmaker without much of a track record managed to support himself, much less buy so much pricey equipment. But I hadn't thought of black-mail as an option. I figured maybe he came from money. Or was really good at getting grants."

"We'll be looking into that." He entered a few more words in his notebook. "And now I need to go see if your dad can tell me anything else about the murder weapon. But after that I'll want to start talking to possible witnesses. Any chance you can give me a list of everyone who's been spending time here?"

"I'll send you my list of the cast and crew." I pulled out my phone. "It's got their emails and cell phone numbers, and I think—yes, it also shows where they're bunking. Emailing it now."

The chief had pulled out his own cell phone.

"Then I have a list of history professors and students that I can send you," I said, as I navigated the files on my phone. "I didn't compile it, so I can't guarantee that it's one hundred percent accurate—I got the History Department to put it together so I'd have some idea who was officially participating in their *Macbeth*-related research projects and who was just showing up for the free food. I'd definitely talk to Dean Braxton and Professor Cohen, both of whom were at the video event to see Goodwin's attempts to show them in a bad light."

I emailed that list off as well.

"Then you've got professors Philpotts and Kroger," I continued. "From the English Department. Kroger was here complaining to me yesterday, and Philpotts is the one Goodwin had on video sneaking into our house. If either of them was here last night to see Goodwin's show, I didn't spot them, but it was a big crowd, and even if they weren't here—well, if I were as petty and vindictive as Philpotts I'd do my best to insinuate a spy into our midst. It wouldn't be hard to find a history grad student who needs a little extra cash, or maybe an undergrad who'd like a guaranteed A in one of Philpotts's classes next semester. I don't have their contact information, but I'm sure they won't be hard to find. If we find Goodwin's video, can we charge Philpotts with trespassing? I told you about him sneaking into our house."

"It might be difficult to prove," the chief said. "He could

claim that you told him you'd leave the door open for him."

"Then why was he behaving so furtively?"

"Because he was uncomfortable entering someone else's space, even with permission?"

"I don't buy it," I said. "But yeah, a good defense attorney could run with that. Maybe he'll turn out to be the killer or the vandal. Or both. He'd get time, wouldn't he, even if it's only for the vandalism?"

"Up until now, I'm afraid it would have been a misdemeanor," the chief said. "Jail time only, if that—the local courts tend to let professors off with community service. For destruction of property, the damage has to be a thousand dollars or more to qualify as a felony. But if the same person also vandalized Mr. Goodwin's trailer, that would undoubtedly be a felony. Getting back to contact information—I'll also need to talk to the folks out at Camp Birnam. I suppose it's too much to hope that you have any information about exactly who's out there."

"I'm not even sure they know themselves," I said. "But if I had to tackle them, I'd start with a woman named Sally. No idea what her last name is, but she seems to be a lot more practical than most of the reenactors. She might be taking advantage of MacLeod's misdeeds to seize leadership of the group, and I wish her luck with it. They'd all be a lot better off."

"That's useful." He stood up and glanced over toward where Dad and Horace were still at work. "Just ask for Sally?"

"Or look around for a short, sturdy woman in her forties," I said. "Slightly better dressed than the rank and file. And if you hear anyone giving sensible orders, that will probably be her."

"High praise coming from you." The chief smiled. "After the time I spent yesterday with those reenactors, I look forward to dealing with someone you consider sensible. And by the way—that knife of yours."

"It'll probably turn up in the prop box," I said.

"But if it doesn't, let me know. It could be just a coincidence, your knife disappearing the same night Mr. Goodwin was murdered."

"But I know you're highly suspicious of coincidences," I said. "I'll let you know when I've found it."

"And just in case we run across it, can you give me a description of the missing dagger?"

"I can do better than that." I still had my phone open, so I sent him one of my pictures of it. "Check your email."

"Impressive," he said after he'd tapped his phone a few times to view it. "And it looks sharp. Is that usual with a stage weapon?"

"It's absolutely verboten." I explained about using an existing, already sharpened blade. "That's part of the reason I'm stressed—I shouldn't have let it out of my hands still sharp."

"They're all grown-ups," he said. "They should know by now not to play with knives."

"Except for Josh and Jamie," I said. "Who aren't grown-ups but very definitely know that."

"But I can understand your worry," he said. "I'll see what we can do to help find it."

With a nod, he headed back out into the pasture.

I settled back into the wrought iron chair. It was a very comfortable chair—as well it should be. I'd been working for years on perfecting the design. And right now, where I was sitting just outside Rose Noire's shed was a very good spot for keeping my eye on what was going on. If I turned my head to the right, I could see the pasture where Dad, Horace, and the chief were now talking. Turn left and I could catch a glimpse of Goodwin's trailer, where my friend Aida Butler, one of the chief's deputies, was standing guard. And straight ahead I could see the tents that housed most of the cast and crew, and beyond them the back of the house.

I could even keep tabs on what was happening around me if I closed my eyes and listened. Not that I needed a nap, but I'd been up earlier than usual, and it hadn't exactly been a stress-free morning. Suddenly I felt strangely tired. Yes, I could close my eyes and take a few deep, calming yoga breaths . . .

"Meg?"

I started and opened my eyes to see Tanya standing in front of me. She had her huge straw purse over her shoulder—had I slept so long that it was time for the actors to take off for rehearsal?

"Oh, God, did I wake you?" She looked guilty.

"If you did, it's probably a good thing—I don't want to nap away the day." I pulled out my phone and glanced at it. I couldn't have been asleep long—maybe fifteen minutes. But I felt groggy. If only I could reclaim the energy I'd felt when I'd started the day.

Tanya had taken one of the other chairs and was lifting her face to the breeze and inhaling deeply.

"This is nice," she said. "Do you think Rose Noire would mind if I came over here to relax sometimes?"

"I'm sure she wouldn't mind," I said. "She'd probably be flattered. Just ask her. And if she shows any sign of hesitation, just tell her that for some reason you find it easier to breathe over here. You could even say it has a relaxing aura, or just good vibes. She'd love hearing that."

"Okay." She chuckled. "And actually, it's true. I wonder if it has something to do with all the plants."

"Very likely—especially the lavender." I waved at the nearby expanse of purple flowers and gray-green foliage. "That's one of Rose Noire's favorites, and she planted an extra-large amount of it this year, because of the play."

"Lavender's good for theater?"

"It's supposed to be good for creativity," I said. "Also for relieving stress, anxiety, and insomnia. And headaches. And promoting harmony. And there's even science to back some of those things."

"Damn," she said. "I should spend a lot more time over here. Better yet, how about if we buy a bunch of industrial-strength fans and blow the lavender fumes over toward your yard? Because there was already a lot of stress and anxiety, and the news about Goodwin is only going to make it worse."

"No one's feeling just a little relief that we won't have him snooping around anymore?" I asked.

"A little?" She snorted. "More like a lot. But gone is one thing; dead's quite a different kettle of fish. No one wanted that." She looked thoughtful for a moment. "Well, obviously almost no one."

"True," I said. "And killing him was over the top. We could have just kicked him out. Told him he didn't have permission to film here, or over in Camp Birnam or out at the zoo. It's all private property. Having him here was the History Department's idea, not ours."

"Yes, Michael had sort of implied that."

"And last night we decided it was time to get rid of him," I said. "Not by killing him, of course," I added, seeing a look of surprise on her face. "We were just going to kick him out. Wish we'd done it a few days ago."

"Yeah," Tanya said. "Maybe he'd still be alive. Then again, I bet we're not his only enemies. Someone who has nothing to do with the show could have followed him here and killed him."

"I'm sure the chief will keep that in mind," I said. "After all, he'll be getting everyone's impressions of Goodwin."

"Okay." She nodded. "But I'll mention it all the same. You know, I think the first time Michael said he could get rid of Goodwin if we wanted, everyone was like 'No, let him stay, we want to be on the screen!' But after seeing his footage—well, last night someone suggested that we take a vote in the morning on whether to ask Michael to kick him out. I'm not saying it would have been unanimous in favor of that, but it would have been a solid majority. Maybe even a landslide."

I nodded. Could knowing that Goodwin was likely to get kicked out in the morning have had anything to do with the murder? What if someone who had a grudge against him decided to strike while the filmmaker was still within easy reach?

The chief's problem, not mine.

Although I'd make a point of mentioning it to him.

Tanya and I sat and inhaled the lavender scent for a minute or two. An ambulance arrived, and we watched as the two EMTs took out the stretcher and headed our way. They were moving briskly, but not with the kind of purposeful haste they'd have shown if there were still a chance of saving someone's life. I knew both of them, and greeted them by name as they passed. Then I closed my eyes and focused on my breathing.

"Actually, I wanted to ask you something," Tanya said.

"Ask away."

"I sort of need to know what to do about something."

"What?" I opened my eyes. She sounded—and looked—troubled.

"Do you think someone could be trying to poison Celia?"

Chapter 17

That undid most of what little relaxation the lavender and the breathing had accomplished.

"I don't know," I said. "What makes you think that might be happening?"

"You know how she is about hydration," Tanya said. "She's always got a bottle of water going."

I nodded.

"And leaving half-finished bottles around during rehearsal. I mean, we all do that to some extent, but she's the worst. And it's mostly disposable bottles—she has one or two reusable bottles, but she misplaces them all the time, so she snags disposable bottles wherever she can. And people give her a hard time about the environmental impact, so then she reuses them over and over, which they say you shouldn't do because then they're like petri dishes for bacteria."

"I know," I said. "And nasty chemicals. Don't get my dad started on that subject."

"So I'd been wondering if maybe that was the reason for her stomach problems," Tanya said. "What if she picked up some kind of gastrointestinal bug and kept reinfecting herself with her water bottles?"

"You could be right." Now that I thought of it, you almost always saw Celia with a water bottle in her hand or at her elbow. And when she wanted a sip of water, she tended to commandeer any glass or bottle in sight—I'd lost my own supply that way a time or two. "Have you tried suggesting that to her?"

"Well, I didn't think she'd react well if I marched over and said 'Celia, you idiot, I think you're poisoning yourself.' I was looking for a way to sort of bring it up naturally in conversation."

I nodded.

"Only I started to realize that she doesn't have conversations that include me." Tanya looked not so much hurt as annoyed. "She doesn't socialize a lot with anyone, but ever since I've been trying to find a way to mention it to her, I started noticing that she goes out of her way to avoid me. If I join a group, she leaves."

"I don't suppose that has anything to do with the fact that Michael has you fill in for her when she's too sick to rehearse."

"Of course not." She rolled her eyes. "Anyway, I was thinking maybe I should try to get someone else to talk to her about it. I was going to see what you thought."

"I think it's a good idea," I said. "I could suggest it to my dad."

"That would be great," she said. "But then this morning something else came up. Just now I helped Rose Noire fix up Celia's room a little so it's ready to welcome her back whenever the hospital releases her. We changed the sheets and towels and brought in a vase of fresh flowers. Rose Noire said she'd go up again later to dust and vacuum— Celia probably hasn't had much time for that since she's been here."

I nodded. I didn't get the impression dusting and vacuuming were high on Celia's priorities at home, either—or for that matter, picking up anything she'd thrown on the floor—but that was neither here nor there.

"And I found this in her room." Tanya reached into the straw purse and pulled out a bottle—a pretty ordinary bottle of Deer Park spring water.

"She buys those by the case," I said.

"I know." Tanya looked impatient. "Rose Noire and I

must have collected a dozen empty or half-empty bottles, and she had most of a case sitting on her dresser, still in the plastic wrap. This was in the case—but look at the cap."

She held the bottle closer and I could see that the white plastic cap had been cracked open.

"Someone opened this bottle and then put it back in the case?" I asked.

"Exactly." Tanya set the bottle down on the wrought iron table between us. "And maybe she did it herself—like maybe she cracked it open, and then realized she already had a bottle going and put it back. But look at the water—does it look different to you?"

I leaned closer so I could peer at the bottle. It looked like water.

"Different how?" I asked.

"I don't know—it's more obvious if you hold it next to another bottle. A little more . . . not exactly cloudy. Viscous, maybe."

I peered at the bottle again.

"I'd have to have something to compare it with," I said.

"Maybe you could do more than that," she suggested. "Isn't your cousin the forensics expert? You think maybe he could test it to see if there's anything there that shouldn't be?"

"I could ask," I said. "Although it could be a while before Horace has time to do any forensic work apart from what's connected to Goodwin's murder."

"This could be connected," she said. "You saw the video last night—did you notice the bottle swapping scene?"

"Bottle swapping scene?" I shook my head.

"Remember the scene where she was doing her 'Out, damned spot' speech and suddenly doubled over in the middle of it?"

I nodded.

"It was in that scene. There was a half-full Deer Park water bottle sitting at the far edge of the shot, and then a hand comes in and takes it out and puts it back in again a little later. Or maybe puts in a different bottle of the same brand—I wasn't sure the water was at the same level."

"I didn't notice that," I admitted. "I was probably too focused on Celia."

"Well, it was pretty subtle," Tanya said. "I'm not sure I'd have noticed it if I hadn't been already hyperaware of Celia and her wretched water bottles and the possibility that she was making herself sick with them. And okay, maybe it wasn't her bottle. Maybe it belonged to someone else, and they picked it up, took a swig, and put it back. But what if it was her bottle? What if someone swapped it for a different bottle—one with some kind of poison in it?"

"What did the hand look like?" I asked. "Male or female? Big or small? Pale or tanned?"

"No idea." She shook her head, and the little metal beads in her braids made soft tinkling sounds. "The camera was focused on Celia, so the hand and the bottle weren't really that clear. Plus I was focused mostly on her and didn't realize what I was seeing until it was almost over. I was planning to suggest to Michael that someone take a closer look at that part of the video. But I guess that's a no-go, if whoever killed Goodwin also destroyed all his video."

"Well, Horace is still processing the trailer," I said. "I suppose we can always hope that he might come across a flash drive or something that the killer missed." I decided not to mention the possibility that Goodwin might have backed up his video online. Maybe I was being paranoid, but the less said about that the better—what if the killer figured out where the online backup was and got to it before the chief did? "But yeah—in the meantime, I'll turn the water bottle over to him and see what he can find out."

"Thanks," she said. "I'll leave it with you. It'd be nice to stop worrying about Celia and go back to being annoyed with her." She frowned and looked as if she was trying to decide whether to say something. "She acts as if I'm trying to steal her part," she said finally. "I'm not. But there's a big difference between trying to cut someone out and being ready to pitch in when asked. If she's too sick and Michael asks me to fill in, I'm not saying no. Not for a rehearsal, and not for the whole show. I wish she'd get that."

"The show must go on," I said. "To coin a phrase."

"Yeah. You must think we're all horrible," she said. "Me quivering to step into Celia's role if she gets sick enough. Macbeth and Banquo doing their best to upstage each other. Fawn constantly trying to make her boss look bad in the hope of replacing her."

"Fawn the costume assistant?"

"Yeah. Maybe she doesn't do it around you, but when she's around us she's always criticizing Maeve's designs and complaining that Maeve hasn't told her stuff and whining about how much work there is to do with Maeve never here."

"Why in the world would we want the costume designer full-time during the rehearsal period?" I asked. "We wouldn't need Fawn if Michael didn't want everyone to get used to moving in cloaks and robes and whatever. Taking care of the rehearsal costumes isn't exactly a full-time job."

"Well, she's also supposed to keep Maeve from having to come all the way down here whenever she needs a measurement or wants someone to try on a costume," Tanya added.

"True," I said. "But again, very far from a full-time job. If Fawn's overworked, she needs to find a different job." And the very inexperienced Fawn was clueless if she seriously thought she had a chance of replacing Maeve—an award-winning costume designer who had worked successfully with Michael at least a dozen times in the past decade.

"Oh, I think Fawn knows she's got it cushy—she's just a recreational whiner." She stood and stretched. "And now that I've handed over that water bottle to you, I'm going to go focus on getting ready for rehearsal."

She nodded a farewell and headed back toward the house. Looking very cheerful now that she'd passed along her worries to me.

I studied the water bottle for a moment. Then I got up and peered inside the shed. Yes, there were a few water bottles there—mostly partly empty ones. Rose Noire collected all the abandoned ones she found lying around, used the leftover water for her potted plants, and recycled the plastic. I grabbed one with the water at the halfway mark, so I wouldn't mistake it for the one Tanya had brought me. I set it on the wrought-iron table and studied them both.

Yeah, the full one did look different somehow. Or was it only my imagination?

"I say half empty," came Horace's voice from behind me. "But that's probably because I'm a cynic."

I glanced up to see him and the chief returning from the pasture.

"I work very hard on seeing the bottle as half full," the chief said. "Think positively—that's my motto."

"I'm more interested in this one that's definitely almost full," I said. "And maybe you will be, too, when I tell you about it."

"I'm listening." The chief took the chair he'd been occupying before.

"You want me, too?" Horace asked.

When I nodded, he also took a seat, and I told them both what Tanya had related about the water bottle. Long before I'd finished, Horace pulled out a pair of gloves and an evidence bag and began formally securing the bottle as evidence.

"Of course she handled it," Horace said. "I hope you didn't."

I shook my head.

"We can use her fingerprints for exclusionary purposes," the chief said. "Because we will be getting everybody's fingerprints."

Horace sighed.

"Chief," I said. "I've only known Tanya for a few weeks. I like her, and I'm inclined to believe what she told me. But . . ."

"But none of us is an infallible judge of character," he said. "And what if Ms.—"

He frowned and glanced down at his notebook, trying to be casual about it.

"West," I said. "Tanya West."

"Thanks." He looked up from the notebook. "Rather a lot of names to take in this morning. What if Ms. West knows her colleague is being poisoned because she's the one who's been doing the poisoning? She might think it would be a good idea to tell you about it to divert suspicion from herself."

"Plus if she planted the bottle and isn't sure she was careful about fingerprints, now they're on it in a non-incriminating way," Horace said.

"Exactly," I said. "I have no idea what motive she'd have for killing Goodwin, but then I don't know her all that well. I don't know any of them all that well."

"Did Ms. West appear in Mr. Goodwin's video?" the chief asked.

"Not in any way that sticks out in my mind," I said. "He probably had her in the blooper section—you know, flubbing a line or tripping on stage. Stuff like that. Of course, we have no idea how much more footage Goodwin was planning to show. Celia and her queasy stomach wouldn't have been all that great as a grand finale."

"Yeah," Horace said. "We don't know what we don't know."

"But with any luck we'll get hold of the video one way or another." The chief stood. "Thanks for giving us the water bottle. If Ms. West asks what happened to it—"

"I'll tell her that I turned it over to Horace and he'll test it when he gets a chance," I said.

He strode off toward the trailer.

"It's not even a lie." Horace scribbled a few more words on the evidence bag and got to his feet. "I'll take a sample to do a few quick and dirty tests on my own before sending it down to the Crime Lab in Richmond."

He nodded and hurried off after the chief.

I glanced over at the yard. The cast and crew were mostly up and around. Someone must have made a run to town—Rose Noire was laying out boxes of fresh doughnuts and bagels from the bakery at Muriel's Diner.

I closed my eyes and focused on seeing if I could remember anything else from Goodwin's footage. Of course, the chief wouldn't have to rely on my memory alone. He'd be asking everyone else, too. But the more I could remember . . .

"Meg?"

Chapter 18

I opened my eyes to see Rose Noire standing in front of me with an anxious look on her face. Had I fallen asleep again?

"Is something wrong?" I braced myself.

"I need to show you something."

"Okay," I said. "What?"

She strode off. With a sigh, I stood up and glanced around. Nothing new was happening out in the pasture or over at the trailer, so I followed her. She led me around to the other side of the shed—the side away from the house.

"There."

She seemed to be pointing at where the black Sumatrans were busily pecking and scratching in the herb fields. And many of them happily taking dust baths—nice that someone found something about the drought to enjoy. I was about to ask Rose Noire what I was looking for when I spotted it.

No, them.

"I see we have intruders," I said.

In addition to the expected number of diminutive glossy black hens scratching and pecking among the herbs under the supervision of the rooster Napoleon I spotted two noticeably larger birds. If they were trying to blend in with the crowd for free feed, they'd picked the wrong poultry yard—the two newcomers were at least twice the size of the Sumatrans, with white bodies, red bills and legs, and patches of soft brown on their heads, backs, and bellies.

Also, they were ducks. Ducks, or possibly fairly young geese—it was hard to tell at this distance.

"When did they show up?" I asked.

"They were in the coop when I opened it this morning."

"*In* the coop?"

"Yes. When I let the Sumatrans out of my shed, I opened the door to the coop so they could go in out of the sun later if they wanted and those ducks strolled out."

"Weird," I said. "Should we maybe get a lock for the coop? Because if birds can just appear in the coop, they can also disappear."

"I hadn't thought of that," she said. "Yes, let's get locks for both coops. Because I don't think we've seen the end of this."

"You think it's some kind of trend?" I asked. "A new way of pranking people by inflicting random unsolicited water-fowl on them?"

"I think this has something to do with those people who are casting spells in the woods," she said, in a half whisper.

"We don't know that anyone's casting spells in the woods." I kept my voice calm and normal. "I think it's much more likely to be just a few of the Birnamites sneaking away at night to do something the others don't approve of. Maybe some of them are tired of eating that horrible stew, so they creep off to the woods occasionally to grill hot dogs and roast foil-wrapped ears of corn and have a nice anachronistic pig out."

"Roasting corn isn't exactly an anachronism, is it?" Rose Noire pointed out.

"It is if you're an eleventh-century Scot," I said.

"Oh, good point," she said. "I forgot they're supposed to be pre-Columbian Old World. Most of them are just kind of generically peasanty and dirty. But I don't think that's what they're doing. I'm positive they're out there casting evil spells. What about that grimoire page?"

"From a printed book, remember," I said. "Not someone's

hand-lettered personal magical journal. Maybe someone's doing research on medieval magic rituals so they can give Michael suggestions on how to improve the accuracy of the witch scenes in the play. He'll love that." I rolled my eyes, just in case she missed the sarcasm in my tone.

"You think it's one of the three witches?" Her air of fierce suspicion alarmed me.

"It could be one of the three witches," I said. "They'd be interested in enhancing their scenes. Or Hecate— remember, there's a fourth witch in the play. But it could also be one of the reenactors who's caught sight of a rehearsal and gotten fired up to research the real thing. Or one of the history students. In fact, if you ask me, that's the most likely scenario. All the history students have been doing research, either about medieval Scotland or Elizabethan England. They're all determined to give Michael helpful hints about making the production more historically accurate."

"I barely know any of the history students," she muttered. Her expression suggested that she planned to remedy this omission at the earliest possible moment, and that the history students were unlikely to find the process enjoyable.

"They're mostly harmless," I said. "Michael always listens very patiently, then tells them that he'll keep their suggestions in mind, but that he considers precise external accuracy less important than communicating the inner truth of the historical situation to a present-day audience. He can make it sound not only plausible but downright virtuous and responsible."

"But what if they've gone beyond researching and have started experimenting?"

Getting Rose Noire off a subject could sometimes be harder than taking a stolen chunk of dangerous chocolate away from Spike. Would she feel insulted if I suggested that we had a lot more urgent things to worry about than a bunch of nutcases gathering in the woods to chant "double, double, toil and trouble" around a cauldron?

Then again, maybe we should worry. Rose Noire had good instincts, I reminded myself. And she probably had a better idea than I did what a group of not-so-nice people might be getting up to out there in the woods if they believed in magic. They might go beyond merely chanting spells. I should probably stress that angle when I notified the chief about the mysterious poultry arrival.

But since she knew that however polite he was about it, he didn't believe in spells, auras, and premonitions, would turning the whole thing over to the police satisfy her?

"We'll keep our eyes on them," I said finally.

"How can we keep our eyes on them if we have no idea who they are?" she demanded.

"Actually, 'we'll keep our eyes on them' was short for 'We'll remain vigilant both to detect any future signs of magic use and to identify the perpetrators thereof.'"

She seemed to find that acceptable. She even brightened a little. Then her face fell again.

"If only I hadn't been too tired to stake out that clearing last night." She sighed deeply. "Maybe if I had . . ." She let her voice trail off.

"I can't see how staking out the clearing would have prevented Goodwin's murder," I said. "It wouldn't even have prevented whoever stashed those ducks in the chicken coop. And frankly, I'm very glad you weren't wandering around the woods and pastures last night. What if the murderer had run into you instead of Goodwin?"

She didn't look as if this thought consoled her.

"Meanwhile, we should tell the chief about these ducks," I said. "And then take practical steps to protect the poultry," I said. "Specifically, installing those locks. I could call—damn!"

"What's wrong?" Rose Noire sounded anxious, so I hurried to reassure her.

"Nothing big—I just realized that Randall Shiffley's out of town. Not a problem—we can ask Vern." I glanced around and spotted Vern and Aida talking by the door of Goodwin's trailer.

"I didn't know Vern had anything to do with running the family construction company," Rose Noire said.

"He doesn't," I said. "But he can tell me which of their cousins Randall left in charge when he left town—and motivate them to get the job done almost as fast as Randall could."

I turned to go, then had a thought. I pulled out my phone, opened the camera app, and took a number of pictures of the new arrivals, both from a distance and then from as close as I could get without stampeding them. I made sure to get a few little Sumatrans in for scale.

"Good thinking," Rose Noire said. "In case they disappear as mysteriously as they arrive, we will have proof that they were here."

"I hadn't thought of that," I admitted as I turned and headed for where Vern was now back to standing guard—well, technically sitting guard—outside the trailer. "I was just going to see if I could look them up on the internet—if we knew what kind of ducks or geese they are, we might have an easier time tracking down where they came from. Finding out if they were stolen."

"Also good thinking."

As we approached the trailer, we could see that Vern seemed to be keeping watch not only over the trailer door but also over a small pile of evidence bags that had accumulated on the ground at his feet.

"We could get another deputy to take them down to Richmond," Vern was saying over his shoulder. "Sammy could do it. Unless you're thinking it would be useful to hang out with all your buddies at the Crime Lab."

"Let's see how it goes," came Horace's voice from inside the trailer.

"Hey, Vern," I said. "Got a couple of questions for you."

"Fire away."

"Any chance you could help me arrange for someone from Shiffley Construction to install locks on our chicken coop doors sometime today?" I asked.

"Sure." He looked puzzled, but pulled out his phone. "Any particular reason?"

He left unspoken the question of why I was worrying about this when a murder had just happened in our backyard. I explained about the uninvited ducks.

"That's mighty peculiar," he said, frowning.

"And leads to my second question," I said. "You think I should tell the chief about it?"

"The chief?" He frowned slightly. "Are you thinking these ducks could have something to do with the murder?"

"I have no idea," I said. "And if it doesn't, maybe I shouldn't bother the chief with it."

"I'm almost positive they're tied to the murder," Rose Noire said. "Look at where we found poor Mr. Goodwin's body."

"In close proximity to the chicken coop where Rose Noire found the ducks this morning," I explained.

"Ye-es," Vern said.

"Well, yes, but more importantly, what was he doing out there?" Rose Noire demanded.

"If we knew that—" Vern began.

"The place where we found him is more or less directly on the path he'd follow if he were heading out to take more movies of the spell casting," she said.

"Spell casting?" Vern echoed.

"Remember that place in the woods you went out to investigate?" I asked.

"Where someone was having a dangerous illegal campfire?" he asked. "Because you're right. The spot where we found him's not exactly on the direct path from his trailer to that clearing, but making allowances for the fact that he's not from around here and a city slicker to boot . . . yeah, he could have been heading there. Good thinking," he added, nodding to Rose Noire.

"Just what did you find out there?" I asked.

"Remains of several campfires," he said. "None of them more than two weeks old, and whoever started them was pretty damned careless. Pardon my French, but we were lucky those idiots didn't start a forest fire. The clearing was full of bone-dry fallen leaves, and they hardly bothered to rake them away from the edge of their fire. You can see a place where some of the leaves caught fire and they had to stamp them out. And you could also see they'd been cooking there."

"Really?" I asked. "And how did you know—did you find leftover food?"

"No, but you could see the marks where they set a pot over the flames—one of those old-fashioned three-legged cast-iron pots from the look of it. You could see the indentations of the legs in the ground."

"An old-fashioned three-legged cast-iron pot," I repeated. "What you might call a cauldron?"

Vern nodded.

"They weren't cooking," Rose Noire half whispered. "They were casting evil spells. Brewing up foul potions."

"Evil spells?" Vern echoed. "Why evil? I'd have thought you'd be the last to jump to the conclusion that anything magic is evil. What's to say they weren't out there doing a variation on that rain dance spell you organized a few days ago?"

"No." She shook her head. "There were signs. Show him, Meg."

I pulled out my phone and opened up one of the pictures I'd taken of the scrap of paper Rose Noire had found. He peered at it with a puzzled look on his face.

"The writing's in Latin," I said. "So don't try to puzzle it out—I'm hoping Dad can translate. Just look at the illustrations."

He nodded and continued to stare at my phone for a bit.

"Okay, I see what you mean," he said finally. "I don't much like the look of those drawings. Something nasty about them. Especially that one of the horned dude slitting the rooster's throat. This has something to do with the clearing?"

"I found it there," Rose Noire said. "Right next to where the fires were. And Meg—you saw Mr. Goodwin's video—that scene where those three people were stirring something in a cauldron—he must have filmed it out in that clearing."

"Well, yes, he could have," I said cautiously.

"Wouldn't be hard to figure out for sure if we ever find that video," Vern said. "But maybe we could just ask the three people who were out there."

I glanced at Rose Noire. She shook her head.

"The picture quality was pretty terrible," I explained. "We couldn't tell who it was, much less where."

"But what if Mr. Goodwin was heading out to the clearing in the hope of getting more video?" Rose Noire said. "Taking some kind of film that would work better in really low light."

"Or maybe some kind of night-vision lens," Vern mused. "Yeah, we should definitely tell the chief about that. I don't quite see how the ducks fit in, though."

"Neither do I," I said. "So maybe it's a complete coincidence that two ducks appear out of nowhere on the same night when someone is murdered a few hundred feet away."

"I'm not a big believer in coincidence," Vern said with a chuckle. "And I don't think the chief is, either."

"Maybe the spell casters wanted to perform a ghastly

blood sacrifice," Rose Noire said breathlessly. "But realized we keep too good a watch over our own chickens and
gave up on the idea of stealing one of them. So they stole
two ducks from somewhere else instead, and were on their
way out to the clearing with them when they realized Mr.
Goodwin was following them. And they killed him to keep
him from revealing what they were up to, and didn't think
it was safe to go ahead with the sacrifice, so they stuffed
the poor ducks into the chicken coop and went home."

Vern and I looked at each other. It sounded pretty
crazy, but then so was the sudden, apparently random appearance of the ducks. And I'd seen the footage of the
three women—well, three people—stirring the cauldron
and dancing around it. She hadn't made that up. However crazy it sounded—well, there could be people crazy
enough to do it.

"You could have a point," Vern said. "Maybe I should
take a look at these critters. If I knew what kind of ducks
they were, maybe I could find out if anyone's missing any."

"I took pictures." I pulled out my phone and showed
him. He took the phone and peered intently at it.

"I think those are geese, not ducks," he said finally.
"Pretty small for geese, but look at the bills—ducks have
broad flat bills for straining food out of the water. Geese
have shorter, sharper bills for pecking people with. And
each other. I'm sure if we asked your granddaddy he'd
give us the scientific reason why their bills ended up that
way, but if you ask me it's just for pure meanness. Never
tangle with a full-grown goose."

"Young geese, then," I said. "Goslings. Do you recognize the breed?"

"No," he said. "And I think I would remember if I'd
seen them around anywhere—they've got pretty distinctive markings. But text me a couple of those shots. I'll ask
down at the feed store—if anyone local's raising geese like
that, you can bet they'll know."

"Can do." I pulled out my phone and sent him the best of my goose photos.

"And I'll call down to Shiffley Construction as soon as I brief the chief on this."

"Brief me on what?"

Chapter 19

We turned to find the chief had returned.

"You tell him," Rose Noire implored me in an undertone. "He'll listen to you."

And she dashed away. Probably just as well. The chief was much too polite ever to show it, but I had the sneaking suspicion that Rose Noire baffled and irritated him sometimes. Her theory would sound a lot saner if either Vern or I explained it. And the more I thought about it, the more convinced I was that she was right—there could be something sinister about the sudden arrival of the geese.

Since I still had my phone out, I texted him the goose photos while Vern filled him in on the unexplained geese, the illicit campfire, and Rose Noire's theory of how they might be connected to the murder. He made it sound not only sane but actually plausible.

"Crazier things have happened," the chief said. "Horace, have you been listening to this?"

"Yes, chief," Horace said. "And before you ask, I haven't yet seen any sign of goose feathers, either here or near the body, but I'll keep my eyes open."

"Good." The chief was studying my goose photos.

"And I'll need to take feather samples from those geese," Horace added. "I'll be putting in for hazardous duty pay."

"Get Rose Noire to help," I said. "Give her a few hours with those geese and they'll be following her around, just like the chickens."

"Good idea." Horace sat down on one of the chairs

just outside the trailer door and mopped his face with his sleeve. "Sorry, boss, but I'm nowhere near finished yet."

"No problem," the chief said. "Anything interesting so far?"

"I'll go make that call about the locks." Vern stood up and ambled off. Forensics discussions were not his cup of tea.

"Actually," Horace said, "the pattern of destruction is pretty interesting."

"There's a pattern?" I muttered, glancing involuntarily at the portion of the mess visible though the open door of the trailer.

"Oh, yes." Horace's normally placid face was animated—you never saw him with that keen a look of pleasure and excitement outside a crime scene, and I got the impression this was turning into a more interesting crime scene than most. "Look around—at first glance, it looks like the vandal attacked everything. Food, dishes, toiletries, clothes, books, papers, electronics—all of it swept onto the floor and stomped on."

The chief and I both nodded.

"But if you start looking more closely . . . the books are fine, except for the ones that fell into the spilled food or the beer. No pages ripped out. There's broken glass and china, but only a little, and only from things that would probably have shattered when they fell—no suggestion that the vandal stomped around to break more of them. Doritos and Cheerios are pretty easy to crush, but you could probably sweep up a couple of bowls full of unbroken ones in there if you wanted, although I wouldn't recommend eating any of them because there could be broken glass mixed in. The vandal didn't rip any clothes or towels or papers. It's all pretty much 'make the place a mess, and do it fast'—until you get to the electronics."

"The vandal targeted the electronics, then?" the chief asked.

"Big time." Horace nodded vigorously. He took off his right glove, reached into his pocket, and took out a little gadget that I recognized as a laser pointer. "For example, see those bits of red plastic."

He turned on the laser pointer and aimed its little red beam at a scattering of bright red plastic shards just inside the doorway.

"Used to be the case of an external hard drive," he said. "An older one, the kind that uses a rotating metal disk as a storage medium. This is probably the disk that used to be inside it." He moved the beam over to indicate what looked like an unmarked CD that had been broken into a dozen jagged fragments. "Whoever did this didn't just stomp on the hard drive by accident. Those things are sturdy. They broke open the case, pulled out the disk, and then shattered it. Probably with a hammer—I recovered a hammer from Goodwin's tool chest that has some sugges-tive traces. We might be able to prove it was used on the electronics."

"And not just on this hard drive, I gather." The chief looked grim. "All the electronics."

"Well, no—not all the electronics," Horace said. "Only the electronics that have any kind of memory. From the fragments I've found so far, my best guess is that they did in two laptops, four external hard drives, half a dozen SD cards, and a flash drive or two. And it's obviously some-one with at least a basic idea of how these things work. One of the laptops was solid state, and at least one of the hard drives—the data isn't stored on disks but on a series of computer chips. The vandal pulverized the chips—see there?" The pointer beam darted over to some debris that I wouldn't have recognized as the remains of computer chips if Horace hadn't told us.

"So whoever did this knew what he was doing?"

"Seems like it. See that?" Horace moved the pointer to another bit of debris. "That used to be a flash drive. Like a solid-state hard drive, it uses chips for storage. And right beside it you can see the remains of an SD card—that's the kind of card you use in a digital camera. The camera it came out of looks fine." The pointer indicated a large and complicated-looking Sony video camera with hardly a scratch on any of its gleaming black surfaces. "And the vandal didn't even touch either of those two monitors, or the speakers. I'm assuming because there wouldn't be any data on them."

"What are our chances of recovering any data from any of these broken things?" the chief asked.

"Slim to none." Horace sighed and looked discouraged. "Of course, if Goodwin was smart, he backed up his stuff to the cloud somewhere."

"Which would mean in theory we could recover it," the chief said. "Assuming we figure out what service he used and then go through the tedious process of proving we have a right to see it."

"I'm keeping my eyes open for any clue about that," Horace said. "But I'm starting to get the idea he's one of those people who doesn't write down anything, just keeps it all in his computer and his phone."

"Has the phone turned up here in the trailer?" the chief asked. "Because it wasn't on him."

"Not yet." Horace shook his head. "And I haven't run across his keys, either."

"So last night someone either lured Mr. Goodwin out near the woods or followed him there," the chief said. "And killed him by striking his head multiple times with an as-yet-undetermined object."

"Actually, I have a candidate for the object." Horace moved the red beam back to the Sony camera. "Traces of blood along the bottom edges of that. The strap's the right size to account for the abrasions Dr. Langslow found on the victim's neck. And the break in the strap is recent."

He used the pointer to trace the worn black strap to a point where we could see the clean, slightly ragged edge.

"Suggesting that someone grabbed the camera, causing the strap to break, and then hit him over the head with it," the chief said.

"Exactly." Horace nodded. "Several times."

"And during roughly that same time period, someone entered Mr. Goodwin's trailer and destroyed every electronic data storage device they could find," the chief said. "Attempting to make it look like yet another attack by the vandal who has already been plaguing the household."

Horace nodded again.

"We don't know in what order these two things happened, and we don't even know for sure that the same person is responsible," the chief went on. "The killer could have come back here, bringing the camera used to kill Mr. Goodwin, to ransack the trailer and destroy any device that could store video. Or the killer could have chucked the camera in here and left, with someone else coming in to do the vandalism."

"Could be," Horace said. "Or the killer could have come to the trailer, seen that the vandalism had happened while he was out in the pasture killing Goodwin, and decided it was a good place to chuck the murder weapon. Still, I'm betting it was the same person."

The chief nodded and turned to me.

"Was there a reason Mr. Goodwin's trailer was so far from the house?" he asked. "It certainly would have been more convenient for him to have parked closer to the house or the barn."

"He was parked closer to the house the first couple of nights," I said. "But it turned out he was a chronic insomniac who whiled away his sleepless nights listening to heavy metal music and watching horror movies. After the second night we bought a two-hundred-foot extension cord and made him park as far away from the house as he could and still get power from the barn."

"And the distance was enough to eliminate the noise problem?"

"Well, that and the fact that we warned him if he woke us up again, we'd kick him off the property entirely," I said. "And explained that if we evicted him, we'd let everyone in the county know why, so fat chance of getting anyone else to let him park in their yard, much less use their electricity. He was still noisier than seemed quite necessary, but he wasn't keeping everyone up all night, so we could live with it."

The chief nodded. Then he turned back to Horace and gestured toward the trailer.

"The noise from smashing the electronics wouldn't have carried to the house?"

Horace glanced back and forth between the house and the trailer and shook his head.

"Not that well," he said. "And even if anyone heard it, by now they'd probably gotten used to ignoring a certain level of nuisance noise from this direction."

The chief nodded.

We all three stared at the trailer for a minute or so.

"So, Horace," I said. "*You* can't extract data from any of those ruined devices."

"And I'm not sure anyone can," Horace said. "But I know what you're about to suggest. Chief, it might be worth checking to see if any of Rob's people could figure out how to do it."

The chief nodded. I had to suppress a chuckle. By "Rob's people," Horace meant the tech experts who worked for my brother's company. Although Mutant Wizards had started out as a computer game company, it had gradually expanded into a multifaceted technology powerhouse and its Data Wizards division was rapidly making a name for itself as a leading provider of forensic technology and cyber security services.

"I'll give him a call," the chief said.

"Actually, Rob's on vacation," I said.

"Again?" Horace muttered.

"Again," I said. "Didn't you hear why he's taking so many vacations?"

"Because he can afford to?" To Horace's credit he sounded more philosophical than envious.

"Well, there is that," I said. "But he and Delaney announced that they're not going to set a date for their wedding until they figure out where they want to go for the honeymoon. That's why they've been traveling so much— they're test-driving possible honeymoon destinations."

"So what's the latest candidate." The chief looked amused, which was a nice change from the grim look he'd worn ever since he'd arrived.

"They're doing a repeat visit to Maui," I said. "And Grandfather went with them—not that he'll be going along on the actual honeymoon, but he's taken a sudden interest in volcanos, and this was a good excuse to visit some. Anyway, keep your fingers crossed—we could have a winner in the honeymoon sweepstakes. The point is—there's a six-hour time difference. No way Rob would be awake unless he hadn't fallen into bed yet, so it could be hours before he gets back to you. But our nephew Kevin is running most of Data Wizards these days—you could just call him."

"If you think your brother would be okay with that," the chief said.

"Better yet, I'll contact Kevin," I said. "And shoot Rob an email to let him know I did it. So if he's not happy, he can blame me."

I had pulled out my phone and was already texting Kevin.

"Urgent!" my text said. "Chief Burke needs your help

on a murder case. Can you come out to where Damien Goodwin's trailer is parked on the road near our house?" And then I composed and sent a very short email to Rob to tell him that I was enlisting Kevin's help.

"Done," I said. "And I told Kevin to come to the trailer—I assume you'll be here a while longer?"

"Quite a while longer." Horace nodded. "Which is a good thing, since Kevin's not exactly a morning person."

"Kevin takes not being a morning person to completely new levels," I said. "If you see him before noon, it's probably because he stayed up all night working."

"Or running a Dungeons & Dragons game," Horace added.

"Or doing both simultaneously," I said. "He also takes multitasking to new levels. But contacting him directly should still be faster than waiting on Rob."

"Remind me not to use either of you two as character references."

Chapter 20

Kevin's voice startled all three of us, but the chief managed to hide it better than either Horace or I could.

"Mr. McReady," the chief said. "Meg and Horace were just saying that if anyone could assist us it would be you. Horace, if you could brief him on our problem?"

Kevin draped his lanky frame over one of Goodwin's lawn chairs and cocked his head expectantly.

"You heard about Goodwin's show last night?" Horace began.

"I was there," Kevin said. "Up on the balcony," he added, seeing my look of surprise. "The jerk really knew how to tick off everyone, didn't he? It's a wonder no one knocked him off long before this."

"Then you would share Meg's suspicion that Mr. Goodwin's video might hold a clue to his murder?" the chief asked.

"Yeah," Kevin said. "Only question is whether one of them did it or whether they all got together and did the whole *Orient Express* thing."

"The chief would really like to see that video," Horace said. "Just one problem." He stepped aside and indicated the open door of the trailer.

"Wow." Kevin craned sideways to get a better view. "Somebody did a number on this place."

"The chief is wondering if there's a chance of retrieving data from any of this," Horace said.

Although Kevin usually guarded against showing anything that resembled enthusiasm, he pried himself out of the lawn chair speedily and followed Horace to the door of the trailer.

The chief and I watched as the two of them scrutinized and discussed various collections of debris. I could see Kevin was getting interested in the challenge. When he turned back to talk to the chief, he had what I called "the look." I'd seen it often enough on Dad's face when he'd encountered some new medical oddity. Or on Grandfather's face when an animal was in peril.

"I have no idea if it's possible to recover data from any of these media," he said. "But it would be a really cool experiment to find out. Could be a real breakthrough if we figure out a methodology. And if it's the video you're hoping to find—that's even harder, because they're big, complicated files."

"So it might be impossible to recover any of Mr. Goodwin's video," the chief said. "And even if it is possible, it will take time."

"Yeah," Kevin said. "An unpredictable but almost certainly non-trivial amount of time. Still, it's worth a try. But have you considered—"

Then he stopped.

"Considered what?" the chief asked.

"Not that I want to tell you how to go about your detecting," Kevin said. "But have you considered that he might have backed up some of his stuff to the cloud? Assuming he wasn't a complete idiot, of course."

"We thought of that," Horace said. "The problem is that so far we have no idea what cloud services he might have used."

"Once we get his financial information we can probably figure out which ones he had accounts with," the chief said. "And even before that, once the county attorney gets me the paperwork I can contact some of the more commonly used cloud services."

"But all that's going to take time, and meanwhile the

killer's hanging around here," Kevin said. "I might be able to help you figure out where he backs up—he was using Meg and Michael's Wi-Fi when he first got here."

"Until you kicked him off," I said. "You never did explain exactly what he was up to."

"Well, for one thing, he was trying to visit some pretty dodgy sites that I blocked him from going to," Kevin said.

"What kind of dodgy sites?" I asked. "Unusually disgusting porn sites? Sites where he could have picked up malware and brought it into our network? Sites that might have brought law enforcement down on our necks?"

"Yeah," he said. "All of the above, actually. I didn't let him get away with anything. With so many new people using the guest Wi-Fi, I was keeping a pretty close watch on traffic. I shut him down hard and didn't let him go anywhere he shouldn't have. And after that I watched him like a hawk, so I noticed when he started trying to set up a bunch of networked wireless video cameras. Only in a couple of the public areas of the house, but I didn't figure you wanted him spying on people anywhere—and what if he decided to expand into the bedrooms and the bathrooms and such?"

"I wish you'd told us," I said. "If I'd known he was doing that, I'd have insisted on kicking him out long ago. And I remember when you changed the guest password, but how do you know he hasn't talked one of the other guests into giving him the new password and gotten back on our network?"

"I knew that was a possibility," Kevin said. "Either someone would feel sorry for him and give him the password, or someone would have written it down and wouldn't be careful. So I made sure all his devices were blocked, and I kept an eye out in case he tried to get on with any new ones."

"That's good," I said.

"Good and bad," he said. "Kept him from getting up to

anything that could cause problems, but it also meant he couldn't use your Wi-Fi to back up his video to the cloud."

"So maybe he hasn't backed up recently," I said. "Damn."

"Not from your Wi-Fi," Kevin said. "He'd have had to go someplace with readily available public Wi-Fi. Here in Caerphilly, that would pretty much come down to the library or the coffee shop. No way he could do it on his cell phone connection—especially not out here in the middle of nowhere." He glanced around with a faint frown, as if suddenly noticing how many hundreds of suspicious-looking trees were looming over him.

"I can check to see if he's been hanging around at either place." The chief was nodding with satisfaction and scribbling in his notebook. "Let's hope it was the coffee shop, because you know how Ms. Ellie is about protecting the privacy of her patrons. Even if all they're doing is abusing the free Wi-Fi."

"Yeah," Kevin said. "But we might not even need to bother her. Unless he was a total idiot, he'd have done some backing up in the first couple of days, before I kicked him. So even though he might have had to move to some other Wi-Fi, he'd be uploading to the same place—wherever he had an account. I'll check the traffic on Meg and Michael's server for those first couple of days. If I see that he uploaded any honking big files, I can tell you where to look."

"That would be very helpful," the chief said.

I pulled out my phone and checked the time. Rehearsal would be starting soon.

"I'm going to go back inside and do useful things," I said. "Unless you need me for anything."

"I'll let you know if we do," the chief said.

Back in the kitchen, I set to work making lunches for Michael and the boys—ham sandwiches, fruit, bowls of tossed salad, and cookies. Most of it left over from last night's dinner; nothing that wouldn't keep if the cast decided to celebrate Friday by ordering in pizza for lunch. Probably less likely to happen today—even those who didn't like Goodwin probably wouldn't feel much like celebrating.

Michael dashed in.

"My god, are you all right?" He gave me a quick, fierce hug. "I heard you found Goodwin's body."

"Rose Noire and I did," I said. "And I'm fine. I did have a bad moment when I thought maybe whoever killed him might have used my creepy dagger."

"Which creepy dagger?"

"The new one," I said. "Do you know where it is?"

"It's not in your forge?"

"No." I shook my head. "Last time I saw it was when you and the cast were having such fun playing with it. I'm hoping the prop master locked it up with the rest of the daggers."

"Not what I told her to do, but yeah. She might have. I'll ask her. And if she doesn't have it, I'll make sure she finds it."

He gave me a quick kiss and dashed out the back door.

I went back to packing the lunches. When I'd finished them, I set the three insulated canvas lunch bags on the kitchen counter and looked around for my notebook. Time to reorganize my thoughts. Today probably wouldn't be a particularly productive day by my standards. Still—

"Mom?"

Chapter 21

I turned around to see Josh and Jamie standing in the kitchen doorway. Looking anxious. It was like an indoor replay of that moment when they came to tell me that they'd found a body. Was that really only yesterday?

"What's up?" I asked.

"We found something we thought maybe you or Dad should see," Josh said.

"Or maybe Chief Burke," Jamie added. "But we thought we should show one of you guys first."

They both had their hands behind their backs, in what was intended to be a casual pose, but Jamie appeared to be holding something.

"Okay," I said. "Shoot."

They exchanged a look. Then Jamie pulled his hands from behind his back to display their find.

A book. Specifically, a copy of *Alice's Adventures in Wonderland*—a deluxe edition bound in purple leather, with the title and author's name and an ornate art nouveau–styled border illustration stamped on it in pastel shades of pink, blue, and yellow. The Cheshire Cat stared out from the spine, and on the front cover a distinctly grumpy Alice sat in an ornate armchair, flanked by Humpty Dumpty and the Mad Hatter.

Curious. Jamie was using two paper towels to hold it by the corners.

"I knew we had several copies of *Alice in Wonderland*," I said. "But I don't recall seeing that one before."

"We haven't seen it, either," Josh said.

"And pretty sure it's not ours," Jamie said. "Take a look."

He set the book down on the kitchen table and handed me his paper towels. I used one of them to flip the book open.

Someone had hollowed out the pages to create a space inside, about four by six inches. In the space rested a plastic baggie containing white powder.

"No," I said. "I don't think it's ours. Where did you find it?"

"In the library," Josh said. "Do you think it's . . . dope?"

"He means heroin," Jamie added helpfully.

"Or cocaine," I said. "I'm no expert. Let's turn this over to the chief, shall we?"

I pulled out my phone and dialed his cell.

"Is something wrong?" the chief asked. I could hear "I'm busy, so this had better be good" in his tone. I should probably be flattered that he'd answered at all.

"Jamie and Josh may have found some important evidence," I said. "Can you meet us in the library?"

A slight pause.

"See you there."

I hung up, then carefully picked up the book by the edges, using the paper towels, and set off.

The chief was already waiting for us when the boys and I entered the library—he'd probably come in through the sunroom. And no one else was there, that I could see. Although we hadn't noticed Kevin lurking upstairs during Goodwin's video.

"Can you guys check to make sure no one's up on the balcony?" I asked. "Or hiding anywhere else?"

Josh scurried up the small circular stairs to the balcony while Jamie did a quick check on all the nooks and crannies downstairs, and even checked under the tables.

"All clear up here," Josh called as he practically slid down the staircase.

"Just us," Jamie agreed.

I turned to the chief—who had been studying the book in my hands with a puzzled expression.

"The boys found this." I put the book down on the nearest table. "I was going to ask them where and how, but I thought it would save time if they told you at the same time. Unfortunately, we've all handled it."

"Just the outside," Josh said.

"As soon as we realized it could be evidence, we got some paper towels to carry it with," Jamie added.

"And I only touched it with the paper towels," I said. "Check what's inside."

The chief pulled a pair of gloves out of his pocket and put them on before flipping open the book. His eyes narrowed.

"How did you happen to find this?" he asked looking up at the boys.

"We didn't just happen to find it," Josh said. "We went looking for it."

"Well, not this specifically," Jamie said. "But we were pretty sure we'd find something."

"You know how Mr. Goodwin's video kept showing Mr. Brainard coming in and out of the library?" Josh asked.

"He couldn't possibly know," Jamie pointed out. "He wasn't here, and they can't find the video."

"Your mom told me about it." The chief's mouth twitched and I could tell he was suppressing a smile.

"Good," Jamie said. "But I wish you could see it. It was really funny how he kept sneaking in and sneaking out."

"And looking really guilty," Josh added. "In one of the shots he was standing at the foot of one of the library ladders."

"This one." Jamie slapped the nearest rolling library ladder.

"So we decided to try to figure out what he was looking for."

"Or what he was hiding there," Jamie said. "And as soon as we saw this we knew it wasn't ours."

"The family does have a copy of *Alice in Wonderland*," Josh said loftily.

"Several, in fact,"

"But not this one."

"I should hope not." The chief bent to study the plastic bag more closely. "You had to touch the book to take it off the shelves and open it—but did either of you touch the bag?"

They both shook their heads.

"Good." The chief was pulling out his cell phone. "We'll get your cousin Horace to take a look at this. He can tell us what it is."

"Mom thinks it's cocaine rather than heroin," Josh said.

The chief, his ear to the phone, arched an eyebrow at me.

"No, I said it *could* be cocaine rather than heroin," I corrected. "They're both white powders."

"Horace?" the chief said into the phone. "Can you grab your kit for field testing potential drugs and meet me in the library . . . thanks."

"On television the detective wets his finger and tastes a little bit of the drug and knows immediately what it is," Josh said. He and Jamie were frowning, as if suspecting the chief of being derelict in his duty.

"We never actually do that in real life," the chief said. "For one thing, what if the powder contained something quite dangerous—fentanyl, LSD, ricin, strychnine. Would it be smart to taste any of those?"

The boys shook their heads.

"And for another thing, most drugs aren't pure. The dealers often cut them dramatically." Seeing the boys' look of puzzlement, he elaborated. "That means they mix in a lot of cheap stuff to make the buyer think he's getting a lot of drugs when really it's just a lot of filler."

"Ah," Josh said. "Like Aunt Mabel's meatloaf."

"She gives you huge helpings, but she puts in more crumb than hamburger," Jamie explained.

"I see," the chief said. "I think every family must have an Aunt Mabel. So anyway, you'd taste the filler more than the drugs. But most important, you don't want a police officer getting up on the stand and saying, 'well, it sure *tasted* like heroin.' That's no proof. You want someone like your cousin Horace giving scientific results. Here he is now."

Horace popped into the library, looking expectant and carrying a small leather case.

"You've found a controlled substance?" he asked.

The chief indicated the book, still lying open on the table.

Horace whistled and scurried closer to peer at it. The boys beamed proudly at this reaction to their find.

Horace took out his pocket digital camera and snapped rather a lot of photos of the book from various angles. Then he opened up his case and studied its contents for a few seconds.

"By the look of it, I think we could start with the Scott Reagent Modified," he said.

The chief nodded as if he knew what that meant. He probably did.

Horace took out a sealed plastic pouch containing a little vial half full of pink liquid and a small flat thing like a McDonald's coffee stirrer. He picked up a tiny bit of the white powder on the coffee stirrer and popped it into the vial. He closed and shook the vial and then held it up. As we watched, the pink liquid turned blue.

"Whoa!" Josh exclaimed.

"Awesome!" Jamie breathed. "Does that mean it's drugs?"

"Cocaine," the chief said.

"Probably cocaine," Horace said. "This is only a presumptive test. We'll have to send the rest to the state crime lab for full analysis."

"Still, Mom was right," Josh said.

Horace gave me a puzzled glance.

"And now that you've seen Horace test the powder, you should get ready for rehearsal," I said. "Unless the chief has any more questions?"

"Not for now," the chief said.

"Then you have—" I glanced up at the library clock. "Yikes, fifteen minutes before your dad will be taking off. Go get your lunches and your dad's—they're on the kitchen table."

"Thanks, Mom," Jamie said.

They both leaped up and headed for the door.

"Boys," the chief called.

They turned on the threshold.

"Please don't tell anyone about your find," the chief said. "Not even your dad, because you have no idea who could be listening in."

"You think the cocaine belongs to someone in the play?" Josh asked.

"They're all suspects," the chief said. "Right now, everyone's a suspect."

"For the drugs and the murder," Jamie said softly.

The chief nodded.

"Pretend you never saw this thing." I waved at the book. "And avoid being left alone with anyone—stick together, and preferably with your dad."

"We will," Jamie said.

"Book? What book?" Josh assumed a look of complete innocence.

"Thank you," the chief said. "You handled this well."

The boys grinned, then stampeded out of the library.

"Incidentally," I said, when they were out of earshot, "I didn't say the powder *was* cocaine—I only suggested that it could as easily be cocaine as heroin. Although now that the boys aren't here, I will add that unless I'm very mistaken about the behavior of drug users, cocaine did seem the more likely. I haven't seen any of our guests nodding off, but I could name several who sometimes seem to be bouncing off the walls, and I'm not naïve enough to assume it's all artistic temperament."

"Yes," the chief said. "And if I were to ask you to name those cast and crew members who sometimes seem to display an excess of artistic temperament, would this Mr. Brainard the boys mentioned be on the list?"

"At the top of it," I said. "And he's sleeping in a tent in the backyard, which means he'd have no secure, private place to keep his stash. Of course that last point goes for most of them. Only four of the cast and crew are in the house. One's staying with a friend who lives in town, six are in the barn, and the rest are in tents behind the barn."

The chief nodded. He and Horace studied the bag briefly.

"Not exactly a tiny bag," the chief said. "Rather a lot for personal use."

Horace nodded.

"Oh, great," I said. "So maybe we have not just a coke user but a dealer?"

"Maybe just a heavy user," Horace said.

"Or a user who realized before coming down here that he could be out of touch with his regular supplier for some weeks," the chief said.

"And stocked up, just in case?" Horace rolled his eyes. "An organized coke addict?"

"We'll figure that out when we determine who this belongs to," the chief said. "Horace, can you process the book right here for prints and DNA and anything else you think would be useful? We'll seize the cocaine, of course, but I'd like to put the book back up there on the shelf and see if someone comes to claim it. The owner may have seen the boys find it, or may have come looking for it after they took it to show Meg, but with luck whoever it belongs to doesn't know we've found it. Worth trying."

"Of course, they might barge in any time," Horace said. "Or if we lock them out, it could make them suspicious."

"The chief will be using Michael's office for the time being," I said, addressing a bit of empty air as if talking to the actors. "And Horace is storing the evidence collected in Goodwin's trailer in the library until they can arrange transport to the station. They'll be gone by the time you get back from rehearsal, but stay out of their way for now."

"Good." The chief focused back on what Horace was doing with the book. Then he looked up again. "And tell me if anyone seems unduly distressed that the library is unavailable."

"Will do."

I went into Michael's office and found spare keys to it and the library. I locked the door between the library and the rest of the house. Then, once I'd handed the keys to the chief, I went out through the sunroom and looked around.

Russ Brainard was sitting at one of the picnic tables, holding a coffee mug in one hand and a doughnut in the other. As I watched, he gestured with the doughnut hand, shedding powdered sugar on himself and every-thing around him. He seemed to be—well, "his normal self" probably didn't apply. Toward the manic end of the range of behavior I'd seen in him. Which probably meant he had already made a visit to Wonderland this morning.

I strolled over to the picnic tables and made my an-nouncement about the temporary unavailability of the library.

"If any of you left anything in the library that you need for the day, knock on the door and ask Horace or the chief about it," I said in conclusion.

No one jumped up to race over to the library. And no one seemed alarmed or suspicious. Not even Russ.

Of course, Russ—or whoever had hidden his stash in our library—probably considered himself pretty secure.

Hiding the cocaine inside one book out of thousands must have seemed like a brilliant idea. Goodwin's video, with its threat of exposure, must have come as a nasty shock. But now that Goodwin was dead and his video destroyed, Russ—or whoever the cocaine belonged to—might be thinking they were home free.

Instead, thanks to the boys' ingenuity, they might just have shot to the top of the chief's suspect list for Goodwin's murder.

Chapter 22

Since I obviously wasn't going to learn anything from the cast at the moment, I headed for the kitchen.

Tanya got up, gathered a few empty plates and bowls, and followed me inside.

"What about this afternoon's lecture?" she asked. "If the police will be using the library, won't you need to find another place for it?"

"Yikes," I said. "I think postponing it would be more sensible, since I doubt if we can get away with canceling it entirely. Thanks for reminding me."

"Don't pretend you'd forgotten," Tanya said. "I know you had it in your notebook-that-tells-you-when-to-breathe."

"Yes, but I'd deliberately blotted out all consciousness of it," I said. "Were you at his last one?"

"Alas."

"Then you understand. Anyway, thanks." I pulled out my cell phone as I headed back for the kitchen. "Probably good to give him as much notice as possible."

Professor Cohen didn't react well to the postponement of his lecture. He'd probably have spent a lot more time arguing with me about it if he hadn't reacted even more badly to the notion that Chief Burke might want to interview him.

"That's ridiculous," he said. "I had nothing to do with that man's murder and I can't imagine what he thinks I could contribute. Tell him that, and what's more, tell him—"

"Dr. Cohen," I said. "You seem to have misunderstood—I

wasn't relaying any kind of official summons from Chief Burke—just giving you the courtesy of a heads-up that he seems to be planning to interview everyone who was here at our house the night of Goodwin's murder. Of course, it's a long list, and I think it's probably a good sign that you haven't already heard from him. And with luck he'll identify the killer long before he gets to you."

"Hmph." He sounded only slightly mollified. "Still seems like a waste of time. So when can we reschedule my lecture?"

So much for my hope that he'd be so offended by the postponement that he'd cancel this and all future lectures.

"Would next Friday work?" I asked. "Of course we don't know if the murder will be solved by then, but I think we can be reasonably sure they'll have finished using our library."

With much grumbling about how much he hated having messy crossed-off entries in his daily planner, he agreed to next Friday. I restrained myself—with difficulty—from pointing out that if he made his entries in pencil, he could erase instead of crossing off when life took an unexpected turn—as life so often does. He probably also did crossword puzzles in ink.

I pulled out my own pencil and moved his lecture to next Friday. Then I texted Mother to let her know so she could reschedule the ringers. While I was doing that, Rose Noire drifted in through the back door and began wandering around in the kitchen, tidying things that didn't actually need tidying.

"What's up?" I asked.

"I've been thinking about those geese," she said.

"What about them?" I asked. Probably not wise to admit that I'd—well, forgotten all about them was probably not accurate. Filed them away under problems delegated—to Vern and the chief.

"What if the Birnamites did it?" she asked. "Put the

geese in our chicken coop, I mean. They could have, you know. A lot of them were over here for the movie."

"You're thinking that it's the Birnamites dancing around that cauldron in the woods?" I asked. "And that they were somehow prevented from using the geese in whatever sinister ritual they were performing."

"Well, it's possible," she said. "And very worrisome. But I think the Birnamites could have left the geese in our chicken coop for a completely different reason."

"Such as?"

"Well . . ." She frowned slightly. "It's a little difficult to explain. I mean . . . it's subtle."

I assumed by '"subtle" she probably meant either convoluted or offbeat. Possibly both. But not necessarily wrong. I'd already figured out that Rose Noire's way of seeing things was a lot closer to the Birnamites' worldview than mine would ever be. I waited while she sorted out her theory.

"MacLeod is going to claim that our finding the sheep and the heifer at Camp Birnam doesn't mean anything, right?" she asked finally. "That the animals just wandered into their camp and they were only keeping them safe until they could figure out who they belonged to and take them home."

"Which we know is a lie from Goodwin's video," I said.

"But the video's gone," she said. "So the chief's case is a lot weaker, right?"

"He's still got witnesses," I said. "Although I suppose MacLeod could try to intimidate them. MacLeod or the dwindling number of reenactors loyal to him."

"Exactly!" she exclaimed. "So what if they decided to steal a couple of geese and plant them in our chicken coop? They could be hoping to use that to weaken the case against them."

"By suggesting that Caerphilly is a place where resentful farm animals routinely run away from home and get themselves penned up as part of a sinister ongoing plot to frame innocent bystanders for grand larceny?"

"Well, that's a little fanciful," she said. "But they could be trying to say, 'hey, they're charging us with theft, and they're doing the same thing'—in the hope that we'll drop the charges."

"Yeah, I can see them trying to pull that," I said. "It's called 'tu quoque' and it won't fly in a court of law, but that doesn't mean they won't try it. But can you really see them pulling that off without leaving any evidence the chief could use to prove they did it instead of us?"

"No," she said. "But I think they're crazy enough to try."

"Not they—MacLeod," I said.

She nodded.

"I'm not worried about getting in trouble because of someone planting hot geese on us," I said. "Even if we couldn't prove the Birnamites did it, we could take the geese back and explain to the owner what we think happened. We've got credibility with the local farmers—they all know how much time we spend dragging Seth's sheep back to him."

She nodded again. Not looking convinced, though.

"But something else does worry me a bit," I said. "What if in addition to planting the geese MacLeod also decided to confront Goodwin? Convince him to erase the footage of him stealing the heifer?"

"And got into an argument with Goodwin and killed him," she whispered.

"Yes." I nodded. "I can see that happening,"

"We should ban him from the house," she said. "Until we find out for sure if he's the killer."

"We could do that," I said. "And warn everyone to stay away from him. But we'd have a hard time enforcing the ban, unless we want to put guards on every door. And even if we banned him, there are all the other reenactors. How could we be sure he hadn't recruited some of them to his cause?"

"Or some of the cast and crew," she said. "Or the history students. They could have come under his influence."

She was a lot better at this paranoid thinking than I was.

"Even the professors," she said. "Not so much the history ones. They seem—well, normal might be a stretch."

"Crazy in a good way?" I suggested. "Or at least in a way that's harmless and not hard for us to understand."

"Yes," she said. "They're very enthusiastic about the strangest things, but that's fine. Those two English professors, though—the ones who keep dropping by. They're so . . . hostile. Is the whole department like that?"

"Most of them are perfectly nice," I said. "It's just a few of the old-timers like Philpotts who resent the Drama Department for winning its independence."

"He's the one Goodwin showed sneaking into your house, isn't he?" Rose Noire said. "Do you think he could be responsible for the vandalism?"

"Well, yes and no," I said.

She rolled her eyes.

"I'm not trying to avoid the question," I said with a chuckle. "I don't think he personally committed any of the vandalism."

"Why not?" She sniffed slightly. "Seems totally in character."

"Some of those pranks required a certain amount of imagination to think up, plus daring to pull off," I said. "I don't think he's got a scrap of either. But I could be wrong. And what if he enlisted someone else to do it? A student or a younger professor? I can absolutely see him telling them to hang around and do whatever they could to make our lives miserable. And before you say we need to keep our eyes on the English students—as far as I know, we don't have any English majors or grad students hanging around here—but how many students do you know who make it through college without taking a single course from the English Department?"

She nodded and sighed heavily.

"Try not to worry about it," I said. "The chief's back, and while I'm sure he'd have done what he could to help catch our vandal in any case, the possibility that the vandalism might be linked to the murder will give him a lot more incentive."

"And we should help him in any way we can." She turned to go.

"Without interfering in his investigation, of course," I added. "The best way we can help him is by staying out of his way."

"I plan no interference." She assumed her most dignified expression. "I'm going to start by doing a cleansing. There's such a lot of really negative energy built up here. Dispelling that would help clear the way for the chief to succeed."

"A cleansing?" Her cleansings usually involved burning enough sage and lavender and other herbs to fill the afflicted area with a dense cloud of smoke. "Just what are you planning to cleanse? The house? Goodwin's trailer? The field where we found the body?"

"All of it," she said, with a sweeping gesture. "The house. The yard. The nearby fields. I'll work in a huge circle that takes it all in." She frowned, probably because it was dawning on her exactly how huge a perimeter this would involve. "I probably ought to include Camp Birnam."

"Do them separately," I suggested. "Do the house and yard first. And then when you do Camp Birnam, maybe you can add in whatever herbs you'd need to give them a mild case of homesickness. Not enough to make them miserable—just enough to make them decide they've had enough camping for now."

Either she was too absorbed in her thoughts to hear my suggestion or she was deliberately ignoring it.

"I need to go check on my supply of sage," she said. "I may need to buy more."

With that she dashed out of the kitchen.

I opened the refrigerator and found that both the lemonade and the iced tea pitchers were empty. Normally Rose Noire kept those full, but obviously she was too distracted right now. I fixed another batch of lemonade and was trying to decide if I should bother with the tea when the doorbell rang. Nice to know it was still working.

"What now?" I muttered as I ambled toward the front door. Ambled because the odds were high that the caller would be someone I'd find annoying.

Chapter 23

I opened the door to find Ms. Ellie Draper, Caerphilly's head librarian, standing on our front porch, with her purse on one shoulder and an overstuffed tote bag on the other. Her purple Caerphilly Zoo t-shirt—the twin of mine—brought out the purple highlights in her casually cropped hair.

"Meg?" She frowned slightly. "Is this a bad time?"

"That depends on whether you're me or the late Damien Goodwin," I said. "My morning's all the better for seeing you—come on in. You heard we had a murder, I assume?"

"I'll be honest enough to admit that's partly why I came to see you instead of just calling," she said as she stopped inside. "Are you sure now's a good time? You looked annoyed when you opened the door."

"I probably did." I chuckled. "I assumed you'd be someone else entirely. Come on, let's get some lemonade and then we can sit on the back porch and watch the investigation."

"That's an offer I can't refuse," she said.

I closed and locked the door behind her and led the way down the hall.

"I only heard about poor Mr. Goodwin an hour ago," she said.

"We only found him a few hours ago," I said. "Nice to know the town grapevine's on the job."

"And it's terrible news," she went on. "And I wouldn't be barging in when I know you're probably pretty busy, but

I thought you could tell me whether I have something to add to the investigation."

"Like what?"

"I may have tracked down the book from which that little scrap of paper was torn."

"That was fast," I said.

"Well, I was worried," she said. "My Latin's not as good as your father's, but I was able to puzzle out enough of the words on that scrap to get an idea what it was about."

"And that worried you?" I handed her a glass of lemonade. "What was it about? Rose Noire and I assumed it was from a book of spells."

"It is," she said. "Unfortunately not a particularly nice one."

"Rose Noire said she thought it was evil," I said. "I figured she was just overreacting."

"No, evil's not too strong a word," she said. "Rose Noire has a lot more common sense than we give her credit for sometimes. But let's get settled on your back porch so I can tell you the story properly."

I was puzzled. Ms. Ellie hadn't previously shown any hostility to magic. She let the local Wiccans hold meetings in the library conference room. In fact, I was pretty sure she'd joined in last week when Rose Noire tried to combat the drought by holding some kind of rainmaking ceremony—surely that counted as magic. What was it about this spell book that had so obviously aroused her disapproval?

She led the way outside and we sat down in a pair of plastic lawn chairs—placeholders for the elegant, comfortable wrought iron ones I was going to make for us when I had time. I'd only been saying that for about two years now.

Vern Shiffley was sitting at the far end of the yard, presumably combining guard duty over the trailer with his lunch break. He was biting into a large sub. He and Ms. Ellie exchanged waves.

"Anyway," she said. "As soon as I translated the first few words on your scrap of paper I realized it was . . . well, not a book I'd really want in our library here. Or if I did have a copy, I'd be keeping it under lock and key. So I reached out to a group of librarians I belong to. One of them was able to identify the book."

She pulled out a couple of sheets of paper and handed me the top one.

It was the cover of a book. The title, *Spells of Power and Revenge,* was printed in dark red against the glossy black of the cover, and there was something vaguely fungal or reptilian about the shape of the letters. The cover was also adorned with half a dozen creatures that looked as if they'd been lifted out of a Hieronymus Bosch painting and then gussied up by a modern artist with more slick attitude than talent. The general effect was creepy and . . . well, vaguely obscene.

"Ick," I said. "I sort of want to wash my hands after touching that, and it's not even the real book."

"What's inside is worse," Ms. Ellie said.

"I'll take your word for it." I set the printout of the cover carefully on the small plastic table at our elbows. "Should I be impressed or appalled that one of your librarian friends was able to identify this book so quickly?"

"Oh, impressed, definitely," she said. "She's a legal librarian—the only reason she recognized it was that the big law firm she works for is suing the publisher for copyright infringement."

I had to laugh at that.

"Seriously," she said. "The publisher who put this out is mostly known for producing glossy, expensive pornography—some of which appears in this book. They stole most of the spells verbatim from books put out by more legitimate publishers and adapted them slightly to fit their theme—imagine taking, say, *Jane Eyre* and adding in a graphic sex scene every chapter or two. Only *Jane*

Eyre's not under copyright—all the books these idiots stole from are."

"Okay, maybe I should have at least a vague idea of what's inside." I held out my hand.

I took a quick glance at the pages she handed me, grimaced, and thrust them back at her.

"Double ick," I said. "Not something I want the boys finding. I know what I'll be doing while the rehearsal is on."

"Searching the house from attic to cellar?"

"Starting with the library," I said.

"Good thinking," she said. "Because what better place to hide a book than in the middle of a whole lot of books."

I nodded. She was right—and she didn't even know about the phony *Alice in Wonderland* we'd already found. I pulled out my phone, took a picture of the cover, and then shoved the printout back toward her.

"You're welcome to keep the paper copy," she said.

"I'd rather not," I said. "I can delete this from my phone at a second's notice, but I'd have to go to either Michael's office or my own to shred the paper."

"You might want to snap a picture of this, too." She held out another sheet of paper. "It's the page about this book from the publisher's catalogue. Gives the size, which might speed up your searching—it's an odd size, and fairly large."

I nodded and took her suggestion.

"And we identified where the scrap of paper you found was torn from," she went on. "A page in the section about how to cause pain and suffering to your enemies."

"I hate it when Rose Noire gets to say I told you so," I muttered.

"You thought she was overreacting when she called it evil?"

"I thought she was letting her imagination get the best of her when she kept insisting that someone was casting evil spells out in the woods."

"She could be right," Ms. Ellie said. "You know me—I'm a bit of a skeptic about magic."

"But you're very good at humoring Rose Noire."

"Her heart's in the right place," she said. "So whether or not her magic works, if it makes her and other people feel better, I see no harm in it. And if there is something to the idea of positive energy, she definitely has it."

I nodded.

"But this." She gestured at the printout of the book's cover. "There's a nastiness about this that I find very disturbing. It's . . . well, evil, dressed up in exotic trappings to fool the gullible. Someone who'd try to use that thing to cause pain and suffering to their enemies—what happens when the spells don't work and they still want to hurt someone?"

Her voice trailed off and she shook her head.

"You don't disapprove because it's magic," I said. "You disapprove because it's evil."

She nodded.

"I think you should definitely tell the chief about this," I said. "Because for all we know it could have something to do with Goodwin getting killed. And even if it doesn't, it could still help him find the scofflaws who have been breaking the fire ban. Just because he's got a murder case on his hands doesn't mean he's going to ignore lesser crimes."

"And if I'm right about the bad intentions of whoever owns this—well, I'll let the chief decide what to make of it. You know where he is?"

"I think he's still in the library," I said. "Let's head over there. You can show him the disgusting spell book, and I can get started searching the shelves."

It might have been faster just to walk through the yard, but I decided to lead the way through the house. I assumed the chief would stake out the library after Horace finished fingerprinting *Alice in Wonderland,* thinking that the owner of the cocaine would probably visit his stash sooner or later. In fact, maybe that was why Vern was having such a leisurely lunch in a place where he could keep an eye on the sunroom entrance along with Goodwin's trailer. I liked that idea. The sooner they caught the owner the better, and he'd probably avoid the library if he saw hordes of people coming and going.

The door between the library and the rest of the house was locked. Ms. Ellie looked puzzled but said nothing when I knocked instead of pulling out my key.

The chief answered the door.

"Ms. Ellie has some possible evidence to show you," I said as I stepped aside for her to enter.

But I followed her in and stuck around while she showed the chief her finds. I wanted to hear how he reacted, and then make sure he was okay with my searching the whole library for the nasty book.

Meanwhile I studied the shelves nearest me—although if I were the owner of that book and wanted to hide it in plain sight in our library, I'd choose a more remote spot. One of the far corners. Better yet, somewhere on the balcony.

Horace had been doing something to the library ladder when we entered, but he finished up while Ms. Ellie was talking and came over to inspect her finds.

When she finished, the chief turned to me.

"Any idea who this rather offensive volume belongs to?" he asked.

"Only suspicions," I said.

"Your suspicions would also be helpful."

"Well." I took a deep breath. "My suspicion is based on the idea that the book has something to do with the people who are setting those fires in the woods—which isn't proven, but seems likely."

He nodded.

"There was a section of Goodwin's video showing three

women out in the woods stirring a cauldron—well, three people actually; the quality was downright lousy thanks to being shot in low-light conditions, and I might be assuming they were women because the witches in *Macbeth* are. Although I did think I recognized one of them, but I was going to see if Goodwin would let me take a closer look at it, and maybe ask if he had any other footage that would make it easier to identify the participants. I'm betting he chose that footage because the participants would know it was them, but everyone else wouldn't be able to identify them for certain."

"I will take all those factors into consideration." His voice sounded grave, but I thought I detected a twinkle in his eye. "On whom did your suspicions light after viewing Mr. Goodwin's highly unsatisfactory video?"

"Gina," I said. "I can't remember her last name, but she's on your list of cast and crew—she plays the second of the three witches in the play."

"Any particular reason?" He was scribbling in his notebook.

"One of the figures in the video was the right size and shape, and although the voices were muffled and distorted, one of them could be hers." When I said it aloud it sounded very tenuous indeed. "But I could be prejudiced against her," I added. "She seems to be the leader of a little clique I think of as the Mean Girls. They're always sitting together giggling and gossiping—especially about Celia."

"The woman who wrecked her car last night."

"Yes," I said. "From things I've overheard, I think Gina thinks she should have gotten the part of Lady Macbeth, and she isn't just envious of Celia—she's downright hateful about her. So maybe she's taking out her ill will against Celia by casting spells to hurt her."

"You think she really believes the spells will work?" The chief sounded curious.

"No idea." I shrugged. "I confess, I haven't spent much

time talking to her. But if she did believe in spell casting—well, Celia's gastrointestinal woes have been getting steadily worse, and now she's wrecked her car and maybe given herself a concussion. If it's Gina who's playing with magic out in the woods, she just might be getting the idea her spell book's working out pretty well."

He nodded. He was opening his mouth to say something when his phone rang. He held up a finger as if in apology and answered it.

"Yes?" Whatever his caller had to say, it was definitely not making him any happier. His frown grew steadily more thunderous.

"No, I think it's time to put out a statewide BOLO for him . . . Yes . . . No, make it wanted for questioning in connection with a homicide . . . That's right. Thanks."

He hung up and turned back to us.

"Sorry," he said. "Mr. Miller has gone AWOL. The one who's been calling himself Calum MacLeod," he added, seeing our blank looks. "According to the rest of the reenactors he never went back to Camp Birnam last night, and this morning his car wasn't in the field they use as a parking lot. Which didn't worry me all that much until he missed an eleven o'clock hearing on the theft and animal abuse charges. His court-appointed attorney showed up, but hasn't heard from him since yesterday. We've had a countywide BOLO for him for over an hour now, but I think it's time to expand that."

"You think he's the killer?" Ms. Ellie asked.

"He's a suspect," the chief said. "We don't have any evidence against him."

"Not yet," Horace said. "But I'm working on it."

"Of course, so far we don't have evidence against anyone else, either," the chief added. "But this doesn't look good,"

"We have to remember that he was already facing some pretty serious charges," Horace put in. "He could just be running from that."

"Yes," the chief said. "Possible prison time on the theft of farm animals. Could be that he left town before the murder even happened. Maybe he was under the delusion that we wouldn't try to track him down if he skipped out on his bail. We'll find out when we catch him. But in the meantime, I should go take care of some of the blasted paperwork he's causing."

"Wish we could make that a crime," Ms. Ellie said. "Willful destruction of innocent trees by causing unnecessary paperwork."

The chief nodded with a slight chuckle.

"Look," I said. "Getting back to this book Ms. Ellie has identified—if it's okay with you, I want to search for it. Starting here in the library, because the owner of the hollow *Alice in Wonderland* might not be the only person who thinks we wouldn't notice one more book among thousands."

The chief pondered for a moment.

"That would be acceptable," he said. "Provided you promise that if you do find it, you'll refrain from touching it if at all possible, and call us immediately."

"I promise," I said.

"We'll leave you to it, then," the chief said.

"I'd offer to help you," Ms. Ellie said. "But I've already been away from the library longer than I'd like."

"I'll show Ms. Ellie out," the chief said. "And let you get on with your search."

They went out through the door to the house, which the chief locked behind him. Horace shouldered his forensic bag and headed out through the sunroom.

And then reappeared moments later.

"Um . . . do you have any idea what Rose Noire and those other people are doing?"

"Rose Noire and what other people?" I followed him back out to the sunroom to see for myself.

"Don't know the others." He pointed to where Rose

Noire and four other women were gathered in the backyard. "But they're lighting torches, like the mob does before it storms Dracula's castle."

"I think those are sage smudging sticks," I said. "Long ones, because they're going to do a big space cleansing."

"Argh," Horace groaned. "Please tell me they're not going to do the whole house. I was hoping to make it over for tonight's dinner and that sage smoke makes me sneeze."

"I think they're going to smudge a perimeter around everything," I said. "The house, the yard, the field where we found Goodwin. Don't worry," I added. "I reminded her that she needs to keep well away from any part of the crime scene."

"Let's hope she listened to you," he said. "I'd hate to arrest her for interfering with a police investigation."

I watched while Rose Noire and the other women set off, humming in three-part harmony and trailing graceful curls of smoke.

Then I went back inside the library and looked around.

Chapter 24

As I stood looking at the thousands of books, my spirits sank. For a second, I wanted to walk back out. I could recruit a crew—a crew of reliable and reasonably unshockable adults—to help me look for the book.

No. I wanted as few people as possible to know about the spell book. And I could do this. If I stopped dawdling, I could probably even get it done by the time the boys—and all the rest of them—came home from rehearsal.

So I squared my shoulders and marched over to the corner where the wrought iron spiral staircase wound its way up to the second-floor balcony.

I started at one end of the balcony, with the shelves closest to Michael's office.

It was slow going. Fortunately the nasty spell book was somewhat oversized—tall for a hardback, though not quite as big as most coffee-table books. Some shelves contained only books obviously too short or thin to be the book I was looking for, so I could tell at a glance that it wasn't there—although with all of the shelves, even the ones containing only small books, I'd pull out enough volumes to make sure there was nothing hidden behind them. Other shelves went more slowly. When I came to a dust-jacketed book that was even remotely close to the nasty book's size, I'd check to make sure the dust jacket matched the book inside. And remembering *Alice in Wonderland*, I opened up every really big book to make sure no one had brought in another fake book—or worse, carved out a hiding place in one of our books.

At one point I broke off and ran up to the bedroom to fetch my laptop. Occasionally I'd run into books I wanted to send emails about, like a novel Horace had been wanting to read or a decorating book Mother was afraid she'd lost. And while I appreciated having the ability to tap out an email on my phone, it was so much easier on a larger keyboard.

I emailed Horace and Mother and returned to my search. I was halfway down the wall when I heard the door from the sunroom open and close again.

I wasn't keen on having to explain what I was looking for. Luckily, I was working on a lower shelf, and somewhat shielded from the view of anyone downstairs, since I was behind one of the quilts Mother had hung on the oak railing. The new arrival couldn't easily see me.

Of course, neither could I see them. Since I was on my hands and knees anyway, I crawled to where I could peer around the edge of the quilt.

Russ Brainard was standing in the library, looking around as if expecting someone to leap out and accost him.

But he wasn't looking up. People rarely did, I'd noticed. I hadn't been trying to stake out the library, but had that been my intention I couldn't have picked a better hiding place.

Apparently satisfied that he was alone, he sidled over toward the nearest ladder—the one that was still close to where we'd found the fake *Alice in Wonderland*. He started climbing up.

And he was looking down to watch his footing, so I quietly crawled a little farther until I was right above him. I planned to accost him. I'd wait until he pulled the book off the shelves, so I could testify that he'd gone straight to the book and purposefully pulled it off the shelf, not run across it by accident while browsing. But I was going to accost him.

I peered through the railings. His head was level with
Alice now. He braced himself. reached out, pulled the
book off the shelf, and flipped it open. He frowned when
he saw the empty compartment. He looked back at the
shelf, as if wondering if he'd pulled out the wrong copy of
Alice. Then he looked back at the book and stuck his hand
in the compartment, as if testing to see if its emptiness was
an optical illusion.

I stood up and leaned over the railing.

"Looking for something?" I asked.

He shrieked, let go of the book, and lost his footing on
the ladder. He fell backward and landed on one of the
library tables.

"Russ?"

He didn't answer. Damn. I'd wanted to accost him, not
bump him off.

I raced for the stairs, pulling out my phone as I went.
Probably not a good idea to call 911 until I'd safely navigated the wrought iron spiral staircase.

When I reached the ground floor, I ran into my friend
Deputy Aida, entering from the sunroom.

"I'm calling nine-one-one," I said.

"Good idea." She strode over to where Russ was lying
on the center library table. "Damn, girl. Remind me not
to tick you off."

"I didn't shove him," I said. "I just startled him."

"I know." She was checking Russ's pulse. "I was watching."

Russ was making strangled groaning noises. At least he
wasn't dead. And at least he hadn't landed on my laptop,
which wouldn't have been good for either of them.

Debbie Ann answered my 911 call.

"What's your emergency, Meg?" she asked

"Someone fell off the balcony in our library," I said.
"Can you send an ambulance?"

"Can do." Keys rattled. "How bad is it?"

I repeated the question to Aida.

"No visible injuries," she said. "I think maybe he's just got the wind knocked out of him, but we should definitely have the medics check him out."

I relayed the information to Debbie Ann and hung up. Russ was still making gasping groaning noises. I hoped that was a good sign.

"How did you get here so quickly?" I asked Aida.

"Like I said, I was watching," she answered. "Your nephew Kevin set up a bunch of cameras so we could keep an eye out for someone coming to claim the drugs. So yeah, I know you didn't shove him. He just let go and fell back like a Japanese beetle."

"Like a Japanese beetle?" Not a metaphor I'd heard before.

"My mama's rose bushes are infested with them," she said. "Best, safest way to get rid of them is to pluck them off, but half the time, when you reach out to grab them, they let go and fall backward." She performed what I assumed was an imitation of a falling Japanese beetle, flinging out her arms, throwing her head back, and making a little "ahhh" sound. "So you learn to hold a bowl of soapy water underneath to catch them all. He just let go and fell back exactly the way the beetles do. Damnedest thing."

"She scared the hell out of me," Russ wheezed. "I was just looking for something to read and—"

"Yeah, right," Aida said. "You're under arrest for possession of a Schedule II controlled substance. You coherent enough for me to read you your Miranda rights?"

"Go ahead and do it." The chief appeared in the door from the sunroom. "And then you can go with him down to the hospital. I imagine they'll want to check him out there before we take him over to the jail. And if they give you any medical reason why the Miranda wouldn't have taken the first time, you can do it all over again. Meg, can you let Michael know Mr. Brainard will be unavailable for rehearsal?"

"Can do." I pulled out my phone. "For how long?"

"Possibly as much as ten years." The chief contemplated Russ with the same pleased look Grandfather usually wore when inspecting a new arrival at his zoo. "Assuming we're able to prove possession with intent to distribute."

Russ groaned.

"Although Mr. Brainard could improve on that outcome considerably if he cooperates with our investigation."

Russ looked unhappy, but I saw no sign that he was in pain. Still, we twiddled our thumbs for a few more minutes until the EMTs showed up with their rolling stretcher.

"Ooh," one of them said. "Got a live one this time."

They gave Russ what seemed like an admirably thorough examination before moving him onto the stretcher and rolling him out with Aida by his side.

The chief and I watched them go.

"Hidden cameras in our library," I said. "Wish I'd known."

"Your nephew set it up." He looked sheepish. "I meant to tell you. It was before we knew you'd be searching the library for that book. Frankly, we didn't expect anything to happen until the actors got home from rehearsal. Or do they usually get off this early?"

I glanced at the library clock. Only four o'clock. Surely it had to be much later, given everything that had happened today.

"They don't usually get off until five or six," I told the chief. "I suppose they could have let Russ go early if they were only going to work on act five. He's got a pretty big part up until he gets killed in act three, and of course his ghost shows up a couple of times after that. But not in act five."

"Break the news to Michael gently. About his arrest, I mean." The chief turned to go.

"Chief," I said. "Do you think maybe he could be the killer?"

He turned back.

"No idea," he said. "From what I've heard about Mr. Goodwin's video, he certainly could have motive. But we don't yet have any evidence that points to him. Or to anyone else for that matter. But it's early still."

"No sign of MacLeod or whatever his real name is?"

He shook his head.

"You never know," I said. "He often showed up at dinnertime. If that happens, I'll call you. I assume it's okay if I keep looking for that book Ms. Ellie told us about?"

"Absolutely," he said. "But if you find it—"

"Don't touch it."

"Right." He turned again and followed Russ and Aida to the ambulance.

I pulled out my phone, then paused. Should I wait until Michael got home?

No. He'd want to hear the bad news right away. I hit the button to dial his number and strolled out into the sunroom to stretch my legs.

Michael answered before the second ring had finished.

"What's up?" he asked.

"Is this a bad time to talk?" I asked. "I mean, if I'm interrupting—"

"Now's a fine time," he said. "We were about to rehearse the banquet scene, but no one can find Russ. He went for a bathroom break, and disappeared. I've got half the cast out combing the zoo, looking for him."

"You can call them off," I said. "He came back here."

"To the house? What in the world—well, I can ask him that. Tell him to get his sorry self back here pronto."

"He's not here anymore," I said. "Aida and the chief just arrested him and set off to take him down to the jail."

Michael was speechless, and that wasn't something that happened very often.

"Damn," he said finally. "So he's the one who killed Goodwin?"

"Possibly, but the jury's still out on that one," I said. "He's definitely the one who hid a fairly substantial amount of cocaine in a hollow book in our library, where it was found by two innocent minors. Minors we happen to share DNA with."

"You're not kidding, are you?"

I told him as succinctly as possible about how Josh and Jamie had found the hollow copy of *Alice in Wonderland*. "And we warned them not to tell anyone but you, and not even to tell you unless they were absolutely positive no one could overhear. I gather the day has been too busy for a private talk."

"It's been crazy," Michael said. "And he's out. Russ, I mean. He may be a fine actor, but he's been distracted and unreliable ever since rehearsals started. I'm sure his contract includes a morals clause, and we'll be exercising it. I'll call up Arena's business office right now. And after that—well, I'm going to try to get a little more work done, but there's a good chance we might be getting back early. I'm not sure anyone will be able to concentrate once they hear this news."

"I'll probably be in the library," I said. "Which is still off limits to cast and crew for the time being. I'm not sure Horace and the chief are finished here."

"Check."

"And by the way—MacLeod has gone on the lam. If you see him, call nine-one-one."

"Is the chief thinking he might be the one who killed Goodwin?" Michael sounded eager. Was it only because he was eager to get the murder case solved, or would he be relieved to find out the killer wasn't a member of his cast?

"Too early to tell," I said.

"Well, I don't wish him ill," Michael said. "But I do wish him elsewhere. In case he has the nerve to show up again, can we get your mother and dad on record that he's permanently banned from their property as well as ours?"

"Can do."

With that we hung up.

I figured the news that someone might have hidden an evil spell book in our library could wait until he got home. With luck I might even have found the book by then.

As long as I was out in the sunroom, I took a glance around before heading back inside.

In the distance, I could see Rose Noire and party stolidly marching through the fields on the far side of her shed, waving their sage smudging sticks. It looked as if they were heading for the woods, probably to avoid treading too close to the chief's crime scene. I wondered if they'd be finished by nightfall.

Goodwin's trailer was swathed in yellow crime-scene tape, and the door was secured with a heavy chain and a padlock.

Horace and the chief were sitting on one of our picnic tables, discussing something with solemn faces. They'd probably stop talking if I went out and approached them.

There are few things I hate more than not being able to do anything to fix whatever problems are going on. So I focused on the one problem I might be able to fix.

I went back to searching for the nasty book.

I had finished the one long wall and was working on the bookshelves directly above the French doors when Dad dashed in and looked around wildly as if expecting to find someone or something.

Chapter 25

I stood up, eased my back, and leaned over the railing.

"What's up?" I asked.

"The chief asked me to meet him in the library," Dad said. "Do you—ah, here he comes."

I decided to go down to the main floor. Either the chief had invited Dad to the library because he knew I was still here and wanted to talk to us both, or he'd be kicking me out anyway.

"Thank you for coming," the chief said, as he strode in. "No luck yet, Meg?"

I shook my head.

"Then I'll make this quick, so you can get back to your search." He sat down at the closest library table, and Dad and I joined him.

"I've sent that water bottle Meg found off to the Crime Lab in Richmond for testing," the chief began. "But Horace kept a sample of it to do a little unofficial testing of his own. And he's got some interesting results already. The bottle contained arsenic."

"Of course!" Dad exclaimed.

"What do you mean 'of course'?" the chief asked.

"Well, being odorless, colorless, and tasteless, it's one of the few poisons that could successfully be administered in water," Dad said. "And arsenic perfectly accounts for Celia's symptoms—vomiting, diarrhea, abdominal pain. Of course, those are also the symptoms of any number of gastrointestinal ailments—everything from minor food poisoning to cholera and stomach cancer. But I should have thought of arsenic."

"It wouldn't be my first thought," the chief said. "You don't see that many arsenic poisonings these days."

"Actually, it's still a big problem in many places," Dad said. "Globally there are millions of people in developing countries exposed to it because of naturally high arsenic levels in their drinking water."

"I stand corrected," the chief said. "But I was thinking of deliberate arsenic poisonings. You just don't see that much of it in modern police work. So while I know arsenic poisoning's the gold standard for classic mysteries—"

"Especially Agatha Christie," Dad said, with alarming enthusiasm. "She used poisons much more often than most other mystery writers—of course, she had so much professional experience with them."

"Professional experience?" The chief frowned, as if worried that Dad was about to shatter his image of Dame Agatha by revealing her as a serial killer who specialized in poisons.

"She trained as a dispenser, you know—an apothecary's assistant," Dad said. "Around the end of World War One, and then she volunteered for similar work during World War Two, so she'd have gotten updated training then. In those days, most prescription medicines were made up to order in a local pharmacy by assistants like her. And of course medicinally speaking, arsenic was much more widely used in those days than it is now."

"Is it used at all now?" The chief sounded genuinely curious.

"Oh, yes." Dad brightened, and I wondered if the chief would come to regret the question—he'd hit on one of Dad's pet topics. "For example, there's an arsenical compound called melarsorpol that's the only effective treatment for one form of late stage sleeping sickness. And scientists are testing arsenic trioxide as a treatment for leukemia."

"Presumably you need a prescription for those uses," the chief said. "Isn't arsenic somewhat difficult for the average person to acquire nowadays?"

"Not if you know where to look for it." Dad was warming to his subject. "You'd be surprised how easy it is to acquire poisons. With arsenic trioxide, I think the most amusing way to acquire it would be to roast some arsenic ore—you can sometimes find that on eBay, and it would be an interesting chemical experiment."

"Please tell me you haven't mentioned this in front of the boys," I murmured.

"But the easiest way would be to keep your eyes open when visiting flea markets, junk stores, and yard sales," Dad went on. "Some years ago I started buying up antique medical paraphernalia, including old patent medicine bottles. They add a nice note of authenticity when I set up my medical tent at a period event. But I have to check them out—better yet, clean them out thoroughly—before giving the public access to them. You'd be surprised how many of them still contain some portion of their original contents."

The chief nodded. He'd seen Dad's medical tent at several recent Civil and Revolutionary War reenactments.

"So I'd hit the junk stores," Dad went on. "If I were looking specifically for arsenic, I'd keep my eye open for Fowler's Solution, although you might also find solutions that are bluntly labeled as arsenic. And one of the nicest items I have in my collection is a bottle of Arlington's Arseniated Hemaboloids—they contain not just arsenic but also strychnine. That's another poison you can get rather easily in old medical bottles—"

"Stick to the arsenic," the chief said. "Are you saying that if I wanted to commit a murder using arsenic, all I'd have to do would be to browse the local junk shops?"

"Or possibly the feed and farm supply stores," Dad said. "And local farms. Up until recently, most commercial poultry growers added arsenic compounds to the feed to promote growth and fight disease. I think that's been banned nationwide now, but only within the last decade, and I have no idea whether or not it's still used in various other countries. And once an agricultural chemical's banned, disposing of it properly becomes difficult and expensive, so you'd probably find a lot of that kind of stuff lurking on the back shelves of poultry farms and the smaller agricultural supply shops. And the landfills—good heavens."

"And then there's taxidermy," I prompted. I'd heard Dad on this topic before.

"Oh, yes." Dad brightened at the thought. "Arsenic used to be part of the standard process of taxidermy up until the nineteen eighties. Ever seen a taxidermied animal that's sort of giving off a white powder?"

"There's an old deer head back at the station that's doing just that," the chief said. "Are you telling me the thing is oozing arsenic?"

"Could be," Dad said. "You should have it tested immediately. I'd have suggested it myself if I'd noticed—where is it hanging?"

"We keep it in a cardboard box in the very back of the evidence room," the chief said. "It wasn't a particularly successful bit of taxidermy as far as I'm concerned—you've never seen an angrier expression on the face of a deer, and although I'm not a fanciful man, I could all too easily imagine that thing jumping off the wall and seeking vengeance. I'd have thrown it out years ago, but that wouldn't be very diplomatic—my predecessor shot it and taxidermied it himself. We used to get it out and hang it in my office on those rare occasions when he'd come back to visit, but he's getting along now, so it's been a few years since he did that."

"We can have Horace test it to confirm it's dangerous,"

Dad said. "If it is, I can arrange for safe disposal. Unless you want to have it treated to remove the arsenic. Which would be expensive, but—"

"I'd rather have it gone," the chief said. "Skip the testing—even if it's not contaminated, we can use that as an excuse for getting rid of it. I will authorize Horace to work with you to get that done, and if my predecessor ever comes by and notices its absence, we'll explain about the arsenic. But let's get back to the question of where someone could get arsenic in this day and age. I will keep in mind the possibility that the culprit has access to either vintage taxidermy or banned agricultural chemicals, but I think what you suggested as the easiest option would also be the most likely—that the perpetrator acquired the arsenic at a yard sale, flea market, junk shop, or antique store."

Dad nodded.

"But however easy it is for someone to get hold of arsenic in that way, what is the likelihood that a layperson would know this?" the chief asked.

"Very likely," I said. "If they happened to have been living here the week before last and attended Dad's lecture on poisons."

The chief's face fell.

"Very true." Dad's tone was apologetic.

"So any of the cast and crew members could easily be in possession of this knowledge," the chief said.

"Yes," I said. "This was the first week everyone was here. Now we bring in ringers, so the cast and crew can focus on the play, but that first week most of them attended. Plus a lot of the reenactors."

"And several of the history professors," Dad said. "Which was flattering. And also that English professor—the one who looks like a startled walrus."

"Professor Philpotts," I said. "Startled walrus is good. I've always just said he looked like Teddy Roosevelt."

"Who looked rather like a startled walrus himself," Dad said. "He was definitely there—Philpotts, not Teddy. He asked several remarkably unhelpful questions."

"That was back when we were still trying to charm Professor Philpotts into working with us," I said. "But he was so rude and disruptive at Dad's talk that I told him not to come back."

"So you gathered most if not all of my suspects together and carefully educated them on how to acquire arsenic and other illegal substances." The chief sounded more bemused than upset.

"Well, at the time I didn't know they were going to be your suspects," Dad pointed out. "And the focus of my talk was more on protecting themselves against poisons whose existence they might be unaware of. It's not just arsenic and strychnine—I go into the importance of not mixing acetaminophen and alcohol, for example. Or eating green potatoes. Or keeping lilies in the house where cats could chew on them. Or—"

"I'm sure if whoever did this hadn't attended your lecture, they'd have found something else to poison Ms. Rivers with," the chief said. "And possibly something both more lethal and harder to detect."

"You're only saying that to be kind," Dad said.

He was probably right.

"The important thing now is to find the culprit," the chief said. "Would I be correct in assuming that these different forms of arsenic would have slightly different chemical profiles? So that you could work with Horace, or possibly with the Crime Lab in Richmond, to eliminate at least some of these potential sources?"

"Oh, yes." Dad brightened. "I'll get to work on that right away."

"And then we may know whether to focus on interrogating poultry farmers, junk store owners, or taxidermists," the chief said. "Meg, I don't suppose you have any idea whether any of your houseguests have been frequenting the local junk stores."

"Probably a lot of them have," I said. "Struggling actors on a budget, you know. I remember one dinner when a couple of the women came back from a trip to the Second-hand Rose and were showing off their clothing finds and marveling over what choice pickings there were, particularly at the thrift shops near the campus."

"Which ones? Which actors, I mean."

I closed my eyes and tried to remember. And winced before answering.

"Tanya—the one who found the bottle," I said. "And Gina—Second Witch. And the costume designer, who wasn't down here last night. At least not that I know of—she said she was going back to D.C. for a few days, but you can check on that—her contact info is on the list I gave you. And I think all the women and a lot of the men were taking down the names and addresses of the choicest shops—including Celia herself. It's been a recurring topic of conversation."

"It figures." He sighed, then straightened his spine. "Thanks." With that he nodded and strode out of the library.

"Perhaps it's just as well I didn't mention arsenic-treated lumber," Dad mused. "That might have upset him even more."

"Is it possible to poison someone with arsenic-treated lumber?" I asked. "I mean, how would you extract the arsenic?"

"Soaking in water would do it," Dad pointed out.

"But then it would taste like old lumber," I said. "Instead of being tasteless and odorless."

"You could burn it," Dad suggested. "The arsenic wouldn't burn, so it would be concentrated in the ash."

"But there goes colorless," I said. "I think Celia would

notice if someone had been sifting wood ash into her water bottle."

"True," Dad said. "Anyway. I'll go find Horace and see what we can do about identifying the source of the arsenic."

He turned to leave. He was moving a lot less briskly than the chief. Just for a moment, I wanted to run after him and tell him it was all right. He wasn't to blame if someone took the helpful information he'd tried to share and turned it to harm.

And then it occurred to me how I could distract him.

"By the way, Dad," I said. "Am I correct in suspecting that those geese belong to you—the ones that were in the chicken coop this morning?"

"Oh, my goodness!" His face lit up. "With everything that's happened this morning, I completely forgot. I should—wait. What do you mean 'were in the chicken coop'—where are they now?"

"Don't worry," I said. "Rose Noire let them out and they're hanging around with the Sumatrans, foraging in the herb fields."

"Oh, that's good," he said. "Is it okay if I leave them there a little while longer? It's going to be such a busy day."

"Fine with me," I said. "I was just wondering how they ended up in our chicken coop in the first place."

"I can't believe I forgot to tell you!" Dad sounded more triumphant than apologetic. "It was like this: I'm sure some people were getting tired of my agonizing over which heritage breed of geese I should get."

He was right, but it wouldn't be polite to say so.

"Well, we all knew it was a big decision for you," I said instead.

"I'd pretty much taken Cotton Patch and Shetland geese out of consideration, because they're the best fliers, and I don't think your mother would stand for geese getting into her flower garden. And Cotton Patches are the least productive when it comes to eggs—sometimes only a dozen a year! The Chinese are the most productive, but then we don't yet know how many goose eggs we'll be able to use, do we? I'd hate to see them go to waste."

I thought of asking if goose eggs tasted noticeably different from ordinary hen's eggs, but decided that would reduce my chances of getting an answer to my original question in under an hour.

"And the Steinbacher is prone to goose-on-goose aggression," Dad went on. "So I was worried about whether they'd coexist peacefully with all the ducks and chickens. I'd pretty much narrowed it down to either Pilgrim or Pomeranian geese. The Pilgrims are famous for being sweet tempered, and the Pomeranians are supposed to be reasonably docile, yet they still make a lot of noise to greet visitors, which makes them good watch geese."

I couldn't help thinking that even if the Pilgrims were sweet tempered for geese, they might still have been too feisty for Mother's taste. And had Dad thought about how Mother would react to having a flock of birds so noisy that they made good watch animals?

I'd let him worry about that.

"Of course," Dad was saying, "once I'd narrowed it down to those two, I realized I had a problem—you have no idea how much demand there is these days for heritage breeds! I've been on the waiting list with half a dozen goose breeders for months, and I was beginning to wonder if I'd ever get my geese. Then a breeder called and said he'd had a buyer fail to show up twice, and if I'd come and get them right away, he'd be happy to sell me a pair of Pomeranian goslings. So I jumped on it."

"Congratulations," I said. "So is the plan to have them live with our Sumatrans?"

"Heavens, no," he said. "They need a pond. But I had to drive all the way to Maryland to get them, and I only just barely got back in time for poor Damien's viewing last night. Oh dear—is that the right word? I don't think so.

Viewing sounds more like going to see him at the funeral home."

"Video showing," I suggested. "So you stuck the geese in the chicken coop instead of bringing them into the library with you—good decision."

"And once the showing was over, I realized it was probably a good idea to pick them up in the morning," he said. "After all, they'd had a long, tiring day. They were bound to have gone to roost. And the Sumatrans, too, and I'm sure they were all just as happy I let them get a good night's sleep. But then this morning, after you found poor Goodwin's body—well, I didn't exactly forget about them, but I wanted to make sure I took care of anything the chief needed first so I'd have plenty of time to get them settled in their new home once I got them there. But I should have warned you."

"No harm done," I said. "Rose Noire and I were just worried that it might be the work of the vandal—stealing someone's geese and hiding them in our coop to cause trouble."

"Oh dear—I'm sorry." Dad looked contrite. "I didn't mean to worry you."

"Not a problem," I said. "But see if you can't take them over to your farm sometime today—let them get settled into their permanent home."

"I will." With that he dashed off.

I wondered, briefly, if Mother knew they were acquiring geese. If she didn't, or if the geese turned out to be noisier than she could put up with, Dad's geese might end up staying indefinitely with the Sumatrans.

I'd worry about that if it happened.

I went back to searching our shelves for the nasty spell book.

Chapter 26

If I'd been searching for something more pleasant, I might have found spending time in the library relaxing. There were no sounds but the steady ticking of the library clock; periodically I'd take a break and walk out into the sunroom to stretch my back and check on what was happening in the backyard. Rose Noire and her sage-bearing allies had disappeared into the woods. I expected it would be a few hours before they reemerged somewhere down the road on the other side of the house.

On one of these trips I spotted Vern Shiffley sitting at one of the picnic tables. It occurred to me that I hadn't yet found a chance to ask him about the campsite, so I strolled out and joined him.

"Hey, Meg." A clipboard lay on the table, and he was obviously trying to fill out the form that was on it.

"Just tell me to get lost if I'm interrupting."

"Interrupt all you like." He stifled a yawn. "I'm thinking maybe I should go home and get some shut-eye. Fill this thing out when I wake up again. 'Course, it's kinda sorta your fault I have to fill it out in the first place. Report on last night's surveillance."

"Surveillance? Do you mean the clearing with the campfire?"

"Yeah." He nodded. "Went out there just after dark and set up my portable deer stand in a tree. Picked a place where I'd be well-nigh invisible from the ground."

"Oh dear," I said. "Were you there all night?"

"I decided to knock off around two or so," he said. "And

then once I headed out of here, I stopped to check the ditch, just out of habit, and spent another couple of hours dealing with Ms. Rivers and that car of hers."

"Sorry you had to waste time on the stakeout," I said.

"Wasn't time wasted," he said. "Can't expect to catch them the first time out. And it was kind of peaceful just sitting out in the woods. Like deer season."

"I'm trying to figure out what—if anything—this has to do with Goodwin's murder," I said.

"Who knows?" He shrugged. "You're thinking maybe the firebugs weren't out in the clearing because they were back here killing Goodwin? Could be. Or maybe they had nothing to do with it. Most likely, given all the commotion that took place over that video of Goodwin's, they decided to lie low last night. But that's okay. Odds are they'll be back, and sooner or later I'll get them." He yawned again, and this time he didn't even try to suppress it. "But not tonight, I think. If I were them, I'd wait till the police activity here died down a bit. It can wait. And there's no reason why these reports can't wait, either. My pillow's calling."

He stood up, nodded in farewell, picked up his clipboard, and sauntered through the backyard to his cruiser.

I returned to my search in the library.

I finished up a little after five and sat down in one of the comfy chairs to regroup. The nasty spell book wasn't in our library. At least it wasn't in here right now. I texted Kevin.

"Do those surveillance cameras cover both entrances to the library?" I asked.

"Of course," he texted back.

"Good. Thanks," I replied.

Presumably he had seen me searching the shelves. And theoretically he could alert me—or the chief—if someone came in carrying a moderately large book and tried to hide it on the shelves.

But would he?

I pondered for a few minutes. Then I texted him the cover of the nasty spell book.

"Someone here at the house may have a copy of this," I said. "Chief wants to see it. And I don't want the boys to find it."

He didn't reply. At least not right away. I let myself out of the library through the door to the house, locked it up again, and was heading down the long hallway to the rest of the house when I heard the faint ding of a reply.

"Understood," it said.

Should I push a little farther—enlist him to use his superior technical knowledge to help me figure out where the book was hidden?

I could work on that later, if my own efforts continued to be fruitless.

The actors weren't back yet, and there were no re-enactors hanging around—thank goodness. But half a dozen cousins and uncles were already firing up the grills for our usual Friday night cookout. No doubt Mother was in the kitchen, supervising the rest of her minions.

And the farthest picnic table—farthest from the house, and thus closest to Goodwin's trailer—had become the de facto operations center for the police. At one end, Horace and Sammy were inventorying evidence bags and packing them into the plastic milk crates Horace kept in his trunk for hauling large quantities of evidence. At the other, Aida was discussing something with the chief, who had dragged a comfortable lawn chair to the head of the table. As I watched, Rose Noire dashed out of the kitchen, deposited a pitcher of lemonade on the police table, grabbed the empty pitcher that had been standing there, and scurried back inside.

I nodded my approval. But while lemonade was all very well . . .

I went outside and strolled over to the picnic table, trying to walk slowly and noisily, so they'd notice me approaching and could break off any confidential discussions before I came within earshot.

"Meg," the chief said when he saw me. "Aida has good news for you."

"News, anyway," Aida said. "Not sure how good it is. I just ferried Lady Macbeth back here from the hospital. Your dad hasn't cleared her to work just yet—he thinks she should be on bed rest for another day or two. But neither the arsenic nor her own driving did her in, so the show can eventually go on."

"That's good news," I said. "I should check on her." I probably didn't do a very good job of sounding like a concerned and caring hostess.

"I'd leave her be," Aida said. "Like Garbo, she wants to be alone. She's already snapped at Rose Noire just for asking if she needed anything. She'll probably be just as rude to your dad when he drops by in a bit to get her vitals."

"I'll let Dad deal with her then," I said. "Actually, I came out here to invite all of you to stay for dinner. I know you've all been putting in double shifts and long hours today and probably haven't had as much time for meals as usual."

"I have to take all this down to the Crime Lab in Richmond," Sammy said.

"Then stick your head in the kitchen before you go," I said. "We can make you a fabulous carryout dinner. And that goes for anyone else who can't stay to eat."

"I'll ask Debbie Ann to organize the dinner breaks so everyone can drop by at least for a little while," the chief said. "And speaking of dropping by—apparently Josh and Jamie are planning to camp out tonight to guard your chickens, and they invited Adam to join them. I assume they cleared it with you?"

"No," I said. "But they've been at rehearsal with Michael all day, so they probably cleared it with him." Or maybe, since the boys and the chief's youngest grandson spent so much time in each other's houses, they were getting out of the habit of asking. "Of course, that's assuming you're okay with Adam camping out so close to your murder scene," I added.

"I'm pretty sure this wasn't some kind of random killing," he said. "And it's not anything that could be a danger to the boys—although I assume you'd have no objection if I had the officers on duty cruise by here a little more often than usual."

"I'd be delighted," I said. "Come on, Sammy—let's get you fixed up with that gourmet doggie bag."

In the kitchen, Mother was supervising the dozen or so relatives busily preparing for the evening's cookout. Although they all seemed to be giving the kitchen table a wide berth. Mother was standing there, frowning down at something.

No, at someone. Celia was sitting at the table, glaring up at Mother. She looked ghastly and her face was pale and drawn. Her shoulders were hunched and both hands gripped something on the table in front of her.

A can of Vienna sausages. Hot and spicy Vienna sausages.

"Yes, dear," Mother was saying. "But that really isn't the best thing for your stomach, you know. You'd be much better off with some nice saltines, and perhaps a little clear broth. Something that spicy—"

"I'll eat what I want to eat." Celia sounded like a two-year-old on the brink of having a meltdown.

"For heaven's sake," I said. "Someone's been trying to poison her. Let her eat whatever she feels safe eating."

Celia shifted her glare to me. She didn't look the least bit grateful for my intervention.

"If you like, I've got a few other factory-sealed things that might be a little easier on your stomach," I went on. "How about a can of applesauce? One of those mini-cans? They're vacuum-sealed, so if you don't get that whooshing sound when you open it, you'll know not to trust it.

Or how about some crackers? I've got some of those little individual serving packets we put in the boys' school lunches sometimes. You could hold them under a sink full of water, and if they don't get soggy you'll know no one's tampered with the wrapper."

She didn't actually spurn the suggestion, so I went into the pantry, grabbed two small cans of applesauce and half a dozen small packets of crackers. I put them on the table near her.

She looked at them, frowning slightly.

A cousin was coming forward, holding out flatware and a plate.

"No, she won't want those," I said. "I expect she'll want to eat things with her fingers, right out of the can. Safety first."

The cousin scurried away. Celia was starting to look a little less hostile.

"Michael's decided not to have any full cast rehearsals this weekend," I told Celia. "He'll be doing some of the problem scenes and also working with people who want individual help. So he'll check with you once Dad clears you to get back to work."

She nodded. She stood up, picked up her can of Vienna sausages. She paused, then added one of the applesauce cans and two of the cracker packets to her stash. She nodded at me, and silently left the kitchen.

"Don't you think that was a little cold?" Sammy said. "Talking to her about getting back to work?"

"I think she's terrified that her illness is going to cost her one of the best roles she's ever landed," I said. "I think she has been for weeks. So if that was cold, maybe cold is what she needed."

"Does she really think we'd try to poison her?" Mother asked.

"Seems a little paranoid to me," a cousin said.

"Someone *did* try to poison her," I said. "We just don't

yet know who. So maybe she's being paranoid, or maybe she's only being careful. We may know none of us are mad poisoners, but how well does she know us?"

"True." Mother shook her head, wearing what was clearly meant to be her "more in sorrow than in anger" expression.

"If she still feels the same way tomorrow, let's help her out," I suggested. "If her car's still in the shop, one of us can take her to the grocery store and help her pick up whatever canned goods she'd like."

"I suppose you're right," Mother said. "The poor thing has had a terrible time."

This pronouncement seemed to turn the tide of public opinion, at least here in the kitchen, and everyone dived back into working with more cheerful faces.

Everyone except Rose Noire. She slipped out into the hall. I found her there at the foot of the stairs, staring upward.

"Don't worry," I said. "Give her time. She'll get over it."

"A little ginger tea would do wonders for her stomach," Rose Noire said.

"Not if she's worrying that with every sip that you might be poisoning her," I said. "And of course we understand that you'd never do anything like that, but she doesn't really know you, does she?"

"No more than we know her." She sighed. "We don't know any of them all that well. Any one of them could be involved in that horrible evil magic out in the woods."

I could have added that any one of them could also have killed Goodwin or poisoned Celia, but I didn't think that would improve her mood.

I knew what would, though.

Chapter 27

"By the way, I've got something to tell you." I tried to give my voice a conspiratorial tone.

She looked at me glumly, as if she suspected I was only trying to distract her. I slipped into the living room, which was empty. She followed me.

"You can't say anything about this to anybody," I warned her.

She pursed her lips as if to suggest she knew how to keep them closed.

"But your concerns about those people casting evil spells in the woods?" I glanced around, more to impress her with the need for secrecy than from any fear that someone might be eavesdropping. "The chief is taking them seriously. He had Vern stake out the clearing last night."

"I'm sure it's the fires he's taking seriously," she said. "He doesn't believe spells do anything."

"Probably not," I said. "But what does that matter? If he figures out who's lighting the fires, he'll figure out who's casting spells, and he'll do what he can to stop them from doing either."

"True." She frowned. "Vern didn't see anything last night?"

"No. He sat up in a tree on his portable deer hunting platform from shortly after dark to about two a.m. Nothing. He suspects all the fuss from Goodwin's video showing may have scared them off."

"Yes." She nodded. "Or maybe they spotted him."

"Spotted Vern?" I chuckled. "In the woods? When he didn't want to be spotted? I expect the tree he was sitting in barely knew he was there."

"You're right," she said. "And yes, it probably was too chaotic for them to get in their spell casting. But he's going out there tonight, isn't he?"

"I don't know." I realized immediately that this was a mistake. I needed to reassure her that the suspicious clearing was under surveillance, not reignite her interest in staking it out by herself. "Of course, he wouldn't tell me if he was. And the odds are he is. The chief might think the stakeout is just as important as the murders—a bad fire could take lives. And he might even suspect that there's a connection between the campfires and the murder, in which case he'd prioritize the stakeout."

Had I succeeded in reassuring her?

"I hear you," she said. "If—oh dear. Did you see that?"

She pointed to one of the front windows. I didn't see anything but our front yard.

"One of Seth's sheep just trotted by," she said, heading for the archway. "I should haul the poor thing back before anything untoward happens to it."

"The reenactors haven't been invited tonight," I pointed out. "And MacLeod seems to have skipped town—no one's seen him all day. The sheep shouldn't be in any danger."

But she was already gone, and I wasn't sure if she'd heard me. Or if she'd really gotten the point I'd been trying to make about leaving the stakeout to the police. Heard it, definitely. But agreed with it?

I'd have to keep my eyes on her.

Back in the kitchen, Mother and her troops were trying to talk Sammy into taking along three or four times as much food as he could possibly eat for his dinner. Sammy was protesting that he couldn't possibly eat so much.

"Share it with Horace's friends at the crime lab," I said.

"To thank them for coming in on the weekend to receive our evidence."

Sammy liked the idea, and stopped protesting. Unfortunately, the notion of his sharing the food down at the crime lab inspired Mother and the assembled cousins to increase the quantities.

I left them to it.

When I stepped outside, several dozen heads swiveled to stare at me, and then gradually lost interest when it became obvious that I wasn't about to do anything interesting.

The troops were definitely ready for dinner. Apart from Celia and Russ Brainard, all the cast and crew were there, swilling iced tea or lemonade. No uninvited reenactors trying to lose themselves in the crowd—not even the one who usually hung out with the other Mean Girls. They looked a little lost without her.

Those visiting relatives who were neither grilling nor helping out in the kitchen were mingling, some with the actors, others with the larger-than-usual cadre of history professors and students. We usually got a smattering of them on Fridays or Saturdays, but not this many. Curiosity about the murders had probably inspired more than usual to take advantage of their open invitation.

Over at the police table, I caught Horace yawning, and remembered that he, too, had gone straight from night shift on patrol to a busy day of forensics. I hoped the chief remembered this.

Just in case he needed reminding, I ambled over to the police table.

"Roger," Horace was saying. "But if you need me—"

"I need you rested and sharp," the chief said. "Skedaddle."

"Thanks, boss," Horace said. "See you later, Meg."

Rose Noire deposited a tray on the police table, containing an antipasto plate, a dish of homemade pickles, and a platter of raw vegetables and dip. The chief shut his notebook and stretched before reaching out and grabbing a pickle.

I took a seat on the bench and helped myself to some of the antipasti.

"I'm glad you decided to stay for dinner," I said.

"I'm glad you invited us," he said. "Minerva's taken the choir down to Richmond for a concert. And while I'm perfectly capable of cooking a decent dinner for myself and the boys—"

"After a day like today you shouldn't have to."

He nodded. He leaned back in his chair, sipped his iced tea, and for a few moments it was as if things were back to normal. He could be here picking up Adam after a day of playing with Jamie and Josh. For years now the boys had been inseparable, and Henry and Minerva Burke had become increasingly a part of our day-to-day circle of friends. We could so easily be sharing a laugh over something silly the boys had done, or making sure the other was up to speed on the latest gossip they'd brought home from school.

Then he frowned slightly and the police chief was back.

"I have to admit, it's been an interesting day," he said. "I try not to assume anything, but I think there's every chance that you were right about Mr. Goodwin's video being a catalyst for his murder. And it's been eye-opening, interviewing several dozen people about what they saw last night."

"Let me guess," I said. "It's like hearing about several dozen different movies."

"That's about the size of it." He chuckled. "There's actually a term in psychology for it—the *Rashomon* effect. Named after that Japanese movie where you see the same events from four different points of view. Or, if you like, a fancy way of saying that uncorroborated eyewitness testimony is pretty darn useless. Today's been like a textbook example of that. I'm thinking maybe, once this is over, I should write an article about it. Maybe for *Police Chief*—that's the magazine put out by the International Association of Chiefs of Police."

"Oh dear," I said. "You aren't getting anything useful from anyone?"

"It's not that," he said. "But I could save so much time if we could just find that wretched video."

"At least then you'd know what people actually saw."

"Well, not really," he said. "I'd still be dealing with the fact that everyone saw it through the lens of their own mindset and experience. But it'd be a little easier to sort the misperceptions from the out-and-out lies. No such thing as gospel truth in a situation like this, but right now I can't even consider something probable unless I hear it from at least two people. Which is normal, of course—witnesses are always subjective. But I don't usually have anywhere near this many witnesses and their stories aren't usually this different. According to the reenactors, the video was mostly a slander against Camp Birnam. The actors think it was almost entirely about their rehearsals and are sure he set out to make them look foolish. The history professors think they were his main target. About the only thing they all agree on was that Mr. Goodwin was prejudiced against them and used all sorts of clever tricks and techniques to make them look bad."

"If you ask me, they're right about that last part," I said. "The more I think about it, the more I am convinced that he didn't just happen to capture unflattering or even incriminating video about people—he went looking for it. Set people up so he could get it. And made sure to show us the worst footage he had."

"I won't argue that point," the chief said. "With luck we'll be able to see that when we get access to his backup files."

"When you get access," I echoed. "That sounds positive. At least more positive than 'if' would be."

"If he uploaded anything, we'll get it eventually," he said. "Young Kevin has already given us the most probable target. It's just going to take an inconveniently long time. And I can't just sit around and wait. So I'm trying to piece together exactly what was on that video he showed."

"Sorry I wasn't more help," I said.

"Don't apologize," he said. "Your account of the video was the most clear and complete version I got from anyone. In fact, offhand I can only think of two bits of potentially useful information I got from someone other than you, and neither of those has been corroborated yet."

"Seriously?"

He nodded,

"I feel a little less useless, then. If you want to interrogate me about the uncorroborated bits, I'm game."

"I'm not sure either of them is important." He was smiling, as if he realized my question was inspired as much by curiosity as by a desire to help. "One was Ms. West's assertion that she saw a hand reach into the video frame, remove Ms. Rivers's water bottle, and then replace it. And I seem to recall that you've already stated that you don't remember seeing that."

"Yes," I said. "I can't prove she didn't see it, either, of course."

"And since Horace has found arsenic in the bottle allegedly taken from Ms. Rivers's room, I'm very interested in anyone who's been playing fast and loose with water bottles."

I nodded. Allegedly. That must mean Tanya was still on his suspect list.

"What was the other thing I didn't spot?" I asked.

"Mr. Goodwin had a scene that showed Ms. Rivers discovering that her script had been splattered with red paint," he said.

"Yes," I said. "He didn't show the epic temper tantrum

she pitched when she found it. I wonder if he was saving that for his grand finale."

"With luck, we'll find out," the chief said. "What he did show, according to one witness I interviewed, was that in the scene of her finding the damaged manuscript, she already had slight red paint stains on her fingers."

"Yikes," I said. "No, I didn't spot that."

"Difficult to find an innocent explanation for that," the chief said. "Of course the one person who reported it could be making it up."

"Yes." I nodded slowly. "Or imagining it."

"Keep it to yourself," he said. "But you might want to keep a close eye on her."

"I will," I said. "Although I can think of one explanation for the red paint stains that would be not only perfectly innocent but highly plausible."

"Really?" The chief frowned. "What would that be?"

"What if Goodwin wasn't there to film her reactions when she found it, and asked her to reenact it for the camera?" I asked. "He did that all the time. Like when we found the dead-man's-fingers in the woods, remember?"

"I remember." The chief looked discouraged. "He didn't even care about having an accurate reenactment. When he found out Josh and Jamie had been the ones to find it, he settled very easily for a completely bogus reenactment by MacLeod."

I nodded.

"But why would Ms. Rivers agree to the reenactment?" he asked. "Knowing he'd do everything possible to show her in a bad light."

"She wouldn't have known that," I said. "The paint-stained script was one of the first things the vandal did. Happened the first week we were here. Back then we hadn't seen any of Goodwin's footage, and we hadn't even started to suspect that he wasn't acting in good faith. And besides, from what I heard, Celia totally lost it when she found the ruined script. Pitched a major temper tantrum. If she found out Goodwin hadn't filmed her meltdown, or didn't have very good footage of it, I bet she'd be eager to film a more flattering reenactment."

"Yes." He sounded thoughtful. "If only her carefully staged reaction had been captured on film, the people who saw her go ballistic would find that no one believed their version. They might even start to doubt it themselves. Blast! I need to talk to that woman. When your father shows up, I'll see if I can get him to sign off on my doing another short interview. Any idea where he is?"

"I'm hoping he went to take his goslings home." Seeing the chief's puzzled expression, I explained about the goslings' mysterious arrival.

"Glad to see another mystery solved," he said.

"And I think I'll take a turn around the yard, play hostess, and see if I can find Dad and send him your way."

"Thanks," he said, before turning his attention to other matters—specifically, the delivery, by Rose Noire, of a plate full of food, and the arrival of an uncle who was a passionate true crime aficionado and doubtless wanted to tap the chief's professional expertise. But since the uncle rarely took the slightest interest in a case unless it was at least a hundred years old, the chief might welcome the distraction.

While playing hostess I spotted Dean Braxton sitting by himself at one of the picnic tables. Curious—usually he'd be surrounded by most of the history professors and students who'd showed up. He was sipping a glass of lemonade, so at least someone had made him welcome. But his face wore an irritated frown, and that wasn't an expression I ever wanted to see on one of our guests, so I strolled over to greet him.

Chapter 28

"Do you expect any of the reenactors to show up?" Dean Braxton asked, once we'd exchanged expressions of pleasure at seeing each other and praised the mildness of the evening. "I was hoping to talk to one of them."

"I doubt if they'll show." I glanced around. "At a normal meal I'd expect to see a few of them, ingratiating themselves into one conversation or another and hoping that we'll invite them to stay and eat. But they seem to have made themselves scarce today."

"Probably hoping to distance themselves from the murder," the dean said. "Or perhaps afraid you'll kick them out on their ears after the trouble they caused yesterday."

"They're annoying," I said. "But we know they're a useful part of the History Department's *Macbeth* project."

"Actually, they're not." He steepled his fingers and tapped his forefingers against his chin—a bit of body language I'd noticed before. It seemed to signal that he was switching gears from social to official mode. "After seeing their antics on video, I did a little checking around. And strangely enough, none of the History Department faculty I talked to seemed to express any interest in their reenactment project. Of course, it's always possible that they want to disassociate themselves from something that has proven to be both embarrassing and unsuccessful. But I don't think so. I think I'm picking up genuine puzzlement over why the department ever approved the project. And possibly a little hostility toward the project itself. And while I can't yet be sure, I think the idea originated with one of our graduate students."

I nodded. I wasn't sure where he was going with this. I didn't like the idea that some poor graduate student might be set up to take the blame for whatever embarrassment the reenactors had caused the department. But if his ire toward Camp Birnam was going to clear the way for us to get rid of the reenactors . . .

"Specifically, a graduate student whose older brother is working on a doctorate in English," the dean went on. "Professor Philpotts is on his dissertation committee."

Okay, this was taking an interesting direction.

"You think Professor Philpotts arranged to inflict the reenactors on us?" I asked.

"You could put it that way." A faint, rueful smile crossed his face. "He certainly does seem curiously obsessed with everything connected to Michael's production. The other day he dropped by my office, ostensibly to discuss some issues raised at the latest meeting of the Paperwork Reduction Committee—there's irony for you, Philpotts being on the Paper Reduction Committee. You'd think the English Department wanted to sabotage the whole scheme."

I smiled in appreciation of his point, but refrained from commenting, lest the conversation stray onto the tedious topic of Caerphilly College academic politics.

"But that's neither here nor there," the dean said, correcting course on his own. "Anyway, Philpotts seemed less interested in the committee than in talking about the pranks someone has been playing here at your house. He was positively gloating."

"He would." I shook my head. "Which is one reason we've been trying not to make a big fuss about the vandal—that would only give him more gloating fodder."

"He must have his sources, then." The dean sipped his lemonade and then glanced at the glass appreciatively, as if he'd been sipping a particularly fine vintage wine. "He's certainly up with all the details—scripts ruined with red paint, ladies' unmentionables strung up in the library, racial slurs spray-painted on the walls—it all sounds very—"

"Wait a second," I said. "He told you about the racial slurs?"

"He did." The dean's face assumed a look of distaste. "And if you ask me, he relished having an excuse to repeat them. The man's clearly . . . well, an unreconstructed Confederate would be an exaggeration, I suppose. But I've never felt confident that his views on a number of social issues were entirely consistent with the enlightened and progressive views the college seeks to promote."

Which was as close as the politically astute dean would come to calling Philpotts an out-and-out bigot.

"That's interesting," I said. "Because no one's supposed to know about the racial slurs."

"Why not?"

"You know how the police don't make some aspects of a crime public?" I explained. "Usually to smoke out false confessions."

He nodded.

"The police were keeping the racial slurs quiet," I said. "I was alone in the house when I found them. Apart from me, only Deputy Vern Shiffley ever saw them—well, apart from whoever wrote them. Vern helped me paint over them before anyone else came in. So how does Professor Philpotts know about them?"

The puzzled look on Dean Braxton's face gave way to a curiously blissful smile.

"You think he did it?" he asked.

"I have a hard time imagining him spray-painting graffiti in our house," I said. "But he could have instigated it. Suggested it to someone."

"Either way, he'd be responsible." The dean was almost purring. "For a singularly heinous and insensitive act. I note that there are several persons of color among

Michael's cast and crew—imagine if they'd found those scurrilous writings."

I nodded.

"Now that the chief's home, are they making any progress in solving the vandalism?" he asked.

"Unfortunately, he's had to prioritize the murder for now," I said.

"True." I got the feeling the dean wouldn't have criticized the chief if he'd let the murder slide a bit to focus on bringing down Professor Philpotts.

"But on the positive side," I added. "I think the murder means they're able to throw a lot more resources at investigating anything that's been going on at our house. After all, it's possible that the vandalism is related to the murder."

"Yes," the dean mused. "Unable to cause enough consternation with minor, if highly offensive, pranks, the vandal escalates to murder. Sounds plausible to me."

I suspected any scenario that ended up with Philpotts in handcuffs, or at least departing in disgrace from the college, would sound both plausible and desirable to him.

"Would you be willing to fill the chief in on that conversation with Professor Philpotts?" I asked. "It might help him solve the vandalism case."

"I'd be delighted to." He did sound delighted. "Very capable man, the chief. And he's right over there—do you suppose now would be a good time to talk to him?"

He pointed toward the table where the chief was now chatting with Dad and Aida.

"If it's not, you could always arrange a mutually convenient time," I said. "Just don't mention the racist graffiti in front of my dad."

"You haven't told your dad?" He looked amused.

"He gets carried away sometimes and forgets what's public information and what's supposed to be secret," I said. "And he always feels terrible afterward. So we have a standing arrangement that we don't tell him anything that he'd get in trouble for spilling."

"Smart."

I decided not to mention that on at least one occasion the chief had deliberately told Dad something he did want to get to the right ears.

I accompanied the dean over to the police table, and managed to draw Dad aside.

"Did the chief mention that he wants to interview Celia again?" I asked.

"Yes, and I was going to go up sometime this evening to see if she seems well enough for a brief interview."

"Do it soon," I said. "In fact, do it now. I can tell worrying about that is really bothering him. And you can make sure she's eating properly."

"Good idea."

He scurried off. I glanced over and saw the chief and Dean Braxton in close conversation.

The picnic wore on. Goodwin's murder was almost the only topic of conversation, and I wanted none of it. Michael and I took our plates over to sit near the llama pen.

"By the way, the missing dagger is not in the prop chest," Michael said. "The prop master is under orders to find it. If she can't, I think we'll need to do a complete search. House, barn, tents—everything."

"That would be a major hassle."

"I don't suppose there's any chance the chief might want to do it."

"I could suggest it," I said. "After all, he'd be the first to say that he doesn't believe in coincidences. Maybe it's just a coincidence that the dagger disappeared the same night that the murder happened, but you never know."

"Brilliant," he said. "Might even work."

"If it doesn't, I'll see if Mother can organize a search," I said. "She's always looking for interesting projects to keep the visiting relatives busy."

He laughed out loud.

"I like the way you think."

Once we'd finished our dinners, Michael got the chief's permission to reopen the library for the evening's entertainment and headed over there to get ready. He was calling the event a watch party, but it was more than that—one of the history professors was going to show excerpts from movies made out of Shakespeare's plays and analyze what was well done and what was anachronistic and unhistorical. In another mood, I'd have found it fascinating, but tonight I was too restless to focus on it.

I checked in the kitchen, but there were more than enough volunteers to do what little cleanup hadn't already been done. I said goodnight to the relatives who'd decided to pass on the watch party and head back to Mother and Dad's for the night. Then I found myself at loose ends. And cranky. I knew the best cure for that.

I headed out to the barn. I checked all the stalls to make sure none of the cast and crew who were sleeping there had gone to bed early. Then I opened up my forge and looked around for something to do. Physical work at the anvil almost always improved my mood.

The creepy dagger.

Just to be certain, I checked the prop box myself. It lived in the garage when it wasn't at rehearsals. The creepy dagger wasn't there, dammit. So much for the theory that the prop master had put it away there by mistake. Had I told the chief about the dagger's disappearance? I thought so, but I was too distracted to remember. I'd ask tomorrow. If it didn't reappear soon, I'd need to re-create it. I could manage that. I still had my sketches. I could get out the clay now.

No. I wasn't feeling creative tonight.

But I did feel like hammering on something. Probably not a good time to start anything big that would require an hour or two of concentrated and noisy labor. But I could do something small. I grabbed the snake dagger, whose sharp edge still needed to be made dull enough for rehearsal use.

As I waited for my forge to heat, and then for the knife blade to reach a temperature where I could work it, I brooded over the missing dagger. Did its disappearance have anything to do with the murder? What if the killer had taken it, intending to use it on Goodwin, but hadn't been able to get it out when they met and had fallen back on whacking him with his own camera? Or was its disappearance simply the vandal's latest effort? I liked that idea better—although for all I knew there was a connection between the vandalism and the murder.

The most logical one being that the vandal had killed Goodwin and destroyed his video because it contained incriminating evidence. What if—

I shoved those thoughts aside, because the knife blade was hot enough for me to work on it, and I had to concentrate on what I was doing—a series of small, cautious taps designed to blunt the carefully honed edge while maintaining the illusion that it was still razor sharp. After half an hour's meticulous work, including a couple of reheatings, I ran my finger carefully over the edge. It would do. The actors would still have to be careful—you could easily poke your eye out with it, although the same could be said for any stage sword or dagger.

But anyone who picked it up with the idea of stabbing someone or slitting someone's throat would be disappointed.

Was I worrying unnecessarily? Maybe whoever had killed Goodwin didn't have any other homicidal plans.

Unless, of course, they thought someone was about to stumble on evidence of their guilt—in which case anyone here could be a target. Me, for example. Or Dad. Or my very inquisitive twin sons.

Dammit, what was taking the chief so long getting access to Goodwin's backup files?

Chill, I told myself. Maybe the chief already had access. Maybe he already knew who Goodwin's video incriminated and was busily building an airtight case against them.

Or maybe there was no backup video. If that was the case, he might not have anything to go on apart from what I and others could remember about the video. If only I could dredge up a few more useful details. I closed my eyes and began trying to re-create what had happened last night in the library. I started with the sensory details. The feel of the library—warm, even though the night was cooling off outside, and slightly stuffy from the crowd. The smell of the popcorn after Josh and Jamie poured the melted butter on it. The salty, greasy taste of it. The popping of corn kernels. The steady buzz of the audience chatting as we all waited for the show to begin. Goodwin standing by the TV screen, watching the audience. Watching all of us, or anyone in particular?

Just then I heard the screen door close—not with the usual vigorous slamming noise that reminded me I should replace the door closing mechanism, but with a furtive tap.

I glanced out the barn door and saw Rose Noire creeping steathily across the yard.

She was dressed entirely in black—black leggings and a flowing black tunic over a tight-fitting black knit leotard-style top. No, not entirely in black—her tennis shoes were deep purple.

My first reaction was surprise—who knew that Rose Noire's wardrobe could supply enough black garments to let her dress up like a cat burglar out of the comics? But then I realized that one of these items looked very familiar. The tunic was almost certainly a burnt velvet one out of my own closet—a little dressy for skulking in the woods. And I wouldn't be surprised to learn that she'd also borrowed the leggings and the knit top from my wardrobe.

I wanted to ask "what are you up to?" But that would be silly. I knew what she was up to.

I could try to talk her out of it, but then she'd probably just pretend to listen and then sneak out again as soon as my back was turned.

I waited till she was past the barn door opening. Then I grabbed a handy empty feed sack and stuffed into it a few items I thought might be useful. I wasn't all in black, but my jeans, black sneakers, and purple Caerphilly Zoo t-shirt were pretty dark. And I'd match my furtive sneaking skills against hers any day.

I peeked out. She was out of sight. I eased out of the door, slipped along the side of the barn, and peered carefully around the corner. She was almost at her shed.

I waited until she disappeared behind it, then quietly made my own way through the tent city and across her herb fields. When I reached the shelter of the shed, I peered around a corner.

She was almost to the woods. I waited until she reached the first few trees. She looked around again and slipped into the woods.

I set off across the fields, aiming at the point where she disappeared. I reminded myself there was no need to hurry. If I lost her I could still find the clearing. I'd sent its GPS coordinates to Vern, and I was sure I could still find them in my phone if need be.

It was a little creepy, passing by the spot where we'd found Damien Goodwin's body. Horace had left a wide circle of yellow crime-scene tape around it. Which was a little odd—I knew from overhearing him talk to the chief that he was pretty sure he'd found everything there was to find there. Was he still holding his options open, in case he thought of some other test he needed to perform?

More likely he just didn't want to take the crime-scene tape down just yet. That would certainly be a note of unpleasant finality. Maybe it was better to leave it for a while.

The wind would whip it about, the sun would begin to fade it in time. Gawkers might eventually grow bold enough to take pieces of it as souvenirs. A gradual rather than a sudden disappearance.

At least for the time being the crime-scene tape helped us avoid walking over the spot where Goodwin had died. Not that I'm overly superstitious, but the idea of doing that bothered me.

So I steered clear of it and slipped into the woods.

For a moment I thought I'd have to take out my phone and navigate to the GPS coordinates, but then I realized that the woods weren't really trackless. Far from it. You could see faint suggestions of paths all over the place, leading in any direction you might want to go. Deer trails, I supposed. I closed my eyes, tried to remember which way Vern had pointed when I'd asked where the clearing was, then took the most likely path.

Eventually I heard slight rustling sounds ahead of me. Rustling sounds and the occasional light thump. I slowed down and proceeded with caution. I came to the clearing—well, a clearing—and peered ahead.

It was the right clearing. I could see the remains of the campfire in the center. The rustling and thumping sounds were from Rose Noire's efforts to jump up and grab a tree branch that was just a little too far over her head. Her back was to me.

I stepped into the clearing with what I thought was a brilliant absence of rustling.

"Would you like me to give you a leg up?" I asked.

Chapter 29

Rose Noire shrieked and whirled around to stare at me.

"Keep it down," I said. "Or you'll scare away the very people you're trying to catch."

"What are you doing here?" she demanded.

"If you recall, I told you I didn't think it was such a good time to be sneaking around alone in the woods," I said. "So I followed you. You're no longer alone. Hang on, and I can give you a leg up to your branch."

She frowned for a moment, then apparently decided it was a good idea. With my help she was able to grab the branch and pull herself up.

"But what about you?" she asked, once she was perched on the branch. "You're not going to go away, are you?"

"Stand by to catch." I reached into my feed bag and pulled out a length of rope. I tossed one end up to her and, once she'd tied it to her branch, I used it to half climb, half walk up the trunk of the tree to another useful branch.

"You came prepared," she said.

"Not as prepared as I might have been if you'd told me you were planning this," I said. "I bet if we gave him a few hours' notice Kevin could have found us a night-vision camera."

"If I'd told you, you'd have tried to talk me out of it," she said. "And it's a good thing I did come—I've already discovered something I should have noticed previously."

"What's that?"

"The herbs," she said. "I must have smelled them before

without really being conscious of it. You kept asking me why I was so sure they were up to no good, and I knew there must be something else I could tell you. The minute I got here I realized what—the odor of the herbs. I figured out where they emptied out their cauldron after the spell and focused on the smells that were concentrated there— and I'm sure of it. They're not using the kind of herbs you'd use for a spell of good intent. They're using foul, bitter, dangerous herbs. That's why I knew they were up to something evil."

For just a second, I was tempted to ask how often her premonitions and aura-detection came down to having a keen sense of smell. But she had a point. The human sense of smell worked like that, unconsciously yet so powerfully that it could almost seem like magic. I could understand why she'd wanted to come back.

Or maybe she'd just gotten tired of waiting for the chief to do something.

"Let's shut up so we don't scare off our prey," I whispered.

She nodded. She closed her eyes and began some kind of yoga breathing. Not, I hoped, a kind that was likely to put her to sleep and make her fall off her branch.

I shifted around until I had the least uncomfortable resting place possible. It occurred to me that if Vern had left his deer stand in place it might make a much more comfortable place to perch. I scanned all the nearby trees, but if he'd left it behind he'd done a great job of camouflage. So I pulled out my phone and texted Michael that I was going out to Rose Noire's shed to help her with a project, and he shouldn't wait up for me. And then I went to my phone settings, switched it to dark mode, and muted all its usual sounds. At least I hoped I'd managed that. The phone screen was surprisingly bright in the dark of the woods, so as soon as I'd finished I turned it off.

Rose Noire's phone dinged. I recognized the sound

most phones used to signal an arriving text. It sounded unnaturally loud in the still woods.

"You might want to turn off notifications for the time being," I whispered.

"Already doing it."

"Anything urgent?"

"Clarence just got back after a rescue mission, and he's dropping off some baby geese for your dad," she murmured. "He wanted someone to know in case your dad had already gone to bed."

"Not urgent then."

She nodded. Nice that my eyes had adjusted well enough that I could see it.

We fell silent. I wondered briefly about the message. Clarence Rutledge, the town veterinarian, often went on missions to rescue cats and dogs from kill shelters. So far Spike's well-known ferocity had enabled us to weasel out of fostering or adopting any of his charges. But if he was expanding his efforts to include poultry and other farm animals . . .

I'd worry about that later.

Time passed. I found myself wishing for something to do. If only I could listen to my audiobook—but I hadn't brought my headphones or earbuds. And my notebook was back at the house—not that I'd have been able to see it in the dark.

I settled on reviewing my memories of Goodwin's video. Maybe I could pick up where I left off, envisioning myself back in the library. I closed my eyes and imagined myself standing beside Michael at the far end of the library, leaning against the bookshelves. . . .

No use. Maybe I could have done it back at the house, in the comfort of the sofa, but here a twig would snap in the woods, or an owl would hoot, or I'd suddenly notice the annoying way a tree branch dug into my thigh, and I was right back in the present. Hearing the night noises of the wood. Smelling the loamy smell of the leaf mold and a faint thread of the lavender essential oil Rose Noire wore as perfume. And seeing the remains of the campfire below very clearly, now that my eyes had adjusted.

I was trying to think of a persuasive way to suggest that we give up and go home when we heard rustling and crunching noises in the distance.

Rose Noire prodded me in the ribs. Did she think I hadn't noticed?

We both froze, and I tried to breathe as quietly as I could.

The noises drew nearer. Eventually three cloaked figures crept furtively into the clearing. They were all carrying bundles of some sort.

I pulled out my phone—shielding it with my hand, since even in dark mode it gave off quite a bit of light—and sent a quick text to the chief. And then one to Vern. Then I began recording video of the three cloaked figures.

The one in the lead walked calmly over and set two canvas tote bags down near the remains of the fire. The other two stood close together at the edge of the clearing and looked around with visible anxiety. Around, but not up.

"It's so creepy out here," one of them said in a hushed voice. Not a familiar voice.

"Bring the cauldron over here," the one by the campfire said. She didn't speak loudly, but her voice had the rich resonance of a classically trained stage actor. Gina.

"Sorry," the third one said. I recognized her voice, too. Fawn, the costume assistant.

Gina was definitely in charge. Her two acolytes scurried to join her. Fawn set down what she'd been carrying—an oversized purse and a bundle of firewood. She arranged the firewood atop the remains of the previous fires. She then began crumbling up sheets of newspaper and wadding them around the wood.

The other acolyte was carrying a cauldron and had a

canvas sack slung over her shoulder. By now I was pretty sure who she was, too—the young woman from Camp Birnam who'd been the third of the Mean Girls. She set down her sack and stood holding the cauldron, evidently waiting until the fire was laid.

Suddenly Fawn stopped and looked up at where Gina was watching her.

"Do we really need to keep doing this?" she asked.

"We need to keep the energy level up," Gina said.

"But why?" Fawn asked. "Calum's's disappeared and I can't imagine Celia will be able to go on with a concussion on top of her stomach problems."

"And your abusive boss?"

"Hasn't been down in days," Fawn said. "She hates it down here. I bet when she hears about the murder she'll quit."

"She hasn't quit yet," Gina said. "Neither has Celia. And I'm sure Zoe wants to make sure her harasser stays away."

"If he tried it again, I could report him to Sally," Zoe said. "She'd deal with him."

"We need to keep the energy going until the end," Gina said. "Or it could backfire."

The other two gave up their protests. Fawn went back to building the fire.

I made a mental note to apologize to Rose Noire, and offer her the chance to say "I told you so." Not only did we now know who had been setting the fires—and yes, casting spells—we also knew why. Gina mistakenly believed that she was a shoo-in for the role of Lady Macbeth if she could get rid of Celia. Fawn had a similar delusion about taking over as costume designer if Maeve, the incumbent, quit. I could easily see MacLeod as a harasser, so I was inclined to feel sorry for Zoe—but did she really think she had no recourse other than trying to cast an evil spell on him?

When Fawn finished setting the fire, Zoe settled the cauldron carefully on top of it.

Then Gina, who had been watching their efforts, strode over to the campfire. She was holding something that looked like a plastic squeeze bottle of dish soap. Probably not soap though. She squirted some of it at the base of the cauldron. Was it my imagination or did I smell gasoline?

Then Gina pulled out a lighter and a twist of paper. She lit the paper, tossed it at the crumpled newspapers, and flames shot up with a whoosh.

Sparks scattered from the fire. Some of them fell on dried leaves and I could see flames flickering up in one—no, two places. None of the three women noticed— they were staring raptly at the main fire.

Time to shut this down.

I grabbed my rope and rappelled down the tree trunk. As I hit the ground I was opening my mouth to shout out some orders when a loud, firm voice preempted me.

"You idiots! Put out that fire!" Sally the Sane strode into the clearing, anachronistically clad in jeans and sneakers, shaking her fist at them.

The women—well, Fawn and Zoe, anyway—gasped and clutched each other.

"What she said," I snapped. "Put it out! Now!" I let go of the rope and raced toward the small but growing patch of burning leaves.

"Angels and ministers of grace defend us!" Rose Noire intoned from her perch on the branch.

For some reason those words seemed to complete Fawn's and Zoe's demoralization. They turned and fled, shrieking. Gina uttered a few pithy but unprintable remarks and took off in another direction.

"God, what idiots," Sally muttered. She joined me, and between the two of us we managed to stamp out the burning leaves. We could hear shrieks and crashing noises not that far away. The would-be sorceresses didn't seem to be enjoying themselves.

When we'd finished putting out the flames, I pulled a

water bottle out of my feed sack and poured its contents over the ashes.

"Good thinking," Sally said. "We should probably wait till the main fire burns down a bit before we try to deal with it."

"Why are you just standing there? They're getting away!" Rose Noire shouted.

Sally and I turned to see her climbing down the rope. I went over to help her.

"Relax," I said.

"They're getting away." She was whipping her head around and seemed poised to give chase as soon as she figured out which direction her prey had taken. "We have to catch them."

"Chill." I grabbed her arm. "Let them go. No sense any more of us getting lost in the woods."

"She has a good point," Sally the Sane was holding Rose Noire's other arm. "We know who they are. We can testify to what they were up to."

"I've got video." I let go of Rose Noire's arm and held up my phone.

"Oooh," Sally said. "I wish I'd thought of that."

"It'll be lousy video," I said. "Even worse than what Goodwin took."

"Enough to prove what they've been doing. Good show." She let go of Rose Noire's arm and stuck out her hand. "Sally Gladstone."

"Meg Langslow," I said.

"I know," she said. "Sorry I haven't formally introduced myself before, but when I'm up at your house I'm usually fully occupied trying to keep my fellow reenactors on the straight and narrow. Speaking of which—unless my eyes deceive me, there was only one of my lot out here trying to incinerate the neighborhood."

"And two of my lot," I said. "The very two I suspected, but now I know for sure who they are."

"Since we've identified the perps, is there any reason for us to hang around here?" Sally asked. "We could pour some water on the fire and vamoose. Not that this isn't a perfectly nice bit of dark, trackless forest, but I have a lovely bed with an anachronistic air mattress waiting for me back at Camp Birnam."

"We should probably wait till the police get here," I said.

"Ooh," she said. "I do like your style. But couldn't that take rather a long time? I mean, I suppose we should call them, but how are they even going to find us? Unless you're thinking one of us could go to the edge of the woods and try to lead them back here."

"I already called," I said. "Texted, actually, which comes to the same thing. One of the deputies is a legendary tracker. And most of the rest were raised around here and probably know these woods like the back of their hands. Besides, they have our GPS coordinates. And would probably have been out here doing this stakeout themselves if the murder wasn't taking up all their time."

"Excellent," she said. "So all we have to do is wait."

She strolled over to one edge of the clearing, toward a large fallen tree that I'd already marked as a possible place to sit and wait. She kicked one end of the log a couple of times then stepped back and stared intently at it for a few seconds.

"Sometimes they have things living in them," she explained.

When she was sure nothing was going to scamper, flutter, or slither out of the log, she sat down with a contented sigh.

I took a place beside her.

Rose Noire glanced over at us, then turned and frowned at the cauldron.

"Don't touch anything," I said. "It's all evidence."

"I just want to get a sense of what they were doing."

As Sally and I watched from the relative comfort of our

log, Rose Noire took a step toward the cauldron, then another, with her head lifted in much the same way a dog's would be if a passing breeze had suddenly delivered a faint but enticing scent.

"There has been evil done here," she intoned. "This whole clearing has a very negative aura."

From the politely neutral look on Sally's face, I suspected she was not a believer in auras.

Rose Noire closed her eyes and stood with a look of stoic suffering on her face. I wasn't sure if she was doing invisible combat with the source of the evil or just enduring the negative aura. I didn't really want to ask.

Sally and I sat on the log, listening. From time to time we could hear the sounds of someone thrashing through the woods nearby—thuds, cracks, and snapping noises—which could possibly be the police on their way. But probably not—most of the thrashing noises were accompanied by gasps or shrieks, which meant they probably came from one of the three fugitives. Which I decided was a good sign—it probably meant one if not all of them could still be wandering around nearby.

After about five minutes, Vern Shiffley popped into the clearing, unheralded by any thrashing noises. Aida Butler was right behind him.

"Evening, ladies," he said. "We hear you caught our scofflaw firebugs."

"Alas, no," I said. "We surprised them, identified them, and got them on video, but I'm afraid you'll have to catch them yourselves."

I waved my arm in a wide semicircle in the general direction of the most recent thrashing and shrieking noises.

"Shouldn't be too hard," Vern said. "Aida, how about if you stay here and take the ladies' statements, and I'll round up our malefactors."

Aida nodded. Vern slipped noiselessly into the woods.

"You guys certainly got here fast," I said.

"We were actually staking this clearing out from a little farther away," Aida said. "Vern was no end put out when Rose Noire showed up—he was sure she'd scare away whoever we were trying to catch. And you surprised him—he says you were almost into the clearing before he heard you coming. Of course, then he claimed a herd of cows could have snuck up on us under cover of all the racket Rose Noire was making."

"I was not making a racket!" Rose Noire protested.

"This is Vern, remember," Aida said. "Anyway, I'd consider it a compliment to Meg. And he did admit that both of you were doing a pretty decent job of staying quiet. So let's get your statements."

She took out her pocket notebook, clipped a battery-operated book light to it, and began asking the three of us what we'd seen.

It didn't take long for Vern to find the three women— maybe twenty minutes all told. He found Fawn almost immediately. Next was Zoe, the young woman from Camp Birnam, who seemed determined to pretend that she didn't see Sally. Aida was just slipping her notebook and book light back into her pocket when Vern led Gina, the Second Witch, into the clearing.

"Do you need me for anything else?" Sally asked. "Because if you don't, I'd like to head back to camp."

"I've got her statement," Aida said.

"You'll be there tomorrow if we have any more questions?" Vern asked.

"Of course." Sally turned to me. "We're kind of cut off from the news out there. Mind if I drop by sometime tomorrow to catch up on what's happening?"

"Any time," I said. "Well, any time that's not too early."

"I may not get up before noon." With that she nodded, turned on a small pocket flashlight, and strode off as if she knew perfectly well where she was going. She probably did.

"You want to question these three here?" Aida asked Vern. "Or take them down to the station?"

"I think we'll all be a lot more comfortable down at the station," Vern said.

One of the prisoners—I think it was Fawn—gave a single short sob.

"We'll head down there in just a minute," Vern continued. "Let's make sure this fire is out first. Meg, you got any more water?"

I pulled another bottle out of my feed sack and handed it over.

"Thank you kindly." He unscrewed the top, but didn't pour it on the fire.

"I just want to wait until—ah, there he is."

Chapter 30

Horace appeared in the clearing, holding his forensic bag in one hand and his cell phone in the other. And looking a little wild-eyed. I got the distinct impression that he wasn't enjoying our woodland adventure nearly as much as Vern and Aida were.

"And of course this couldn't wait till morning," he muttered.

"Valuable evidence could vanish." Vern's tone was cheerful. "Your crime scene awaits. You want me to put out the fire?" He held up the water bottle.

"Let me get some pictures first."

"Good enough." Vern set the water bottle down at Horace's feet. "We'll see you later."

He and Aida headed off, escorting their three prisoners. Horace turned to the abandoned campfire, his hand already reaching into his pocket. He pulled out a small camera and began snapping pictures. His camera's flash was almost blinding in the dark clearing.

"Do either of you have a flashlight?" he asked. "Because once I douse the fire, it'll be pitch dark out here. And keep an eye out in case there are any other crazy firebugs out here. Sammy should be out here to help pretty soon, but I'd just as soon get this done as quickly as possible."

"No problem." I began rummaging in my feed bag for the flashlight I'd thrown in it.

Rose Noire whipped out her phone and shone its tiny flashlight beam on the campfire. I was still digging in my feed bag.

"Well, better than nothing." Horace's cheerful tone rang hollow.

I pulled out my big flashlight and turned its much more impressive beam onto the campfire.

"Awesome," Horace said. "That'll make this go faster."

Rose Noire persevered with her phone's tiny flashlight, moving around so she could give some side illumination.

Once he'd gotten enough pictures of the fire—including several showing how close it was to the highly flammable dry leaves—Horace lifted the cauldron off and emptied the water bottle onto the flames. Then he turned his attention to the objects the three women had left behind. The plastic squeeze bottle of gasoline and Gina's lighter went into evidence bags. So did a large book he found in one of her tote bags.

"Is that *Spells of Power and Revenge*?" I asked.

"Yes." He frowned down at the evidence bag into which he'd put the book. "Looks like a nasty piece of work. But I'm more interested in this."

He held up a small glass bottle filled with clear liquid. A thin cord made of black and red strands braided together was tied around its neck. He unscrewed the top and took a cautious sniff.

"Odorless."

"And colorless," I added. "Wonder if it's tasteless."

"Not planning to find out." He took out and opened a little sealed bag containing a plastic vial. He poured a tiny amount of the bottle's contents into the vial. Then he screwed the bottle's top closed and tucked it into one evidence bag and the vial into another.

"And then we have this." He held up another bottle, identical down to the black-and-red cord. "Gina the witch lady had the full one. This empty one belongs to the girl who hauls the costumes around."

"Fawn," I said.

He opened the empty bottle and sniffed it with the

same caution he'd shown with the other one. Then he took out another little sealed bag, this one containing what looked like a Q-tip—although he probably called it something fancier. Disposable sterile evidence collection tool, maybe. He swabbed the inside of the empty bottle and tucked the swab and the bottle into another pair of evidence bags.

Sammy showed up, hauling several big battery-powered floodlights and panting, which probably meant he'd jogged all the way from the house with them.

"Looks like you're almost finished," Sammy said.

"Wouldn't mind getting a better look at the scene," Horace said. "Just set up one of those things."

Sammy did, and then joined us to watch as Horace swabbed the inside of the cauldron and then dusted it inside and out with fingerprint powder.

"Sammy, maybe you could check and see the fire's completely out," he said over his shoulder.

"Looks good," Sammy said. "But I'll empty my water bottle on it, just to be sure."

"Thanks," Horace said finally. "I think we're finished here."

"Yes, and we should get back to the house," Rose Noire said, looking up from her phone.

I was relieved to hear her say that. She'd been busy with her phone ever since Sammy had showed up with the floodlights—apparently texting back and forth with someone. I was worried that she might be planning something. More herbal space cleansing, perhaps or a spell to counteract whatever evil curse the three women had been casting.

But she seemed content—in fact eager—to head for the house. So with her carrying one of the big floodlights and my flashlight illuminating the path for all of us, we made good time going back. Evidently the watch party had broken up and the cast and crew were settling down for the night—we could see a few lights on in the tent city. We detoured around it to avoid having to answer questions from the curious.

"So should I warn Michael that he might be one witch short at tomorrow's rehearsals?" I asked Horace as we were loading the equipment into his and Sammy's cruisers.

"Yeah, that'd be a good idea," Horace said. "Because I have a feeling the chief's going to want to hang onto them for a bit."

"The way he's hanging onto Russ Brainard," I said. "I noticed he didn't make it home for dinner."

"And for much the same reason," Horace said. "These three have no local ties, which makes them a flight risk, and for all he knows they could have something to do with the murder or the cocaine. And tomorrow's Saturday, remember."

"That's right," I said. "The judges are off for the weekend."

"Well, if he charges them with a misdemeanor, the magistrate could grant bail," Horace said. "But he's not going to do that till he's finished questioning them about all the unsolved felonies. And if they're smart, they won't talk until they have lawyers, and rounding up lawyers is always slower on weekends. So yeah, Michael shouldn't plan on getting them back too soon."

"He'll manage," I said. And he would. Although it would be a headache.

Speaking of headaches . . . I suddenly became aware that my head was starting to throb. It had been a long and rather stressful day.

"I'm going to hit the hay," I said. "Night."

"Night." Horace seemed a little distracted. He seemed to be sorting his finds. He had tucked most of the evidence collection bags into two plastic milk crates in the trunk of his cruiser. But he'd slipped a few into his own kit.

"We could be sending the whole lot of this down to the

Crime Lab." He indicated the two milk crates. "But that could take a while even if it wasn't the weekend. And I want to test the contents of those bottles as soon as possible. Well, the contents of the one and the former contents of the other. The full one looked like plain water."

"But then so did the water bottle in which you found the arsenic," I said.

"Yeah." He nodded and frowned. "Are these the three the chief mentioned, the ones who have it in for Celia Rivers?"

"Yes," I said. "Especially Gina. Celia has a much bigger part, and Gina wants it."

"And if something happened to Celia, Gina would get her part?"

"I doubt it," I said. "But Gina might be deluded enough to think so. Do Dad and the chief still suspect someone was poisoning Celia?"

"Oh, we know someone was poisoning her." He gave a tight, almost humorless smile. "They took blood while she was in the ER, and your dad ordered a test for arsenic. Someone's definitely been trying to poison her."

"Damn," I said.

"So I'm going to see if there's arsenic in this." He held up the little plastic tube. "If there is, we may have narrowed down the poisoning suspects to those three ladies."

"Even if there isn't arsenic in the bottle, I'm sure they were trying to harm her," Rose Noire said.

Horace and I both started slightly. I thought she'd gone indoors after loading the lights in Sammy's trunk.

"They were trying to cast an evil spell over her," Rose Noire went on.

"You're probably right," Horace said. "But unfortunately casting evil spells isn't against the law."

Rose Noire's grim expression suggested that she thought this was a heinous oversight on the part of the Virginia General Assembly.

"But arsenic is," Horace added. "So if they were up to

something nasty, we'll try to see that they get what they deserve. Night."

We wished him goodnight and turned back toward the house. There were no lights on, so we headed for the back door, which should still be unlocked. No lights on in any of the tents, either. I thought of looking to see what time it was, but decided it would only make me feel worse if I knew.

"After everything that's happened today, the thought of sleeping in my own bed is really appealing," Rose Noire murmured as we climbed the back steps. "Do you think with the new locks it's safe to leave the chickens without a guard?"

"Didn't I tell you?" I said. "The boys are having a sleepout in your shed. And they also invited their friends Adam and Mason, so the chickens will have four guards. Six if you include Spike and Tinkerbell."

"Oh, how nice," she said. "I'll thank them in the morning. So the only thing we need to do before bed is check on the baby geese."

"The ones in the chicken coop? I thought Dad was going to take them home."

"He did," she said. "But then Clarence dropped off some more."

"More goslings?"

"Yes." She nodded. "He texted me while we were out in the woods, remember?"

I had forgotten. Or maybe blocked it out of my mind.

"You can check on them if you want," I said. "I'm too tired to go back out to the Sumatrans' coop."

"He didn't put them in the Sumatrans' coop," she said. "He put them in your pantry."

"The pantry?" That didn't make sense.

She nodded.

"Why the pantry?" I asked.

"The chicken coops are locked now—remember?" she said.

"Yes, but we have any number of sheds and outbuild-ings scattered all around the yard—why would he bring poultry into the house?"

"I have no idea," she said. "Maybe he thought they'd be safer in the house. They're babies, remember. And maybe he heard we were worried about the chickens and didn't want to take any chances. Anyway, if you're too tired, I'll take care of them. Make sure they have enough food and water."

"I think you can rely on Clarence to have left them plenty of food and water," I said. "But I want to see what they've done to our pantry."

I led the way into the kitchen and strode over to the pantry door. I could hear a sort of whining noise inside. I jerked it open.

Out poured an ankle-high tide of white-and-gold fur.

"Puppies! How adorable!" Rose Noire cooed. She plopped onto the floor and the puppies, which were only about the size of guinea pigs, immediately swarmed all over her, barking their high-pitched staccato little barks, licking her with their miniature tongues, and nipping at her with their tiny razor-sharp teeth. "But why is Clarence bringing your father puppies?"

"I have no idea." I squatted down to take a closer look. She was right—the puppies were adorable. But there were six—no, seven of them. And none of them housetrained yet, to judge by the state of the newspapers covering the pantry floor.

One, more adventurous than his siblings, bounced over to me, wagging his tail and yipping happily. I sighed. If his bark were any higher, it would be inaudible to the human ear, and it went through my aching head like a laser. He was cute, though. I'd give him that much, I picked him up to get a closer look.

"Oh, great," I said. "I think I just figured out what happened. Those geese of Dad's—they're a heritage breed you know."

"Well, I assumed as much. No, you stay here, you little monster!"

"Dad's acquiring Pomeranian geese," I said. "And these are Pomeranian puppies."

As if to reward me for my correct guess, the puppy I was holding piddled on my knee.

"Oh, my goodness," Rose Noire said. "I think you're right. But how could Clarence possibly have gotten that mixed up?"

"I can imagine exactly how it happened." I stood, still holding the puppy, and went over to get a damp paper towel to clean up my jeans and his hind legs. "You know how Dad tends to start in the middle of a subject, forgetting that the person he's talking to may not be up to speed. I can hear him saying that he's having a terrible time finding any more Pomeranians. And Clarence would say that he'll keep his eyes open, and how many does he want? And Dad would say, 'oh, half a dozen or so.'"

"Yes, that would explain it. Oh, no you don't, you little rascal! No chewing the furniture!"

This, I deduced, was aimed at one of the puppies.

"And it wouldn't even have sounded odd to Clarence," I added, as I returned my fur ball to the pack. "Mother and Dad have a lot of space over at the farmhouse. Half a dozen dogs wouldn't sound like a big deal to Clarence. The more the merrier. And a Pomeranian's just the sort of fluffy, decorative little dog Mother would want if she actually wanted a dog."

Although not if she saw this crew, who were now rambunctiously yipping and tussling all over the kitchen floor.

"We can call Clarence in the morning," she said. "I'm sure he won't have any trouble finding homes for these little angels."

"I hope not," I said. "But they can't stay in the pantry all night. They'll be completely in the way when everyone shows up for breakfast. And the boys will see them. They'll want to keep them."

"Oh dear," she said. "You're right. But where else can we put them?"

I pondered.

"Rob's bathroom," I said. "He and Delaney won't be back from Maui for another week. We can shut them in there. It will be a lot easier to swab a bathroom down than our pantry. And then we can make Dad or Clarence whisk them away as soon as possible in the morning."

So I grabbed an armload of old newspapers and went upstairs to cover the floors in Rob's bathroom, to reduce the need for swabbing down. I also grabbed everything I thought the puppies might find enticing, like the toilet paper, the bath mat, and the toilet brush, and relocated them all to higher ground. Then we each took an armload of puppies and ferried them upstairs.

"I'll stay here a while and make sure they settle in for the night," Rose Noire said.

If she wanted to stay up all night playing with the puppies, that was fine with me. I fetched the several food and water bowls Clarence had provided and left her to it.

Michael woke when I tiptoed into the bedroom.

"Everything okay?" he mumbled.

"Everything's just dandy." Morning would be soon enough to fill him in on our adventures in the woods and the pantry full of puppies.

Although before crawling into bed I wanted to put Clarence on notice that the puppies had to go. I looked around for my laptop, realized I'd left it in the library, and settled for pulling out my phone. I composed an email to Clarence with one finger while brushing my teeth.

"Clarence, it was very sweet of you to find the Pomeranians for Dad," it said. "But he was looking for Pomeranian

GEESE, not puppies. Can you please take these back before everyone here falls in love with them? I will absolutely help you find homes for them, but we CAN'T keep seven puppies."

When I'd sent that and finished with my teeth, I shrugged off my clothes, pulled on a nightgown, and fell into bed.

Chapter 31

Saturday

The house was crawling with rats. They were running around everywhere, squeaking incessantly. I was grabbing them by their tails and slinging them into a giant cage, but the cage was starting to get full, and every time I opened the door to put a new rat in, one or two escaped, and my efforts didn't even seem to be making a dent in the rat population. They were running up the curtains, swinging from the chandeliers, dancing up and down the piano keyboard—

I woke up. I breathed a sigh of relief. The house was not crawling with rats. But the squeaking noise was real. Actually, it was more of a yipping noise. And it sounded a lot louder than it should if the puppies were still in Rob's bathroom.

I jumped out of bed and scrambled into my clothes. Then I opened the bedroom door.

Michael was chasing Pomeranian puppies up and down the hall. The puppies were having a blast. Michael wasn't. But his face brightened when he saw me, and he sat down at the top of the stairs, where he could head off the puppies if they tried to escape to the ground floor.

"Please tell me we're not keeping them," he said. "They're cute as the devil, but I don't think we need a puppy. We certainly don't need a freakin' pack of them."

"They're not staying," I said. "Dad wanted more geese, but Clarence misunderstood and brought these instead." Seeing Michael's puzzled look, I explained about the two kinds of Pomeranians. "Maybe we should take them over to Mother and Dad's for the time being."

"I'd settle for stuffing them back into Rob's bathroom if I could catch them," he said. "I didn't mean to let them out, but I heard the noise they were making and worried that we had rodents—"

"Which they greatly resemble," I put in.

"And the damned things are like greased lightning."

"Let me put on my shoes and I'll help." I was turning to go back into the bedroom when I spotted something that alarmed me. Tinkerbell, Rob's Irish Wolfhound, was trotting briskly up the stairs.

"Look out!" I said. "Tink's here!"

"Tink's fine with puppies." Michael swung his legs aside to let Tink pass.

"But if she's up, that could mean the boys are," I said. "Do you want them to see the puppies?"

"Good heavens, no." He closed his eyes and shuddered at the thought. "Let's catch them quick and—"

But just then Tinkerbell swung into action. The puppies had spotted her and were reacting with predictable excitement. Three scampered happily toward her, yipping in welcome. Two howled in terror and ran up the stairs. Two stood their ground and barked ferociously.

She reached down, carefully picked up one of the welcoming yippers, and began to climb up the stairs with him. The rest of the puppies gave chase—some playfully, some aggressively. Michael and I followed along, standing ready to block off the stairs if any of the puppies tried to come back down.

But no. They all followed Tink down the hall and into Rob's room.

"How in the world does she know where to take them?" Michael marveled.

"I suppose she could smell where they came from," I said.

By the time we reached Rob's room, Tink had herded the puppies into the bathroom and was sitting inside with them. She looked up at us and her tail thumped the floor a couple of times.

"Good girl, Tink." I patted her head.

"Should we leave her here with them?" Michael asked.

Just then heard more barking coming down the hall. High-pitched barking—though not as high-pitched as the puppies.

Spike barreled into the room, still barking. Then he stopped, his barking changed to a growl, and he began approaching the bathroom door with the slow, stiff gait that signaled he was planning to attack. His ears were back, his lips were curled, his head was low—

"See if you can distract him while I grab him," Michael said.

But before we could do anything, Tink turned to face Spike, lowered her head until it was on the same level as his, and growled. Her growl was so deep you didn't hear it so much as feel it, like the rumble of a garbage truck.

Spike was visibly shaken. His head jerked back so hard that he ended up sitting down.

Tink stopped growling, but she didn't move her head and she didn't take her eyes off Spike. The juxtaposition emphasized the fact that her head was approximately the size of Spike's entire body.

I started to feel sorry for Spike, and I decided to give him a way of saving face.

"You stay here and pen up the puppies," I said to

Michael. Then I headed out into the hall, calling "Come on, Spike! Let's go find the boys!"

Spike got up in the most dignified way possible and followed me—but slowly, as if he'd gotten bored with what was going on and was only following me to be courteous.

Michael shut the door behind us. I headed downstairs, and Spike tagged along, as if keeping me company was a normal and expected part of his day. But he didn't hesitate when I opened the back door for him. He trotted briskly outside—no doubt to find the boys.

Horace was sitting at the kitchen table, wolfing down a huge breakfast—bacon, eggs, toast, hash browns, and a bowl of fresh cut fruit.

"Everyone else is outside," he said when he'd swallowed whatever he was chewing. "Some of the cousins are cooking breakfast on the grills."

"But you're not feeling social?" I sat down across the table from him.

"Not feeling like answering a million questions about why I was searching Gina's and Fawn's tents," he said through a mouthful of toast. "And I'm supposed to ask what you know about those two."

"Not a whole lot," I said. "What were you searching for, anyway?"

"Arsenic," he said. "Gina's bottle—by which I mean the one I found in her tote bag—contained water laced with arsenic. The residue in Fawn's bottle suggested that it previously contained the same thing."

"So you know who's been poisoning Celia," I said.

"Well, yes and no." He sighed. "Fawn says she had no idea there was arsenic in the potion—she called it a potion. It was only supposed to contain the focused energy of their spell to drive Celia away, or something like that. If she'd known there was arsenic in the potions, she wouldn't have been pouring them into Celia's water bottles. So—"

"What? She admitted doing that?"

"She did." Horace nodded and took a bite of bacon—but a small one that wouldn't interfere too long with talking.

"And what does Gina say?"

"Denies it. Claims the potion we found in her bag was one Fawn had given her. Supposed to strengthen her against those who wish her ill. Do people really believe in this stuff?"

"You should ask Rose Noire. What does the third one say? You know, what's her name. Zoe. The one from Camp Birnam."

"She confirms that they were casting spells to drive away the people they didn't want around for one reason or another." Horace was toying with the rest of the slice of bacon. "Denies any knowledge of arsenic. Claims she hasn't poured any potions into anyone's water bottles. And maybe she's telling the truth. Sally up at Camp Birnam hasn't noticed anyone suffering gastrointestinal symptoms."

"But maybe they were waiting to see how well the arsenic worked on Celia before trying it on MacLeod and Fawn's boss," I suggested.

"Yeah," he said. "And even if they hadn't tried to poison anyone yet, if they knowingly helped concoct those potions with arsenic in them they could be charged with attempted murder."

"Thus giving them a motive for murder if they thought Goodwin's video was going to expose them."

"Exactly." He was still holding the slice of bacon. "Can we change the subject? All this talking about poison is putting me off my breakfast."

"Sorry," I said. "So are you going to have to haul all that stuff down to Richmond today? Wait—it's Saturday, so I guess the Crime Lab won't be open."

"Actually, a friend of mine's going to go in and receive it today so they can get started first thing Monday," Horace said. "And Sammy's driving it down—I had to come in on not much sleep to handle the evidence from last night's bust, so as soon as I finish this, I'm heading home to bed. Any chance—"

His phone, which was sitting on the table at his elbow, rang. He glanced down and scrambled to answer.

"Yes, chief." He listened briefly. "Actually, she's right here—I'll ask." He looked up at me. "Can you go down to the station to help the chief with something?"

"Sure," I said. "When? And what?"

"As soon as possible, and he'll explain when you get there."

"Let me grab some food to eat on the way and I'll head out right now."

Horace conveyed this to the chief and signed off.

"Any idea what he needs me for?"

Horace, who was finally chewing on that last slice of bacon, shook his head.

I went back upstairs to put on shoes and grab my purse. Horace was gone by the time I came back to the kitchen. I grabbed one of the reusable carryout containers we often used for the boys' lunches during the school year.

In the backyard, things were quiet. Normally Michael had rehearsals on Saturday, although he kept them shorter than on weekdays, but with relatively major cast members unavailable, he'd canceled those. It felt more like a Sunday, when some of the cast and crew slept late, some went into town for errands or church services, and the rest hung around the house and yard, enjoying their day off. A couple of visiting cousins were cooking eggs, toast, sausage, bacon, and hash browns on the grills. They happily piled my carryout container high and refrained from interrogating me about why I had to eat on the run.

I had to remind myself to watch my speed heading into town, since I doubted "the chief wants to see me" would get me out of a speeding ticket.

Then again maybe it would have. When I walked into

the station both Vern Shiffley and Charles, the civilian desk clerk, broke into broad smiles of relief.

"She's here, chief," Charles said into the intercom.

"Send her right back," the chief replied.

Vern started off down the hallway with his long, ground-covering stride. I could barely keep up with him and had no chance to ask any questions. He ushered me into the chief's office, and the chief waved me into one of his guest chairs with a graciousness that almost hid his impatience.

"What's up?" I asked.

"It's Mr. Miller." He frowned. "Or Calum MacLeod as you know him. We've found him."

"Great!" I said. I refrained from asking questions about where or how. If he wanted me to know, he'd tell me.

"Not that great." The chief frowned. "At the moment he's refusing to talk."

I nodded. I still wasn't sure what this had to do with me.

"He says he won't answer my questions until he has a chance to talk with you," the chief added.

"Me?" My jaw dropped. "Why?"

"He won't say. Do you have any idea why he'd want to talk to you?"

"I can't imagine," I said. "I'd have said that next to my mother I'd be his least favorite person in Caerphilly. I haven't had a single interaction with him that didn't involve yelling at him about something he was doing that he shouldn't be doing. The last conversation we had was probably when we found the stolen sheep and I told him one more screw-up and I'd kick him out of Camp Birnam."

"I remember," he said. "I was there. You didn't talk to him after that?"

"I don't think so." I mentally replayed Thursday and shook my head. "No. I assume he spent most of the day here at the station with you. I didn't see him again until he showed up for Goodwin's video, and I'd have avoided him if he tried to talk to me then. He disappeared shortly after the showing broke up. And I didn't see him all day yesterday."

"With good reason," the chief said. "He was in jail."

"In jail?" I echoed. "But I thought you couldn't find him."

"In the Clay County jail," the chief added. "Apparently, he showed up sometime after midnight at the Clay Pigeon."

"Why in the world would he go to the Pigeon?" I said.

"That's one of the things I'd like to find out from him. It's possible that he's already made himself persona non grata in most of Caerphilly's drinking establishments."

"He hasn't even been here a full three weeks," I said. "But yeah, he could have managed that."

"It's also possible that he went over there after one, when every place in Caerphilly would have closed down. I have no idea if they even have closing times in Clay County, and even if they do I doubt the Pigeon pays much attention to them. It's the Clay County deputies' favorite watering hole."

"You'd think they'd pay more attention to closing time, not less," I said. "But then, Clay County's still a cross between Dogpatch and *Deliverance*."

"While there, he picked a fight with an off-duty deputy," the chief continued. "He was arrested for a variety of offenses, some of which he may actually have committed. And then, for reasons they haven't yet explained to my satisfaction—or that of his defense attorney—they kept him there all day yesterday. They claim they gave him the customary phone call, but if they did, he didn't get through to his attorney."

"If you're not careful you're going to get me feeling sorry for him," I said. "And I wouldn't have thought that possible. Staying overnight in any part of Clay County would be bad enough, but the jail?" I shuddered. "Did he at least get an alibi for Goodwin's murder out of it?"

"So far, no. And it's possible he might if everyone over there in Clay County wasn't so all-fired eager to disoblige him. Or me." His face wore a look of disgust. "So far everyone I've talked to over there claims not to remember when he came in. Which is ridiculous. The regulars at the Pigeon all know each other."

"Know each other?" I snorted. "They're all related to each other. An outsider would stand out like a pink elephant in a flock of sheep."

"Precisely." The chief released an exasperated breath. "I find it highly unlikely that no one in the entire bar noticed he was there until he—and I quote—'just appeared out of nowhere and started whaling on Deputy Whicker.' That's from one of their witnesses."

"Which Deputy Whicker?" I asked. "They have several."

"Doesn't matter," he said. "They'll all tell the same story. Anyway. I'd like to get him to talk to me. You'd think he'd be grateful that I rescued him from that pest hole they call a jail and brought him back here where the cells are clean and the food edible, but he doesn't see it that way. Stubborn as a mule."

"Maybe there's a reason he won't talk," I suggested. "Like maybe he'd rather be on the hook for assault in Clay County than murder in Caerphilly."

"Could be," the chief said. "If he didn't kill Goodwin, maybe he can give me some information that will establish his alibi or help me figure out who did. If he is the killer—well, getting him to confess is a long shot, but at least if I felt sure he was guilty I could stop chasing several dozen other possible suspects."

"Can't you get his attorney to explain that to him?" I asked. "Not that I won't talk to him if you need me to, but—"

"He won't talk to his defense attorney, either," the chief said. "Not until I let him talk to you. So let's see if you can convince him it's in his best interests to talk to one of us."

He pressed a button on his intercom. "Sammy? Can you bring the prisoner into my office please?"

He looked back at me.

"Don't give away any information he might not yet know," he ordered. "And before he gets here, why don't you switch to the guest chair farthest from the door and move it over there." He pointed to a spot beside his desk. I hopped into the other chair and scooted it over as ordered, to a spot that was beside the chief's desk rather than in front of it. I liked this new spot. Not only was it farther from the chair MacLeod would soon occupy, it gave the impression that I was on the chief's team.

Which I definitely was.

The door opened, and MacLeod shuffled in. He was wearing an orange jail uniform and his hands were cuffed in front of him. He had a black eye, a bruised jaw, and the pale, seedy, unwell look of someone on day four of a three-day drunk.

When he spotted me, he frowned and his face reddened.

"You selfish bitch!" he spat. "Why—"

"Mr. Miller!" The chief's voice startled MacLeod into silence. "If you cannot speak with civility, I can have you taken back to your cell."

Chapter 32

MacLeod shut up, but he tightened his lips and continued to glare at me.

Sammy steered him into the other guest chair and hovered just behind him.

"You asked to speak to Ms. Langslow," the chief said. "Now's your chance. But watch your language—and your tone."

MacLeod turned to me.

"Why didn't you help me?" he asked. "Why did you abandon me there in that hellhole?"

I noticed, almost absently, that his fake Scottish accent was gone.

"Help you?" I asked. "I assume from the word 'hellhole' that you're talking about when you were locked up in the Clay County jail. But why would you assume it was my responsibility to help you—and more to the point, how was I supposed to know you were there? The whole county was searching for you."

"But I called *you!*" he said, in a tone of righteous indignation. "They give you one call. I was lucky they let me try it again. But first you hung up on me and then you wouldn't answer."

Light dawned.

"Oh, my God," I said. "You called me from the jail, didn't you?"

"And you wouldn't help me." He tried to fold his arms but the handcuffs prevented him, so he settled for glowering at me with the smug, self-satisfied look of someone who has proven something.

I pulled my phone and checked the call log.

"At precisely four-ten yesterday morning, I received a call from an unfamiliar number." I was directing this at the chief. "I could tell it was a local number, but I didn't recognize it, and my caller ID said 'name unavailable.'"

I rattled off the number. Sammy groaned softly.

"That would be the Clay County Sheriff's Department," the chief said. "I asked them once why they don't identify themselves on caller ID. Apparently people don't answer if they know it's them calling. You didn't recognize Mr. Miller's voice?"

"It was four in the morning, and he woke me up from a sound sleep," I pointed out. "I heard an unfamiliar voice— without the laughably bad Scottish accent he's always used in my presence. He was yelling at me. Most of the words I could understand were either profanities or obscenities. I assumed it was a drunk calling someone he was furious at and getting a wrong number."

"But I called back," MacLeod said. "And you hung up on me."

"I only answered the phone in the first place because it was the fastest way to stop the ringing before it woke Michael," I said. "And after the second time you called I blocked the number."

"And left me to rot in that horrible jail for two days."

"Nonsense," I snapped. "When I answered the phone, if you'd said anything that would have given me a clue that you needed help, I'd have done something. But all you did was yell abuse. And why call me, anyway?"

"No one out at the camp has a cell phone," he says.

"Because you won't let them," I said.

"True." He winced slightly. "And I couldn't remember

the name of my court-appointed attorney here in Caerphilly. Yours was the only local number I had."

He looked so pitiful that I almost felt sorry for him.
He probably had been treated pretty badly by the Clay
County Sheriff's Department. For that reason alone, I'd
have tried to help him if I'd known what was going on.
I wouldn't have gone racing over to Clay County in the
middle of the night, but I'd have called an attorney for
him. My notebook contained an entire page of defense
attorneys, both local ones and ones who were members of
the vast Hollingsworth clan. And I had a pretty good idea
which ones were hungry enough for business that they'd
be grateful rather than annoyed at being called out in the
middle of the night.

"Next time something like this happens to you, try starting out with 'help,'" I suggested. "It tends to put people in
a better mood than having the F-bomb hurled at them.
And if you follow it up with 'please,' your odds of being
rescued will soar to unimaginable heights."

"Those jerks in that dive bar got me riled up," MacLeod
said. "Three of them jumping on me, and then claiming
I started it."

If that was supposed to be an apology, he needed more
practice. Still, it did sound as if he had reason to be upset.
Just not at me.

"Do you have anything else to say to Ms. Langslow?" the
chief asked.

MacLeod pursed his lips slightly.

"If you don't want to go back to Clay County's jail, give
the chief a reason to keep you here," I said. "Because if
you're just going to sulk in silence, you could do that in
Clay County."

"No, don't send me back!" MacLeod sounded anxious.
Maybe even scared. "Okay. Just tell me what you want to
know."

"I can call your attorney if you'd like," the chief offered.

"No, don't do that. She's already mad at me for not talking to her after she came all the way down here on a weekend. I'll talk to her later. See if she can help me sue those creeps. I didn't do anything wrong—not here, and not in that sleazy redneck joint in Clay County. What do you want to know?"

"Your movements on Thursday night," the chief said. "After the showing of Mr. Goodwin's video ended."

"It didn't end," MacLeod said. "The bi—um, actress who plays Lady Macbeth terminated it. With extreme prejudice."

"So I gather," the chief said. "What did you do?"

"Made myself scarce." MacLeod sighed, lifted one hand to scratch his nose, and was startled when the handcuffs dragged the other one up as well. "Thanks to Goodwin, everyone at Camp Birnam was mad at me for one reason or another."

I had to repress the impulse to protest that it was pretty rich to blame Goodwin, since all he'd done was reveal MacLeod's misbehavior. I must have made a noise, since the chief glanced over at me briefly before focusing back on his prisoner.

"What do you mean by 'made yourself scarce'?" the chief asked. "Where did you go and what did you do?"

"I went back to the camp. But they were all giving me the silent treatment. Even . . . well, never mind."

The chief leaned back, laced his fingers over his stomach, and waited.

"So I went off by myself," MacLeod went on eventually. "I had a bottle of bourbon, and I took that and went out into the woods. The idea was to drink myself into a stupor, but there wasn't nearly enough left in the bottle. By the time I realized that, it was well past midnight and I knew all the bars in this hick town were either about to close or already had. So I drove over to this Stool Pigeon place."

He stopped and shut his eyes. When it became obvious

that he wasn't planning to continue, the chief closed his own eyes briefly—I could almost hear him counting to ten. Then he opened them and continued in a surprisingly patient voice.

"Had you been there before?"

MacLeod shook his head and winced.

"Then how did you know where to find it?" the chief prodded.

"Someone told me about it," MacLeod said. "Last time I complained about how early Caerphilly rolls up the sidewalk. They said to drive past the zoo and then keep on going until I ran into a few buildings pretending to be a village. And to make sure I had a full tank of gas, because it was off in the middle of nowhere. They didn't warn me the natives were hostile."

"What time did you get there?"

"Dunno. I passed through Caerphilly at twelve forty-five. I remember thinking maybe I could still find someplace open there, but then what if I wanted to keep drinking? So I kept on going till I hit this Clayville place." He shuddered. "Look—any chance I could get some aspirin or something?"

"I think that could be arranged." He glanced over at me. "And let's let Ms. Langslow get back to her day. Unless you have anything else to say to her."

MacLeod shook his head, keeping the motion down to a bare minimum. Probably a good thing for me to leave, before his obvious misery made me start feeling sorry for the wretch.

"Thanks, Chief," I said. "Want me to ask Vern and Charlie about the aspirin on my way out."

"If you would be so kind." He smiled. "And thanks for taking the time to come down here."

I nodded and left his office.

Vern and Charlie looked up eagerly when I returned to the front desk.

"Is he talking?" Vern asked.

"Yes, but I'm not sure he's got anything useful to say." I related what he'd said—to me as well as the chief. Charlie scurried off to deliver the promised aspirin.

"You know, I might have a bit of evidence to corroborate one part of his story." Vern's face was thoughtful. "When I was searching the woods yesterday morning I found an empty Jim Beam bottle. Empty, but still damp, which it wouldn't have been if it was days old instead of hours. So he probably was out there drinking by himself in the woods."

"Which doesn't give him an alibi," I pointed out.

"No, it doesn't," Vern said. "A pity we didn't spot him passing through town."

"You're thinking maybe he'd have been driving erratically enough that you could pull him over?" I asked.

"Wouldn't matter if he was driving erratically," Vern said. "We picked him up on a DUI the first weekend he was here, and it was his third offense. So if I'd seen him Thursday night I'd almost certainly have pulled him over because I'd have known he was driving on a suspended license. Either way, at least he wouldn't have ended up in the Clay County jail. Did you know we had to delouse him?"

"Ick," I said. "I wish you hadn't told me that. I'm going to be scratching my head all day."

"Spare a little pity for Horace, then," Vern said. "The chief called him in when he was on his way home to finally get some sleep, and now he's processing MacLeod's clothes. Got to make sure none of the bloodstains came from our murder victim."

"Double ick." I shuddered slightly. "I am now officially leaving before I hear anything else I don't want to hear."

I drove home, trying to avoid scratching what I knew were only psychosomatic itches. To distract myself, I pondered the chief's overcrowded jail, wondering which one of his prisoners would turn out to be the killer. The problem was that while all of them had a motive to kill Goodwin—the same motive, fear of exposure—the chief didn't have any real evidence against any of them.

Russ Brainard could be facing prison time for possession—serious prison time if he was found guilty of dealing. And even a conviction for possession could have a deadly effect on his career. Motive enough for murder? Definitely. And the murder method, bashing Goodwin over the head with his own video camera—didn't that sound like something a cokehead would do? In his defense, it was hard to imagine Russ being clearheaded enough to think of destroying Goodwin's video, much less doing such a thorough job of it. But someone else could have done that, with or without knowing Goodwin was dead. Russ as the killer, and someone else with a similar motive and a lot more common sense for the video destruction? I could buy that.

But then there were the three Mean Girls. Goodwin had filmed them casting their spells. If he also had proof that they'd been trying to poison Celia, definitely enough of a motive to kill. Especially since they were so blasé about murder that they were apparently willing to poison three people in the hope of inheriting their jobs.

Well, two people. I gathered Zoe's motive for trying to poison MacLeod was that he'd been harassing her. Which made me a little more sympathetic to her than I was to Gina and Fawn. But not a lot. Surely there was some way of getting rid of a harasser short of poisoning him.

And MacLeod. He was such a clueless blowhard that I had a hard time taking him seriously as a murderer. Sheep thief, adulterer, harasser, and drunk—but a murderer?

But maybe that was shortsighted of me. Maybe he had the strongest motive of all. He was a self-centered egomaniac—and Goodwin had seriously embarrassed him. That could be just as strong a motive as any of them.

And there was always the possibility that the killer was someone else. Someone the chief hadn't yet locked up for other crimes. Probably a long shot—what were the odds that we were harboring yet another criminal? But possible.

Halfway home I got a call from Michael. I pulled over beside an apple orchard to answer it.

"Hey, I'm heading over to the zoo," he said. "Hearing about the latest round of arrests has demoralized everyone, so I'm having an all-hands meeting. Discuss what's happened, calm everyone down. Maybe have some informal auditions if anyone wants to make a bid to replace Russ or Gina. Maybe even a little rehearsing—I can use the excuse that we're behind because of all the interruptions from the murder investigation."

"Are you?" I asked.

"Not really," he said. "And even if we were, we need to recast those roles before we can move ahead. But I think it's a bad idea having everyone sitting around fretting."

"Sounds reasonable." I noticed that the farmer who owned the orchard was striding toward my car. I wondered if he lost a lot of apples to passersby.

"No idea how long it will take," Michael said. "But if I let you know when we're about to knock off for the day, can you maybe call Luigi's and have them deliver some pizzas to the house? And by 'some pizzas' I mean the usual enormous number we need for this crowd."

"Sounds like a plan," I said. "Good luck."

I hung up, and waved to the farmer, who seemed to calm down once he recognized me, saw why I'd pulled over, and realized his crop was safe.

I spent the rest of the trip home pondering the irony that I was looking forward to arriving at an empty house. Normally the thought of coming home and not finding Michael and the boys would sadden me. Okay, I'd still miss them. But I knew where they were, and they were safe. And coming home and not finding two dozen houseguests? Bliss.

As I was parking my car I spotted a package on our porch, so instead of taking the slightly shorter way through the backyard and coming in through the kitchen, I went around to the front door.

The package, rather a large one, was for Rose Noire. I texted her to say it had arrived, included the name of the sender—an herbal supply company—and offered to bring it out to the shed if she needed it in a hurry.

"Oh, good!!!" she texted back. "I've been waiting for that. But don't worry—it can wait until I come back to the house."

So I set the package on the floor beside the hall table. And as I bent down to do so, I noticed an envelope on the floor. It was partway under the table and had probably fallen from it. I picked it up and saw my name written on it in an elegant handwriting that almost looked like calligraphy. Not a handwriting I recognized.

I opened the envelope and found a note in the same decorative script and a metallic red flash drive. The note was from Calpurnia, one of the Wiccans who'd helped Rose Noire with the cleansing.

"Greetings," it read. "I found this in Rose Noire's herb garden during today's cleansing ritual. She says it's not hers, and suggests that you could probably figure out who it belongs to and return it. Blessings, Calpurnia."

Today's cleansing? I think I'd have noticed if we'd had another cleansing. So she must have meant Friday's cleansing. Which meant whoever had lost this flash drive had been doing without for over a day. My first thought was that I'd check the flash drive when I got around to booting up my laptop. How much of a rush could there be? I hadn't heard of anyone frantically searching for a flash drive.

Wait—except Horace, of course. Searching Goodwin's trailer in the hope of finding an undamaged flash drive or external hard drive.

I held up the flash drive and studied it.

Calpurnia said she'd found it in Rose Noire's herb garden. The herb garden that you'd pretty much have to pass through if you were going between our house and the spot where Goodwin had been killed. Even if the killer had come from Camp Birnam, they'd have to pass through the herb garden if they'd gone straight from killing him to ransacking his trailer.

Maybe I shouldn't put off checking out this flash drive.

Chapter 33

I stopped for a moment to remember where I'd left my laptop. Probably the library. I couldn't remember using it since yesterday afternoon, during my search for the nasty book.

I stuck the flash drive in my pocket and headed for the hallway that led to the library.

But I stopped short before entering it. The house was supposed to be empty, and yet I heard noises in the hallway.

The hallway where the vandal had already struck once.

I listened. Swishing noises. A couple of soft taps. And then giggling—a strangely mindless, menacing giggling.

I pulled out my phone and opened up the camera app. Then I peered around the corner.

Professor Philpotts was there. He was wearing his usual dapper pinstripe suit, but he'd also donned a clear plastic rain slicker to protect it, and had bright yellow kitchen gloves on his hands. He held a spray can of paint. As I watched, he shook the can vigorously, then giggled as he meticulously sprayed letters on our wall. Letters that spelled out the purest filth.

I pushed the VIDEO button and began documenting this.

After a few seconds he took a step back and contemplated his work with a look of great satisfaction. Then he glanced down the hall, as if checking to see how much more space he had to work with and spotted me.

"You! What the hell do you think you're doing?"

"Isn't that my line?" I asked.

"You do not have permission to photograph me," he blustered.

"And you do not have permission to paint that filth on our walls." I closed the camera and dialed 911.

"I must insist that you delete that immediately!" His face was beet-red with anger, and he looked more than ever like a walrus.

"What's wrong, Meg?" Debbie Ann asked.

"The vandal is back," I said. "I caught him red-handed—literally."

Professor Philpotts threw down the spray paint and charged at me. He seemed to be trying to grab my phone, but I turned away from him and curled around it defensively. At the same time I stuck out an elbow that collided hard with some soft part of his body. He gave up on trying to snatch away the phone. He settled for shoving me aside with his paint-stained gloves and making a dash for the front door.

I let him go and put the phone back to my ear.

"Meg! Are you okay?"

"I'm fine," I said. "I have the vandal on video—it's Professor Desmond Philpotts of the English Department. He just ran out of the house. I assume he's got his car parked somewhere nearby and will be making his getaway in that."

"He won't get far," Debbie Ann said. "Lock the doors in case he comes back."

I heard a car start up somewhere outside.

"I doubt he'll do that. I'm going to sign off so I can send the video to the chief."

"Good thinking."

After I hung up I took a few well-focused shots of the graffiti, then a selfie of my paint-stained self. I emailed them, along with the video of Philpotts caught in the act, to the chief.

Should I change out of my paint-stained clothes? Or

would the chief want to document them as evidence. I sent off a quick question to the chief.

Philpotts had also left behind a roll of paper towels, so I blotted myself enough that I wouldn't drip on anything.

And while I was waiting to find out what the chief wanted me to do—and with luck, hear that they'd caught Philpotts—I'd take a look at the flash drive.

I took the roll of paper towels with me into the library and spread a couple of them on a chair before sitting down at my laptop. I pulled out the flash drive and hesitated for a moment. Kevin was always warning us to be very careful about putting unknown media into our computers. If he were here, he'd probably snatch the flash drive away from me so he could check it out himself.

"I don't care," I muttered. If the mysterious flash drive infected my laptop with malware, Kevin would fix it. In fact, no matter what I found on the flash drive, I'd ask Kevin to check my computer out later today.

I stuck the flash drive into an open USB slot and clicked to open it. I saw a series of directories. Four of them: Birnam, College, Dunsinane, and Rough Cut.

I opened the Birnam directory. It contained three files. They didn't have names, just long numbers. But they were video files!

All the directories contained video files. I picked one of the smallest files and clicked on it. After a short argument with my computer, I managed to start the video.

It was a short video of one of the Birnamites' huts falling down. Goodwin's video.

I'd have two surprises for whoever eventually showed up to check out the graffiti.

I should let the chief know I had it.

But I wanted to see his face when I handed over the flash drive. So I quickly sent a third email, saying. "By the way, are you coming out to see Philpotts's handiwork?

Because I have something else to show you. Something REALLY interesting!"

Then I gave in to temptation and opened up the folder called Rough Cut. I'd already noticed that it contained by far the largest file. If this was what I thought it was . . .

The title graphic announcing "Another Dam Good Production!" appeared on my laptop screen. It was the video he'd shown us,

I sat back to watch.

I thought of skipping ahead to see what we hadn't seen, but I wasn't entirely sure how to do it—and besides, it was interesting to test my memory against the real thing. And my memory wasn't doing too badly. This time around, I spotted the scene Tanya had mentioned. She was right—a hand did whisk a water bottle off-screen and then replace it. But you sort of had to be looking for it to spot it. Or have water bottles on the brain. And yes, in the scene in which Celia found her script daubed with red paint, she did already have a few red paint stains on her hand. But watching that scene, it struck me as just that. A scene. I'd be willing to bet either Goodwin hadn't been there when Celia first found the bloody script or he hadn't gotten good enough footage, so she'd agreed to reenact it. And the second time around, she did it the way she wanted to remember it. Angry, yes, but dignified, restrained, noble in adversity. I hadn't seen the actual finding of the script, but the way it had been described to me was nothing like this. "She screamed like a stuck pig," the actor playing Macbeth had said. "And then started breaking everything in sight. And the language!"

Still, not exactly motive for murder. Anyone who knew what had happened would understand why she was angry, and if her anger was wilder than most, they'd put it down to artistic temperament.

As the video played on, I nodded to myself. I'd done a

damn fine job of describing what I'd seen. And now we were approaching the end of the video, the part I hadn't seen. The part nobody but Goodwin had seen.

Celia puking and cramping. Celia pacing up and down in this very library, talking into her cell phone. The soundtrack didn't include her words, just the Wicked Witch's music from *The Wizard of Oz,* but I wasn't sure I wanted to hear what she was saying. You could tell from her facial expression that it wouldn't be pleasant.

Then the music disappeared and I could hear what she was saying. And it was vile. She was railing against Tanya, and Richard, the Korean American actor who played the Thane of Cawdor, and every other person of color in the cast and crew—hurling a torrent of obscenities and crude racial insults at them. Followed by several disgusting homophobic slurs against the gay actor playing Macduff. And all of it sounding somehow worse in her powerful, well-modulated stage voice—every word clearly articulated and falling like a drop of acid. No, not acid—sewage. I paused the video. I'd watch it to the end—I could see there were only a few more minutes in the file—but I needed a break from the sheer ugliness of her rant.

No wonder Celia had disrupted the showing. If she knew, or even suspected that Goodwin had this footage and might show it with the real soundtrack, instead of the silly insulting music—she'd have to stop him. It could ruin her reputation. It could damage her career. Even if she didn't lose her part in Michael's production—I had no idea if being a bigot violated the morals clause—future roles might become harder to find in the very diverse theater world of the Washington metropolitan area. Who would ever want to work with someone with a mind like this?

I could see her killing over this. But wait—she was alibied, wasn't she? She'd driven off the road shortly after leaving our house.

Unless she drove off, decided she was too mad at Goodwin to let it go, and drove back to murder him. Or maybe she'd driven into the ditch not when she was in an understandable state of emotional turmoil over the embarrassing video but later, when she was in an even more understandable state of emotional turmoil as a result of killing someone.

And what if—

Just then I saw a flicker of something reflected in my laptop's screen. I wasn't sure what it was, but it startled me, and I threw myself sideways out of my chair and onto the floor.

The fireplace poker Celia was trying to brain me with hit my laptop instead of my skull. Slivers of glass flew everywhere.

"Stop!" I scuttled across the floor, rolled to my feet, and began backing away, watching her carefully. She didn't say anything—just stared at me with a crazed look in her eyes and raised the poker, obviously planning to charge forward and take another whack at me.

And she was trying to kill me with a poker I'd made myself. That bothered me almost as much as the fact that she was trying to kill me in the first place.

"The police are already on the way, you know," I said. "I caught the vandal red-handed just now."

"Yes," she said. "I heard you arguing with the walrus man. Lucky for me."

"So you know they'll be here soon to work the crime scene," I said. "You might want to be gone by then."

"I will be. But first I have to get rid of you. And that movie."

She lunged forward and struck at me. I managed to leap aside, and she made a deep gouge in one of our library chairs with the poker. The irrational thought crossed my mind that If I survived this I was going to send her a hell of a bill for damages.

"Stop now, and a good attorney can probably get you off with self-defense," I said as I inched backward. Damn— she was about to trap me at the end of the library closest to Michael's office, where there was no exit. "You accosted Goodwin and demanded that he delete the movies of you. He reacted violently. You were in fear of your life."

She lunged again, and I dodged again, and managed to slip past her. This was better—I could back toward the door to the house, or possibly the French doors.

"Stop now and we can help you!" I pleaded.

She edged closer.

"It's no use killing me," I said. "The police already have the video. Goodwin saved a copy online."

She didn't react.

Why was I bothering? She clearly wasn't in any shape to hear me. She'd probably been in this same state of blind, unreasoning anger when she'd killed Goodwin. I was looking around for something I could use as a weapon. Or the chance to make a break for it. Turning to open the French doors was a bad idea. Should I maybe just hurl myself through them?

Or should I rush her and grapple to take away the poker? I was tempted to try it. But she was my height, or maybe a little taller. And while I doubted that she had the strength my blacksmithing gave me, I suspected she had the wild, crazy strength that came with over-the-top rage.

I was nearing the French doors. Time for a finesse. I glanced back at the French doors, and then turned my back on her as if to open them. As I expected, she charged. I crouched and then hurled myself in her direction. I hit her at knee level and she fell backward, dropping the poker. I scrambled to my feet, rushed to grab it, and then turned to face her, holding the poker between us.

Maybe I should have tried to pin her down instead. She was up on her feet in an instant, and clearly looking around for a new weapon. Or maybe thinking of charging me to regain the poker. I steeled myself. I had to defend myself as ruthlessly as she'd attack. And—

The door to the rest of the house flew open.

"Stop this instant!"

I took a quick glance over my shoulder. Rose Noire stood just inside the doorway, holding Rob's softball bat.

Celia didn't even seem to notice her arrival.

"I said stop!" Rose Noire repeated, shaking the bat.

Maybe Celia didn't even hear her. Or maybe she did, but had gotten to know Rose Noire well enough to share my doubts about whether she could bring herself to do anything useful with the bat.

I'm not sure what would have happened if reinforcements hadn't arrived. The dogs.

All nine of them.

Tinkerbell arrived first. She burst into the library, paused briefly as if to assess the situation, and then strode forward until she was between Celia and us. She lowered her head and uttered a low warning growl. Anyone who knew anything about dogs would have frozen, and maybe muttered a few prayers.

We didn't get to find out what Celia would have done, because the Pomeranian puppies entered hard on Tink's heels. Their tiny brains immediately interpreted the situation as an exciting new game, and they raced toward Celia, yipping and snarling.

Spike brought up the rear, entering slowly and deliberately, as if trying to set the puppies a good example. When he sighted Celia, he went into his familiar slow attack mode, stalking stiff-leggedly toward her and growling dramatically. Celia didn't even glance toward him.

She'd noticed the puppies, though. They were gamboling around her, yipping ceaselessly, sometimes darting in to nip at her ankles or grab her shoelaces. She glanced down, and then lifted her foot as if planning to stomp the next fur ball who came near.

"Don't you dare!" Rose Noire shouted.

"Leave the dogs alone," I warned at the same time.

Tink growled and began slowly stalking nearer.

Spike launched himself into the air and bit into Celia's upraised ankle.

She shrieked and tried to kick him away, but he had a good hold, so all she succeeded in doing was losing her balance. She toppled over. I confess, I was worried less that she might hurt herself than that she might land on one of the puppies, but they all managed to scramble out of the way.

The puppies were delighted to have brought their foe down to their own level, and began yipping and nipping with renewed vigor. Spike remained firmly attached to her ankle. Tink stalked over and stood with her front feet on Celia's chest. She lowered her head until it was almost touching Celia's, uttered one almost inaudible growl, and froze, staring eye to eye with Celia. Who was either sensible enough or stunned enough that she didn't move.

"Meg, are you all right?" Rose Noire asked. "You're bleeding."

"I'm fine," I said. "It's paint, not blood. Gather up the puppies. I'll call nine-one-one."

"I already called it," came a voice—Kevin's voice.

"Kevin?" I glanced around. "Where are you?"

"Downtown, in my office." His voice seemed to be coming from my mangled laptop. "Good thing for you I hadn't gotten around to taking down the surveillance cameras we used to get the goods on your druggie. I happened to see Celia sneaking up on you, so I started messaging everyone I could think of. I guess Rose Noire was the only one close enough to do any good."

"And isn't it lucky I was playing with the puppies when I got your text," Rose Noire said.

"You'll be getting a lot more company soon," Kevin said. "I think Debbie Ann's sending everyone on the force."

"Good." I went over and grabbed a recalcitrant puppy—one that had decided it would be fun to nip at Tink's ankles instead of Celia's. Tink might as well have been a statue.

"Good dog, Tink," I said.

She wagged her tail almost imperceptibly, then continued staring into Celia's eyes. She was still doing it a few minutes later, when Vern and Aida burst into the library, guns drawn, to apprehend Celia.

Chapter 34

The rest of the day was busy.

Michael and Horace arrived a few minutes after Vern and Aida, followed by the rest of the force and every member of the cast and crew not yet under arrest. I lost count of how many times I had to explain that the red stains on my clothes were only paint.

Once he was sure I was okay, Michael brought me a change of clothes and then dragged the cast out to the barn to continue their meeting.

Vern and Aida took Celia downtown so the chief could interview her in the much more daunting surroundings of the police station.

Horace photographed the new graffiti and did whatever other forensics he needed to do with them.

To my astonishment, the president of Caerphilly College and the dean of the English Department showed up while Horace was at work and asked to see the graffiti. Horace gave them a guided tour. He offered to show them the video of Professor Philpotts painting it, but they declined.

"We are already in possession of that documentation," the dean said.

That sounded promising.

They shuddered and exclaimed a while longer over the graffiti, then thanked Horace and departed.

"What are the odds they'll actually do anything about him?" I muttered to Horace, when I'd returned from showing them out.

"Pretty good, from what I overheard," Horace said. "Apparently they've known for a couple of years now that he was not just a bigot but rapidly losing what few marbles he ever had. Only no one ever managed to get any solid evidence and all the witnesses against him got cold feet and recanted. But apparently the multicultural cast Michael picked for *Macbeth* finally sent him completely off the deep end—and thanks to you they've got him on video. He's toast."

As soon as she arrived, Mother called in an order to the paint store and sent a visiting cousin into town to pick it up. Then, once Horace had finished, a mixed crew of actors and cousins began repainting the hallway.

"The whole hallway," Mother said. "Because otherwise it wouldn't quite match, and besides, I thought it would be nice to try a slightly different shade of cream this time."

To me, the new cream looked pretty indistinguishable from the old, but life was more peaceful when we left the decorating to Mother.

Another mixed crew of actors and cousins cleaned up the library—a nasty job, because glass slivers from my laptop's broken screen had gone everywhere. Kevin showed up and took charge of the laptop itself.

"Don't worry," he said. "I'll take care of it." I had no idea if this meant he thought he could fix it or whether he considered ministering to the mortal remains of deceased electronics a part of his mission on Earth. Although I knew that even if Celia had managed a lucky hit and destroyed the hard drive, my data would be safe. Kevin had set up our backup programs. And he'd show up before long, either with my repaired laptop or another one very much like it that he "happened to be playing with," and I'd be back in business.

All the while I held onto the flash drive, so I could hand it over to the chief myself. He was busy down at the station for quite a while, dealing with the formalities of Celia's arrest. Late in the day, he showed up, looking tired but triumphant.

I let him into Michael's office so he could use the computer to watch the video right away. And I left him to watch it alone. I wasn't sure I wanted to watch Celia's toxic rant in the company of someone whose race she was demeaning. And I wondered if maybe the chief would like the freedom to watch it without having to guard his reactions. Me, I think I'd want to curse and shake my fist at the screen and say aloud what I really thought of her, as long as I could do it in privacy and then put on my game face for the world.

He emerged from the office a little grim, but calm enough.

"Of course we'll have an even better chain of custody once we get access to the video files Mr. Goodwin uploaded," he said. "But this will prove useful in building our case—against all of them."

"All of them?" I said. "Damn—I didn't get to watch what came after Celia's monologue. What else was in the grand finale?"

"Mr. Brainard snorting cocaine off the polished surface of one of your library tables, and Ms. Gerrard pouring a potion into Ms. Rivers's water bottle."

"Ms. Gerrard?" I echoed. "Oh—Fawn. I'm still learning some of the names. But hers I guess I won't be bothering with anymore, because even if you decide not to prosecute her, Michael's firing her. Are you hungry? There's pizza."

"If you're sure you have enough for everybody. I wouldn't want to deprive anyone."

"You'll be doing us a favor," I said. "Kevin and Dad both decided to fetch pizza for the celebration. We'll have leftovers for days."

"I can help with that problem," he said with a laugh. "I'll send my three over to help out Josh and Jamie."

"You're on."

"Oh, and by the way—we found this when we searched

the evidence Vern seized last night at the campfire. I should have told you sooner that we had it."

He held out a dagger—my creepy dead-man's-fingers dagger. And held it very carefully, even though it was encased in bubble wrap. I wondered if he or any of his officers had found out the hard way how sharp it was.

"Thanks," I said. "It was bothering me, not knowing what happened to it—and suspecting someone had stolen it for some evil purpose. And if Rose Noire is right, they were probably planning something nasty with it."

"Unfortunately, I suspect she's right," the chief said. "I'm glad we stopped them. And now—"

Just then Vern and Aida appeared in the library door.

"I'll join you for that pizza in a few minutes," the chief said.

I left him to confer with his officers.

The assembled multitude set up a cheer when I appeared. They'd been doing that all afternoon. I waved my thanks once more, grabbed a glass of lemonade, and looked around.

Every single visiting cousin was here. And the entire cast and crew—well, except for the ones who were still in jail. There was even a table full of reenactors, presided over by Sally the Sane. She strolled over to greet me.

"We're here by invitation, in case you were wondering," she said. "Your mother sent the twins up to deliver it."

"I wasn't wondering," I said. "You're welcome."

"All the more welcome now that MacLeod isn't with us, I assume. We've kicked him out, by the way, for flagrant violation of at least a dozen of our rules—especially the one about not bringing the organization into disrepute by any illegal or offensive action."

"Good to know."

"And now that the chief's given us permission to leave town, we'll be breaking up the encampment and taking your suggestion."

"My suggestion?" I couldn't remember making any suggestions to any of the reenactors. Well, except for telling MacLeod to shape up or ship out.

"Your mother told us something you said about how we weren't really serving much of an educational purpose out there in the woods," she said. "A good point. So we're going to join forces with one or two people from the History Department to come up with a demonstration we can put on in the town square a couple of weekends later this summer. Costumes that really are authentic. One or two historically accurate dwellings—I'm thinking tents of some kind. Demonstrations of genuine period music and crafts. We can actually work with the History Department instead of ignoring them, and do something that's both educational and maybe even a tourist attraction."

"Sounds good," I said. "If you need a blacksmith, let me know."

"Will do." She nodded as if sealing a bargain, and returned to the table of reenactors. Very well-behaved reenactors.

"Meg, you did get your father to check you out, didn't you?" Mother asked.

"I did, and I'm fine," I said.

"And wasn't it fortunate that Rose Noire was there to rescue you?" Mother beamed at Rose Noire.

"I didn't rescue Meg." Rose Noire clearly enjoyed the compliment, though. "She had almost rescued herself by the time I got there. I just helped her tie up the loose ends."

"You and the hounds of hell," Tanya said. She was holding a puppy. Many of those present were holding puppies, in what I hope I had made very clear was the last night of the seven Pomeranians' stay at our house. Clarence was picking them up in the morning, and assured me that he already had a waiting list for them and was vetting the top seven would-be adopters.

"And I wouldn't have been there at all if Kevin hadn't been brilliant enough to text me that Meg was in danger in the library," Rose Noire added.

"Actually, I texted pretty much the same thing to everyone I could think of," Kevin said, through a mouthful of pizza. "The chief, Vern, Horace, Aida, Michael, Josh, Jamie, Clarence, Grandpa, Grandma, and I forget who else. Rose Noire was the only one close enough to actually do anything."

"Good thinking on your part," I said. My hand was hovering between two pizza boxes. Sausage or Luigi's infamous Carnivore Special?

"The chief!" went up a cry from the other side of the yard.

Chief Burke strolled over toward our table, with Horace and Aida in his wake.

"Pizza?" Kevin offered. Coming from him, this almost counted as a gracious welcome.

Aida and Horace were already rummaging in the boxes.

"I wouldn't say no to a slice of pepperoni," the chief said.

A scramble through the nearby boxes produced the required slice, and he sat at one end of the picnic table and bit into it with relish.

"You've had quite a busy day," Dad said. His face showed that he was hoping the chief would fill us in on some of the details.

The chief nodded and continued chewing. Dad began to wilt slightly.

Michael took pity on him.

"So how did Celia pull it off, anyway?" Michael asked. "I thought she drove out of here in a raging temper and almost immediately landed herself in the ditch with a concussion. When did she have time to kill Goodwin?"

"Maybe she killed him and then deliberately drove herself into the ditch," Tanya suggested. "To give herself an alibi."

"No, from what I've been able to get out of her, the driving into the ditch was a genuine accident," the chief said. "Once she realized she wasn't hurt and wasn't getting rescued any time soon because nobody could see her car down there in the ditch unless they went looking for it, she scrambled out of the car and headed back to the house. But on her way she went by Goodwin's trailer and saw him leaving. She followed him until they were a safe distance from the house, then accosted him."

"And killed the poor man." Rose Noire shook her head sadly.

"She claims it was an accident," the chief said. "She rebuked him for spying on everyone and tried to take his camera away. He tried to hold onto it, and in the struggle, she accidentally bashed him over the head with it."

Dad pursed his lips but, with a rare show of discretion, said nothing. I deduced that his findings and Horace's might cast doubt on that explanation.

"And to hedge her bet, she also felt physically threatened, and in case neither accident nor self-defense flies, she also hinted that she was so angry she didn't really know what she was doing, and moreover might have been suffering from the effects of concussion." The chief was looking down at his pizza—but did I detect just the hint of a doubting eye roll?

"She didn't show any sign of concussion," Dad said. "And the symptoms she reported were . . ."

He paused, and I could tell his professional ethics were at odds with what he really wanted to say.

"Not adequately researched?" I suggested.

"One might say that," he said, while everyone else chuckled.

"Whether or not her story's entirely accurate, I wouldn't be surprised if she got off with voluntary manslaughter." From the chief's tone, I gathered he wasn't entirely thrilled with this possibility. "Of course, her strenuous and remarkably effective efforts to destroy his video files might undermine that a little. Oddly enough, she might end up serving as much or more time for attempting to murder Meg."

"I approve of that," I said. "One thing still puzzles me— what did she do with Goodwin's keys? And his phone?"

"Threw them into a bramble patch in the woods on her way back to her car," the chief said. "Where Aida found them this afternoon after some five hours of searching with a metal detector."

"My back may never be the same," Aida said.

"What about the rest of your prisoners?" Michael asked.

"Mr. Miller, aka Calum MacLeod, will be doing jail time," the chief said. "His attorney tried to talk us into cutting it down from twelve months to six months plus community service. I couldn't imagine any service he could perform that wouldn't have a negative effect on the community, so we offered him six months if he'd leave the county afterward and never come back. That proved acceptable. They'll be finalizing that arrangement Monday when the courts are open."

"Good riddance," Rose Noire said, in a rare note of negativity. "He has a very unsettling aura."

"What about Gina, Fawn, and Zoe?" I asked. "The evil fake witches."

"Fawn and Zoe have both agreed to testify against Gina," the chief said. "We'll be charging her with attempted murder."

"Two to ten years," Vern added in a cheerful tone.

"Fawn volunteered the information that Gina purchased an antique patent medicine bottle when the two of them visited the Secondhand Rose," the chief added. "The proprietor identified her. And was unaware of the dangers that could lurk in these old bottles."

"And even though my lecture on poisons helped Gina

figure out how to poison Celia, they're not considering me an accessory," Dad said.

I couldn't quite tell from his tone if he was serious.

"But the chief has asked me to create a poison aware-ness program for the county, to educate people about the dangers and help them dispose of dangerous materials safely."

"And so far we've found no evidence to suggest that Mr. Brainard was selling cocaine," the chief added. "If that continues to be the case, we'll be working toward a treat-ment program rather than incarceration."

"And Professor Philpotts?" I asked.

"His lawyer showed up at the station a little while ago and we let him out on bail," the chief said. "Interestingly, it was a private defense attorney, not the firm the college usually calls in to shepherd faculty members through the perils of the legal system. I suspect the college is none too pleased with Dr. Philpotts."

"We've already heard from the attorney," Michael said. "Offering a formal apology and complete financial restitu-tion for the damages he caused."

"Hold out for more," Kevin said. "Make him pay for the pain and suffering you went through."

"We turned it over to Meg's cousin Festus," Michael said. "We'll leave it up to him. He's probably already having martinis with the president of the college and discussing Professor Philpotts's impending retirement. For health reasons. It didn't hurt that the top dogs in the administra-tion were getting a little fed up with him anyway."

"Things appear to be working out well," the chief ob-served. "Although I suppose I should apologize to you for decimating your cast. I hope this isn't going to cause you too many problems getting the show ready in time."

"We've already replaced Lady Macbeth," Michael said, waving a half-eaten slice of pizza at Tanya.

"Is this a dagger which I see before me!" she declaimed, leaping up and holding up a slice of pizza in front of her, to general applause.

"A couple of my grad students are coming back to town to fill Tanya's old part and the Second Witch," Michael said. "And I've offered Banquo to an old friend who found out a few days ago that he's being written out of the soap opera that's been paying the bills for the last few years. He can use the work, and he'll be great."

"Mom?"

I looked up to see Josh, Jamie, and Adam Burke standing in front of me. They were all three holding Pomeranian puppies. I had a sinking feeling.

"The puppies saved your life," Josh said, in an indignant tone.

"We can't just abandon them," Jamie said.

Adam said nothing, but he was cuddling his puppy and watching his grandfather's expression.

"They helped save my life," I said. "And we're not abandoning them. Clarence is going to find good homes for all of them."

"We want to be consulted on that," Josh said.

"Don't you trust Clarence to find them good homes?" I asked.

"Clarence has an awful lot of animals to find homes for," Jamie said. "We want to make sure he finds really special ones for these guys."

Adam, still holding his puppy, had gone over to lean against his grandfather. The chief was studying the puppy with a bemused air.

Farther down, a puppy was sitting on the table in front of Horace, who was holding out small bits of food for the puppy to sniff.

"I wonder if Pomeranians have any potential as search dogs?" he was saying to Vern.

Rose Noire and Tanya, who seemed to have hit it off, were stroking the puppy that had fallen asleep in Rose Noire's lap.

"Yes, she definitely has a very good aura," Rose Noire said.

Even Kevin seemed to have joined the Pomeranian bandwagon. Someone had set a puppy on the corner of the table near him. He was staring down at it with the same sort of look he'd have if he were examining an interesting new bit of computer equipment. The puppy was staring back with a remarkably similar expression. Kevin tilted his head to the left as if to get a better look. The puppy did the same. The puppy took a few cautious steps toward Kevin's not-quite-empty plate. Kevin pushed the plate closer and watched as the puppy began gnawing on a bit of pizza crust.

Clearly making the house Pomeranian-free was going to be a lot more difficult than I had thought.

"Talk to Clarence tomorrow," I said. "I'm sure he has wonderful homes lined up for all of them. Homes with people who would be very sad if they didn't get one of these little guys."

"But we need to check them out," Jamie said.

Josh nodded.

Tink appeared at my side with one of the puppies in her mouth. She gently deposited it in my lap and then curled up at my feet.

"See, even Tink thinks the puppies should stay." Jamie petted Tink and beamed at the puppy and me.

I thought of pointing out that their beloved Spike might feel very differently. And that finding good homes for the puppies didn't necessarily require keeping them. And that a puppy was a lot more work to train and take care of than a full-grown dog. And—

I didn't feel like fighting this battle. Not tonight. Tomorrow I'd tackle Clarence, and see what I could do to limit the number of Pomeranians that would be staying around.

Tonight I just wanted to enjoy being alive, and see life get back to as close to normal as it ever got around our house.

The puppy piddled on my leg, but only a little, before curling up and going to sleep in my lap.

Acknowledgments

Thanks once again to everyone at St. Martin's / Minotaur, including (but not limited to) Joe Brosnan, Lily Cronig, Hector DeJean, Paul Hochman, Kayla Janas, Andrew Martin, Sarah Melnyk, and especially my editor, Pete Wolverton. And thanks also to David Rotstein, Rowen Davis, and the art department for yet another glorious cover.

More thanks to my agent, Ellen Geiger, and to Matt McGowan and the staff at the Frances Goldin Literary Agency—they take care of the practical stuff so I can focus on the writing.

Sometimes I get the details right, thanks to friends who generously share their expertise. This time, that included Deborah Blake, who took time from her own writing to serve as my Wiccan sensitivity reader . . . Mark Bergin, whose writing I interrupted with half a million questions about police procedure . . . Dr. Robin Waldon, who tried to keep me from playing fast and loose with medical facts . . . Doug Minnerly and Kathryn O'Sullivan, who shared bits of theatrical lore . . . and Luci Zahray, who continues to earn her title as the mystery world's Poison Lady. Of course, if I got anything wrong, it was probably something I wasn't savvy enough to ask them about.

Many thanks to the friends who brainstorm and critique with me, give me good ideas, or help keep me sane while I'm writing: Stuart, Aidan, and Liam Andrews, Chris Cowan, Ellen Crosby, Kathy Deligianis, Margery Flax, Suzanne Frisbee, John Gilstrap, Barb Goffman, Joni

Langevoort, David Niemi, Alan Orloff, Art Taylor, Robin Templeton, and Dina Willner. And thanks to all the TeaBuds for two decades of friendship.

And above all, thanks to all my readers who make Meg's adventures possible.